There Came a
Stranger

There Came a
Stranger

There Came a
Stranger

Andrew J. Fenady

A TOM DOHERTY ASSOCIATES BOOK
NEW YORK

THERE CAME A STRANGER

Copyright © 2001 by Andrew J. Fenady

This book is printed on acid-free paper.

Design by Heidi S. W. Eriksen

A Forge Book
Published by Tom Doherty Associates, LLC
175 Fifth Avenue
New York, NY 10010

www.tor.com

Forge® is a registered trademark of Tom Doherty Associates, LLC.

Library of Congress Cataloging-in-Publication Data

Fenady, Andrew J.
    There came a stranger / Andrew J. Fenday.—1st ed.
        p. cm.
    "A Tom Doherty Associates book."
    ISBN 0-312-87752-8 (alk. paper)
    1. Texas—Fiction.   2. Custer, George Armstrong, 1839-1876—
Fiction.   I. Title.
PS3556.E477 T48 2002
813'.54—dc21   2001023123

First Edition: June 2001

Printed in the United States of America

0 9 8 7 6 5 4 3 2 1

For old pal Gary Goldstein
and new pal Karla Zounek
and best pal Mary Frances

One

Adam Dawson rode West.

The red scarf around his neck was streaked with sweat and faded from rack of sun and rain, stained with dried-out battle blood long ago turned brown against the once bright crimson cloth that had been each trooper's flowing guidon in General George Armstrong Custer's charging Wolverine Brigade at Gettysburg, Falls Church, Yellow Tavern, and finally at Appomattox.

But the war was over. The killing finished. The country united. At least that had been the purpose—to unite the states again.

At Appomattox, Grant had refused Lee's sword, shook the great general's hand and proclaimed, "We are all countrymen again."

The soldiers who survived could go home. Those who did not survive slept forever near battles lost and won.

Adam Dawson had survived—but he had no home.

No home. No family. No ties to anything. Homeless as a poker chip. Aimless as a feather in a breeze. A drifter on horseback—riding West.

But Adam Dawson had made the choice to cut loose. One of the few times he had said "no" to his former commander and still his best friend, *Autie* . . . George Armstrong Custer.

Adam Dawson could have been a part of the "Custer Clan" and still tied to the United States Army—with a commission and a command. But the cost was too high. The cost was killing. Killing enemies who were not enemies. Adam Dawson had had his bellyful of that. At battles that helped win the war and at battles that were meaningless—except to those who died and to those who were maimed.

There were times when Adam Dawson had come skin-close to regretting his choice. When, as he moved West with all his chattels—a bay gelding named Ned, the clothes on his formidable frame, cavalry boots and hat, a buckskin jacket, a Colt .44, a Winchester, a passel of cartridges, a handful of coins and a silver watch with an inscription engraved on the back,

> *Adam*
> *Come on, you Wolverine!*
> *Autie*

—during some of these times, Adam Dawson nearly changed his mind. Nearly nudged Ned north instead of west.

The last time was three days ago when he crossed the Red River into Texas. That night he stared at the campfire as he smoked a cigarette and thought of riding again with Autie toward the sound of the guns. Toward glory. Custer saw glory in every campaign. There were always rainbows in Autie's eyes and glory on his mind.

But glory in what? In the coming campaigns Custer would be killing Indians instead of Rebels. Adam Dawson was sick of killing.

He had made a silent vow, so silent that he told no one, no one but himself, not even Custer. Adam Dawson vowed that he would never again take another man's life—unless his own life depended on it.

So he drifted West—along one of the Creator's most rugged and complex creations—the Texas terrain. Dull, flat, monotonous in places where the Lord had stomped the dust off his boots—spectacular, craggy and colorful in other parts where Adam Dawson rode now.

A warm, nomad breeze swept through jagged cliffs and

red stone monuments. Dawson brought the bay gelding to a stop at a precipitous edge without argument from the animal. Man and horse scanned the country below—country that had never heard of hospitality.

Dawson was thirsty. So was Ned. There was water in the canteen. He thought about taking a swallow, dampening the scarf and moistening the horse's mouth and nostrils. The canteen was about half full or half empty, depending on your outlook. As he looked out over the landscape there was not a river nor a stream. No sign of water on the ground below nor from the gunmetal sky above. He decided to save the water in the half full/half empty canteen. If he took a drink the canteen would be more than half empty or less than half full. No dispute about that. And at this time, in this place water was among Dawson's most precious possessions. There could be some doubt about which item was the most precious—his horse, his guns, his boots, even his hat— but they were all vital and he had to care for each of those items—so they could care for him.

Dawson ran his dry tongue over his dryer lips and gently heeled Ned's flanks.

"Come on, Ned."

Horse and rider picked their way through the loose shale of the sloping canyon wall. He was a good horseman, a natural horseman. Not as good or as natural as Custer, but then nobody was. Not even Ulysses Simpson Grant who held the title of "Best Cavalryman and Worst Cadet" at West Point until a few years later when Custer came along. Custer exceeded Grant on both counts. Dawson never rode with Grant, saw him only twice. The South wished it had never seen him—wished that Grant had never been born . . . but all of that was behind Dawson.

He tried not to think of the past as he and Ned made their way down the slope, but it was hard not to think about the past—particularly when there wasn't much of a future to think about.

So far the future was only a direction—west. And while there were rainbows in Autie's eyes, there didn't appear to be any rainbow in Dawson's sky—and no pot of gold.

Two men on horseback reined up at the lip of the canyon and squinted down at Dawson's back. Two scruffy, hungry-eyed Comancheros. Dirty men in a dirty trade.

Comancheros they were called because mostly they did business with the Comanches—providing the Indians with guns, ammunition, whiskey, other provisions, and prisoners, mostly women—stolen and kidnapped.

Usually the Comancheros favored better odds than two to one. Ten to one was more like it. The two riders, Diaz and Charly, looked at each other, then at the descending horseman in the distance and pondered the situation. The rest of the band was at their camp too far away. When they had pondered enough, Diaz grinned.

"That's a good-looking horse." He said.

"Let's get it." Charly nodded.

"We will. But not yet."

"Not yet?"

"Not yet."

"When?"

"When we can catch him. Not from up here."

"I think maybe . . ."

"I think maybe you shut up and do what I tell you."

Charly shrugged.

Adam Dawson and the bay moved along the flat, unprotected terrain. With the red scarf he wiped the sweat from his eyes, then from his lean, hard face. He breathed the hot, heavy air and thought about the water in the canteen. But Ned was thinking about something else. The animal nickered, both ears sprang forward, his flesh quivered.

"Easy, Ned," Dawson patted the horse and looked around. Nothing moved. No sound. He urged the animal forward and instinctively touched the handle of the .44, reassuring himself of its ready avail.

When Dawson had first started to ride, the horses were all taller than he was. He had to have a boost to get on. But once aboard he took to it like a Cossack. Adam Dawson rode, owned and traded horses before he began to shave. All kinds of horses with all kinds of temperaments from Tennessee Walkers to Arabians, from knotheads to coursers. In peace and war, Adam Dawson spent more time on horseback than he did on his feet. But he never took to any horse and no horse ever took to him like this bay.

It was in St. Louis after Captain Adam Dawson got mustered out. There were a hundred horses to choose from, all ex-army flesh. But Dawson's eyes went straight to the gelding. The owner of all hundred, Jonas Trapp, had said, "Take your pick. Fifty dollars—except for one."

Dawson pointed to the bay.

"That's the one." Trapp said.

"How much for him?"

"Seventy-five."

"Too much." That was almost half of Dawson's life savings including his mustering out pay and he'd still have to buy a saddle.

"That horse belonged to a general." Trapp remarked.

"Generals usually own their horses."

"Not dead generals. This one died on Ned's back at Petersburg."

"Ned?"

"That's what he's called . . . course you can call him whatever you want."

"Not for seventy-five dollars."

"Then go to your next choice."

"I will."

Adam Dawson started to move away. But the bay gelding nickered and both ears sprang forward, his flesh quivered. And so did Dawson.

Since then it was man and horse in harmony. They had ridden through sleet and snow, rock and sand, rain and heat. At times both were hungry and thirsty, but still in harmony. Companions. Comrades.

From the distance Diaz and Charly, pistols drawn, charged and fired at Adam Dawson. The bay was already galloping,

Dawson's red scarf fluttering past his buffalo shoulders, this time away from the enemy instead of charging toward the sound of the guns. Bullets streaked past, but the pursuers gained no ground. The Comancheros cursed and spurred their mounts.

Dawson reined the bay to the left to avoid an outcrop of rocks that jutted from the earth. The animal's muscles bunched as a bullet broke into its flank. The horse and Dawson buckled, somersaulted and landed hard on the ground a dozen feet apart.

The animal was dead.

Adam Dawson scrambled toward the bay, pulled the Winchester from its boot, used the dead horse for cover, and fired again and again at the oncoming Comancheros. Dawson's first four shots missed but each slug came closer to its target.

The fifth shot ripped through Diaz's hat flinging it off his filthy head. The sixth creased the muscle of Charly's left shoulder. Both men reined in their horses hard, bouncing in their saddles.

"To hell with it!" Diaz hollered. "The horse is dead and he's too good a shot!" Diaz wheeled his mount and rode in the opposite direction. Charly didn't hesitate to follow.

"The sonofabitch!" Charly screamed. "He hit me!"

Twin wakes of desert dust spiraled from the hooves of the Comancheros' horses. Dawson stopped shooting. There was no sense in wasting cartridges.

On one knee Dawson patted the dead horse. It could have been Adam Dawson who took the bullet. He sighed a deep breath, set the Winchester on the ground, started to unstrap the saddle and saddlebag and looked up toward the gray, heavy blanket of sky. Soon a circling pattern of buzzards would appear.

It would have been a cavalier gesture. To bury Ned. But impractical, if not impossible. It would take a shovel—and effort. Dawson had no shovel and he had to save his strength.

A Comanche would have cut out some of the horse's meat and eaten it. Dawson had no stomach for that.

He hoisted the saddle and saddlebag onto his left shoulder, took up the Winchester with his right hand, and turned west.

By the time he covered four miles, more or less, the saddle seemed to have doubled in weight. His face, neck and upper body boiled in his own sweat. His feet swelled in his boots and his throat throbbed from thirst.

He let the saddle drop, untwisted the lid of the canteen and allowed himself two swallows of tepid liquid. He could see that the stillborn, ragged, beige desert had begun to give way to a less hostile, if not yet friendly horizon. Scrub grass in spots, mesquite, and clusters of rocks, even boulders, mineral-streaked.

He sealed the canteen, lifted the saddle and saddlebag and headed straight for the boulders.

In less than half an hour he had stashed the saddle among the boulders, taken off his jacket, thought about taking another swallow from the canteen, but didn't. He looked back in the direction from which he came.

Would the two riders come after him—maybe with more riders and guns? To shoot him down, take his gun and rifle, his cartridges, and the silver watch they didn't know he had. He knew he had wounded one of them. Maybe that would discourage them—or maybe not. Maybe that would make them want to kill him.

Dawson had vowed not to kill again—unless his life depended on it.

If they came, his life would depend on it—and kill he would.

Adam Dawson continued West.

Two

The Comanchero camp was isolated within a spectral sanctuary, a mountain meadow between the shoulders of the Santa Margaritas. Years ago it had been a Comanche *rancheria*, a village of close to a hundred Indian men, women and children.

Shortly after Company C, under the command of Captain Amos Kitcher of the U.S. Army, attacked at first light, the dead bodies of ninety-six Comanche men, women and children were counted and buried in a common grave beneath the bloody ground.

A massacre it was called—and as a massacre it was remembered.

What some didn't remember was that forty Comanche warriors from the *rancheria* had, ten days before, attacked a wagon train on its way to Fort Concho—a wagon train carrying wives and children who were to join their husbands and fathers.

No one from that massacre had survived either. One difference was that those bodies—fourteen troopers and thirty-six women and children—were tortured, mutilated and left for the buzzards.

No other Comanche tribe ever moved into that area again, neither did anybody else, until last year when a band of Comancheros led by a man who called himself Corona found it a strategic base from which to do business.

The current population varied from time to time, from

as few as thirty to as many as sixty. Some of the band was composed of scalawags, highbinders, backshooters and all-around no good bastards. The rest were worse.

The worst of all was Corona, so naturally he was the leader. His father Jack Stubbins, whom he never met, was a U.S. Army deserter during the Mexican-American War. Stubbins raped Corona's mother-to-be, a Salazar princess and was hanged for the deed, after his vitals were cut off by the princess's father.

How, when, or why he took the name Corona nobody knew or cared. But they knew that among them, Corona took whatever he wanted, especially the women who lived in the camp.

One of the women, Olita, was pouring whiskey from a bottle onto the wound in Charly's shoulder. Olita was a big woman, about twenty, and handsome by all standards. She wore no clothes on her upper body and unashamedly displayed her womanhood. Charly took notice of the display as she rubbed the gash with a rag.

"Thank you, Olita." Charly grinned.

"Don't thank me. He told me to do it." The woman nodded toward Corona, who watched along with Diaz and some of the other men.

"You stupid sonofabitch . . ." Corona said, "stupid sonofabitch."

"Corona . . . I . . ."

"You shoot a good horse instead of the rider . . ."

"Maybe Diaz shot him . . ."

"I don't think so," Diaz said.

"Shut up both of you. It's lucky you didn't shoot each other . . . maybe not so lucky . . . maybe we'd be better off . . . you're both stupid sonsofbitches. Without me you don't know *nada* about ambush." Corona reached for the bottle in Olita's hand. "Gimme that, you wasted enough good whiskey."

"Bullet went right through," Olita said as Corona grabbed the bottle.

"Should've gone though his stupid head." Corona drank.

"What're we gonna do?" Charly asked.

"About what?"

"Him. The one who shot me. Maybe we could go back and catch him . . . he's got a gun and rifle . . ."

"You couldn't catch snow in a blizzard." Corona swallowed again. The Comancheros laughed their obligatory laugh, all but Charly and Diaz.

"Forget about him." Corona drank what was left of the whiskey. "Olita, get another bottle and come with me."

With every bootstep Adam Dawson knew that he was walking farther away from death and closer to survival.

He remembered the words Custer spoke to him time and again before every campaign, before every battle, before every charge.

"Not today, Adam, not today."

Custer often said that he would know when it was the day he was going to die. That each man's fate was already written in each man's book of destiny.

"I'll know when I come to that page, Adam." He'd repeat. "Not today. Not today." And Custer would lead his Wolverines to glory—and for some of them to death—but not for Custer.

Adam Dawson didn't believe that he, himself, would know the day he was going to die—and he didn't want to know. But when his horse went down, Dawson would not have bet that this wasn't his day, his destiny, to end up buzzard meat in the desert, like Ned.

Even after that, after the bushwhackers turned away and left him afoot, he didn't give himself much more chance than a wax hinge in hell.

But now, with each step toward the crest of the rise, his outlook rose too. In the last hour the desert behind him had melded into darker, richer ground. Splashes of wildflowers scattered from the level table of land upward along the rising flank of the pitted hillock.

Adam Dawson topped out and looked below. A different

world. A world of grass and trees, a trail and in the far distance a willow grove, and most welcome, a stream. Adam Dawson took the last swallow of water from the canteen and moved toward the oasis.

But as he moved on he paused again at the sight of something far ahead, something just off the trail in the shade of the willow grove.

A two-up buckboard hitched to a matched pair of blacks, and beside them a saddled palomino. Even from this distance the saddle looked expensive. And from this distance Adam Dawson could make out more. Two people, a man and woman in each other's arms.

Dawson stepped up his pace and walked toward them. As he came closer it was apparent that they did not welcome the stranger, or for that matter, anybody else.

The woman was young, beautiful, flaxen-haired. The fragile white bonnet didn't conceal very much of her sun gold hair. Eyes blue, two inviting azure pools. The most beautiful woman Dawson had ever seen, more beautiful even than Libbie Custer—and certainly more sensuous than any woman he had ever looked on.

The man's face was almost square with gray, coyote eyes, brown hair graying at the temples, overlarge ears, and his complexion pallid, with skin more suited to the indoors.

Both their heads turned as Adam Dawson approached, and they separated. The woman moved her eyes, then her face away from Adam and toward the stream. The man stepped closer to the palomino, lifted his gray Stetson from the pommel and put it on his head.

"Beg pardon." Dawson said.

The man looked at the tall stranger, but didn't speak. Obviously he resented the intrusion, but he didn't seem afraid. Uneasy but not afraid. Here was an encroacher—afoot, armed, dirty, maybe desperate, a man who could point a gun and take their valuables, even their lives, still the man who had just put on his hat didn't seem to fear—only to resent, and wait in silence.

"There a town close by?" Dawson broke the silence. The

woman glanced at Dawson then looked back toward the stream.

"Pinto." The man said and pointed. "About a mile ahead."

"Thanks."

Even though she wasn't facing him, Dawson tipped his hat to the lady and started walking away, toward Pinto.

"That's a fine looking animal," Dawson said as he passed by the palomino. He didn't expect a reply—and didn't get one. Adam Dawson thought it best to walk away out of ear-shot and sight before he stopped to drink and fill his canteen.

"Brad," she said, after Dawson was far enough away. "Do you think that he . . ."

"Nothing to worry about." Brad said. "Just a drifter. Probably never see him again . . ."

"But he's going into Pinto . . ."

"His kind keeps on going." He reached out. Took her close in his arms again. "Come here."

When the stream crooked to the right and he could not see or be seen by the romantic couple, Dawson went to the wa-ter. He removed the red scarf, kneeled at the bank, cupped both hands and splashed his face, throat and hair. He bent down, dipped his head into the stream and kept it below the surface until he needed to breathe again.

Dawson filled the canteen, drank until his lungs were full, then filled it again. He held the red scarf by one end and let the rest of it soak in the stream—then held it by the other end and let it soak some more.

He rose to his feet and wrapped the wet scarf around his neck.

For the first time in days he knew where he was going. Alone and afoot, but alive and lucky to be, he was heading for a place less than a mile away—a place called Pinto.

Three

Pinto, south of the Red River that divided the Oklahoma Territory from Texas, west of the Sabine that separated Louisiana and Texas, and east of the Brazos that flowed toward Galveston and the Gulf of Mexico, Pinto raddled in an uneven, patternless array of buildings, mostly adobe, once a part of Mexico, later the Republic of Texas, and now a flyspeck in the United States of America.

Adam Dawson, carrying the Winchester and saddlebag, walked down the rutted, somnolent, main street of Pinto. He stopped as he took notice of a sign just far enough ahead to read.

BALDY'S BAR
F R E E   L U N C H

Balm for hunger and thirst. Dawson began to cut the distance between him, the sign, and Baldy's emporium.

Between Dawson and Baldy's Bar Sheriff Ben Vesper leaned back on a shaded Douglas chair in front of his office and jail. Vesper had a frontier face and shoulders to match, bullet eyes the color of lead, and a south-of-the-border complexion. Even without a badge he would have commanded attention, with it he commanded respect. The badge was pinned to the canvas vest he wore. He also wore a .44. He tipped the chair forward on all four legs, but did not rise as he spoke.

"You."

Dawson stopped walking. He turned and looked at the sheriff. Half a dozen other citizens of Pinto who had also heard the sheriff's voice paused and looked at both men.

"Good day, Sheriff," Dawson said.

"Is it?"

"Well," Dawson smiled, "it's a good day to be alive."

The sheriff didn't smile. He didn't speak or move. Dawson started to turn away and walk.

"Just a minute. Don't be in such a hurry."

"I'm not, just thought we were done talking."

"I'll tell you when."

"Sure."

"Yank, huh?"

"Was."

"Where from?"

"North."

"I figured that. Any place in particular?"

"Not lately."

"What happened to your horse?"

"Ambushed. Got shot. Comancheros, I think."

"Dangerous country out there."

"Coulda been worse. Coulda been me."

"What do you want in Pinto?"

"A horse." Dawson shrugged. "Something to eat. Not in that order."

"What happened to the Comancheros?"

Dawson lifted the rifle, just a couple of inches.

"You won't be needing that Winchester . . . while you're here."

"Glad to hear that."

Silence.

"Are we done talking?" Dawson asked.

"For the time being."

"Well, then . . . good day, Sheriff."

Adam moved toward Baldy's. Sheriff Ben Vesper tilted the chair back against the wall.

The half dozen citizens of Pinto who had watched

seemed somehow disappointed that that's all there was to it. Nothing too exciting had happened in or around Pinto for days. No fighting. No shooting. No bloodshed.

It appeared as if this would be just another peaceful day in Pinto. The citizens went about their business—those who had any business. The others just went. All but one. A young, dark complexioned, well-built lad about sixteen who had come out of the nearby livery stable and stood within listening range. Sam Mendez took a step closer to the sheriff.

"What is it, Sam?"

"Oh, nothin', Sheriff. I was just wonderin'."

"About what?"

"That stranger."

"What about him? Ever see him before?"

"No, sir."

"Then what?"

"How you size a man up. I mean how you can tell if a man's . . ."

"What?"

"Well, dangerous. If there's anything about him that . . ."

"Why do you want to know? What's that got to do with workin' in the livery? Afraid he's gonna steal a horse? You don't own 'em anyhow . . ."

"No, sir. But I don't want to keep on cleaning up stables . . . someday I want to be like you . . . a lawman, and I was just wonderin' . . ."

"Sam, stick to the stables or some other profession. The law don't pay much, 'specially around here."

"I don't care about that, the money I mean . . . but how can you tell?"

"Not by lookin' . . . except maybe at the eyes, a little. It's not how a man looks. I've seen the mildest of sorts slit their brother's throat."

"How then?"

"By what he *does*. No use guessin' 'til he makes a move, or starts to. You just got to be ready for anything from anybody . . . and then move fast and first. Comes with experience. If you live. Stick with horses, Sam."

"Not me."

"Suit yourself. But was I you, I'd get back to the stables before you lose the job that you have got, *amigo*."

"Thanks, Sheriff." Sam smiled and moved off toward the livery.

"Lawman." Sheriff Ben Vesper muttered and shoved the brim of his hat lower onto his forehead.

Adam Dawson, still carrying the Winchester and saddlebag, walked through the bat-winged entrance of Baldy's. It looked and smelled like countless other saloons with other names that served the same purpose. Along one side, a scarred and stained bar. Sawdust on a wood floor that hadn't been swept the night before, or the week before. Tin ceiling. Half-dozen tables, all round, with hard-back chairs. A haze of smoke from cigarettes, pipes and cigars curled and settled on anything or anybody it could find. The room was more than half filled, mostly with Mexican ranch hands and idlers from both borders.

As Dawson moved toward the bar, customers glanced up at the stranger, but quickly went back to watching an arm-wrestling contest at the center table.

Two men were seated opposite each other, their right elbows on the table, with hands locked and straining. One man was Mexican, Joe Nueva, the other, Anglo, Pete Sommers. Nueva was handsome, brawny. Sommers, homely, burly.

They strained between two short flaming candles, one on each side of the table. First hand to be flattened would feel the flame and lose the contest.

The Mexicans cheered their compadre, urging him in Spanish to cremate the gringo. The less numerous American contingent countered with similar sentiments on behalf of Sommers.

Both gladiators labored as beads of sweat swelled from their brows and chins, but neither fist wavered in either direction.

Nueva grinned. Pete Sommers grimaced. Still neither fist bent, only quivered.

Dawson stood at the end of the bar, as far away as possible from the competition and noise. He leaned his rifle against the counter.

The woman behind the bar came closer. She was a stone overweight, orange hair—darker at the roots, two raspberry slashes on the surface of her full lips, green eyes a trifle watery, measuring Adam Dawson. He measured back. Despite piled-on powder and paint, there was an unmistakable bonniness about her that came through. She was past her salad days, corseted into a saloon dress that was supposed to match the color of her hair, but she was still palatable and moved toward him with everything she had.

"Hi. I'm Alma."

"Didn't figure you were Baldy."

"That makes you pretty good at figuring. Anything else?"

"Anything else what?"

"Anything else you good at?"

"Beer . . . when I can get it."

"I figure you're pretty good at getting anything you want."

"All I want is a beer . . . for now."

"One beer coming up . . . for now."

Dawson looked at the arm-wrestlers as Alma drew the beer and set it in front of him.

"How long's that been going on?" Dawson swallowed some beer.

"Who knows? Who cares? You come far?"

"Far as Baldy's . . . if there is a Baldy."

"He's in the back," Alma motioned her head. "On his back . . . snoring."

"During business hours?"

"He's the boss. He can do anything he wants."

Dawson smiled at her and took another drink.

"Except that," she added.

Adam Dawson looked from her to the free lunch plate

on the bar. The plate was empty except for a single stalk of celery.

"Hungry?" she asked.

"Isn't half the world?"

"The dumb half."

"I guess that doesn't include lady bartenders."

"I only tend bar part time . . . the other part I sing a little . . . at night." She picked up the free lunch plate and moved toward the kitchen. "I'll get you something to go with that beer."

She walked away with all she had. Dawson followed her movement until she disappeared into the back room. He drank some more beer and looked around the saloon.

All eyes were still on the contest. And the spectators were still exhorting whichever contestant they favored.

All the spectators except one.

Chad Walker sat alone at a nearby table that could've seated six. He sat as if the place belonged to him, not Baldy. And even as he sat it was easy to determine that he must be over six feet tall. Everything about him was big, except his ochre eyes. Thick, broad shoulders spread under a stone face crowned by a top-of-the-line gumbo-colored Stetson. His age was indeterminate, but older than Dawson.

Walker puffed on a king-sized stogie and stared stoically at the arm-wrestlers. Dawson noticed that a couple of times the Mexican arm-wrestler glanced at the big man and smiled. The big man's expression never altered in the slightest. He knocked the tip of the cigar ash into the tray on the table without even looking away from the contest.

Adam Dawson had seen faces like this man's before. Just a few—and all in the war. Dawson looked away. He knew it was unwise to look at a man such as that for too long. Just a glimpse was long enough.

Alma swayed out of the kitchen carrying the free lunch plate now piled with cheese and cold cuts. She set the plate on the bar near Dawson's drinking hand.

"Help yourself, soldier."

"Thanks."

"You know, we don't see many Yanks in Texas."

"I'd've thought you'd seen too many."

Alma shrugged. "All men look alike in the dark . . . almost." She pointed to the free lunch plate. "Eat."

Dawson reached for a piece of cheese.

"Let me put a head on that." Alma picked up the beer mug. "No charge."

The cheers and exhortations in the saloon got louder. Dawson took up a slice of cold meat and slipped it into his mouth as he turned toward the arena.

The Mexican, Nueva, sweated and strained mightily and had gained some advantage. The other man's hand had begun to dip and quake.

With one, final quantum twist, Joe Nueva smashed the gringo's hand onto the table and against the flaming candle.

The room exploded with a torrent of *Vivas* and *Oles*. Some of the customers immediately reenacted the triumph with imaginary opponents. Pete Sommers drooped his head and rubbed his right elbow. Nueva laughed, swept up a mug of beer from the table, chug-a-lugged it, then slapped Sommers on his slumping shoulder.

"Alma!" Nueva hollered and looked toward the bar. "Whiskey! A bottle of whiskey! Loser pays!" He then looked toward the big man seated alone at the table and grinned.

"Yeah, yeah, yeah," Alma said just above a whisper.

"How much do I owe you . . . and Baldy?" Dawson asked.

"Didn't I tell you? First drink's on the house. Why don't you come back tonight? Listen to me sing . . . have some . . . supper . . . huh?"

"Maybe."

"You won't regret it." She smiled through the raspberry slashes.

"ALMA, GODDAMMIT!" Nueva roared.

"Yeah, yeah." She nodded.

Dawson picked up his saddlebag and rifle and turned to leave as Nueva swaggered closer blocking Dawson's path.

"What the hell does it take to get some service around this place?"

"Take it easy, Joe," she said.

"Never mind the easy. You took care of this drifter soon enough."

"Here's your bottle, Joe." Alma set an unopened quart on the bar as Dawson started to sidle past Nueva.

"Excuse me," Dawson said softly.

"What'd you say?" Nueva's face jutted toward Dawson.

"You heard me," he said, no louder.

"I want everybody to hear. Say it again ... louder." He looked around at everyone in the room.

"Joe," Alma said, "for chrissake let it go. Drink your whiskey." She shoved the bottle on the bar toward Nueva.

"You shut up, Alma. Let's hear from your friend. What about it, friend? You got anything to say?"

Dawson brushed past Nueva toward the bat-wings. Nueva shoved him from behind, rocking him against a table, jarring the ashtray and knocking Chad Walker's cigar to the floor.

Adam Dawson instantly regained his balance and faced off with Nueva. Neither man said anything. But Chad Walker did.

"Pick it up!" Walker said in a low growl.

Both Dawson and Nueva looked at Walker, who was still seated. It was unclear as to which of the two men the command had been directed.

Dawson's eyes took in the man at the table but were still acutely aware of Nueva.

"You! Drifter! You dumped my cigar. Pick it up!"

Nueva smiled. Dawson made no move to obey.

"Pick it up," Walker repeated, this time pointing to the smoldering cigar on the floor.

"Not my fault," Dawson said, then pointed to Nueva. "His."

"You hear that, Joe?" Walker asked.

"I heard, Mr. Walker. Now he's going to hear this. You, drifter. You're gonna pick it up like Mr. Walker says."

The men in the saloon were silent in anticipation of the coming showdown.

"Pick it up!" This time Nueva pointed to the floor.

"I do, and I'll stick it in your eyeball."

"Like hell . . ." Nueva threw a swift, hard right, but Dawson blocked it with his saddlebag. He dropped his rifle and jolted a sharp left into Nueva's nose erupting considerable blood. Nueva's head and body shook and he stood stunned. So were his compadres. Only Alma smiled favorably at the result.

Dawson stood still, casting a challenge at Nueva whose eyes were unfocused, with nose still bleeding.

It appeared to be over. Not fast, not slow, Dawson picked up his saddlebag and rifle, turned and resumed his walk toward the bat-wings.

"You gonna take that, Joe?" It was Walker's voice. Even as Dawson started to turn back Nueva made a mad bull charge from behind, managing to get his arms around Dawson and wrestle him to the floor, knocking over a table with glasses and bottles.

Over and under the two bodies tumbled, along with more furniture, glasses and crockery. Dawson's arm became tangled with a fallen chair and Nueva managed to secure a choke-hold on Dawson's throat. But the red scarf interfered with Nueva's attempt to throttle him. Dawson crashed a thudding fist into Nueva's kidney.

Nueva sprang back in agony, but picked up a bottle from the floor and swung it at Dawson's face. Dawson ducked and the bottle shattered against a post, splattering glass shrapnel and cutting Nueva's hand.

Dawson shot a left, then his right fist hard into Nueva's chest and chin. He lifted Nueva to his faltering legs by his bloody shirt as one of Nueva's compadres picked up a heavy spittoon and flung it hard toward Dawson's head.

Dawson saw it coming, ducked, keeping a grip on Nueva, as the spittoon splattered dark juice across the room and smashed through the front window of Baldy's saloon.

Dawson ripped another left and right into Nueva's gut

and face, propelling him across a table and onto the sawdust floor.

It was evident that the fight was concluded.

Dawson wiped at his face and brushed the sawdust from his scarf and jacket.

The bat-wings slammed open and Sheriff Ben Vesper stepped in from the street. At the same time a rotund, hairless man—obviously Baldy—lumbered in from a back room yelling.

"What the goddam hell's coming off here?"

"You!" The lawman took a step toward Dawson. "Come here to start trouble . . ."

"Didn't start it, Sheriff . . . just tried to finish it."

"That ain't all he finished." Baldy said, looking at the shambled saloon. "Look at this place!"

"Shut up, Baldy." Vesper took another step.

"Sheriff . . ." Alma moved closer from behind the bar. "He didn't . . ."

"You too, Alma." The sheriff said, then looked at Dawson. "We got a law in Pinto against vagrants . . ."

"He's no vagrant, Sheriff." It was Chad Walker's voice. "He's a friend of mine."

"Friend? Of *yours*?" The implication was clear. Chad Walker had never been known to call anybody in Pinto a friend. He had been "Mr. Walker" to everyone in and around the territory and had never extended a hand or word of friendship since he came to Texas.

"You heard, Sheriff. A friend of mine."

"Never mind that 'friend' crap." Baldy righted a chair that had tipped over, but the chair tilted unevenly on the floor since one of the four legs was broken. "Look at that! Look at all the damage! I don't care if he's a friend of Saint Jerome's—who's gonna pay for the damages?"

"I'll pay for the damages." Walker said.

It was hard to tell who in the room was the most surprised . . . Adam Dawson, Sheriff Ben Vesper, Alma, Nueva, his friends, or Baldy.

"Well, then..." Baldy began to brighten, figuring he might even make a little profit in the bargain.

"Except for the window," Walker added. "That's on *him*." Walker pointed at Nueva's spittoon-throwing compadre. "He broke it."

"That so, Paco?" Vesper asked.

"I said it, didn't I." Walker's tone was dark.

Paco nodded.

"You gonna pay?" Vesper asked the accused who was looking down at the floor.

"If you say, Sheriff." Paco gulped.

"I say."

"All right," Walker announced in a louder, deeper voice. "I'm standing a round of drinks for everybody. Make it two rounds. That includes you, Sheriff Vesper, now that you've done your duty." Walker came close to smiling. Sheriff Ben Vesper was not amused.

"Don't push it... *Mister* Walker." Vesper cast a parting look at Dawson then proceeded through the bat-wings.

A couple *compañeros* were helping Nueva to his feet and senses, another placed a chair under him when his legs didn't respond positively to the upright position.

Alma and Baldy already were distributing whiskey and beer among the ruins.

Dawson noticed that Walker was looking at him. Dawson nodded. That was as close to a "thanks" as he intended to acknowledge before leaving for he didn't know where.

"Come on over." Walker waved a hawser hand. "Sit down."

"That an order?" Dawson responded.

"Invitation."

Dawson still didn't move.

"You walk out of here now, Vesper'll arrest you for spitting on the boardwalk... or his pride. Come on, sit down."

Adam Dawson took a beat. Then retrieved his hat, rifle and saddlebag, and moved toward Walker's table. He set his possessions on one of the empty chairs, then reached down, picked up the ashtray and cigar, put the cigar into the ashtray, set it on the table and pushed it toward the big man. He sat down near Walker who smiled vaguely. "He's lucky you didn't kill him." Walker looked toward Nueva.

"I'm not in the killing business . . . anymore."

"What is your line of work?"

"Drifting."

Walker studied the stranger as Alma brought them a bottle and glasses. She carried a bar towel draped over her arm and smiled at Dawson.

"Somebody's come to town," she said and handed him the damp towel. "Here, use this, save the wear and tear on your scarf."

"Thanks," he said to Alma as she walked away.

"Yes sir," she added, "somebody's sure come to town."

Dawson wiped his hands and face, breathed deep and looked at Walker. This was the most unpredictable man Dawson had met since the war ended . . . and even before . . . except for Custer.

"Relax, Yank." Walker poured each of them a drink. "We're on the same side."

"The war's over." Dawson drank. So did Walker, who then poured again.

"Not around here." Walker's eyes swept the room. His voice was not discreet. "All these goddam Rebs, redskins and greasers. The place stinks of all of 'em."

"Yeah, well, I'm just passing through."

"Going somewhere in particular?"

"West." Dawson shrugged.

"I see you're still in uniform."

"Partly."

"You that proud of it?"

"I'm not ashamed. Besides, clothes cost money and I don't have much to spare."

"You know there's something about that red scarf I seem to recall."

"That so?"

"What outfit were you with?"

"Michigan Cavalry Brigade."

"You rode with Custer?!" Chad Walker could not, nor did not try to conceal his admiration.

"Nobody rode *with* Custer. We rode behind him."

"I'll be damned!" Walker grinned. "You were with George Armstrong Custer's Wolverines?!"

Dawson nodded.

"What rank?"

"Captain."

"I'll be damned!" he repeated. "Why aren't you still in?"

"Because I'm out."

"Yeah. You know I own a cattle ranch."

"Congratulations. I don't even own a horse."

"You in a hurry? To head West, I mean."

"My life's a clock with no hands."

"Want a job?" Walker's voice bordered on eager. "With me?"

"Doing what? Picking up your butts?" Dawson glanced at the ashtray.

"Know anything about cattle?"

"Some."

"Just sold most of my stock, but I'll be running a new herd. Meanwhile, room, horse to ride, and twenty a month, Yankee dollars . . . and all the beef you can eat."

"Well, I've worked for peanuts. Beef is a big step up."

"Sure it is. Were you with him at Gettysburg . . . Custer?"

"And other places."

"I'll be damned! We got a lot to talk about . . . course I was never any captain."

"So what? I never owned a cattle ranch."

"Let's go."

Dawson rose, hoisted his saddlebag, picked up his Winchester and indicated toward Joe Nueva.

"Why'd you goad him?"

"Nueva? Wanted to see something. Something about you. I liked what I saw. Besides, I never did like that Mex—or any of them."

"Then why'd you hire him?"

"Had to hire somebody—and Mex or not, he was the best 'til you came along, Yank."

"Yeah." Dawson rubbed his chin where one of Nueva's punches had landed.

Chad Walker pushed away from the table. He struggled with painful effort to rise as he pulled two wooden canes from one of the chairs under the table. It was evident that without the support of the canes his legs could not move and sustain the weight of his body. Dawson did his best to contain his surprise and his empathy. He looked away as quickly as he could.

"You don't have to look away, Yank. I didn't get off as lucky as some."

Dawson just nodded, then followed as Chad Walker dragged himself through the room leaving a trail across the sawdust on the floor.

"Nueva." Walker paused in front of the bowed and beaten man, still on the chair, who responded to the sound of the voice.

"Yes sir."

"Pick up your gear at the ranch, Joe. You're fired." Walker motioned to Dawson. "Come on . . . uh, what's your name, Captain?"

"Name's Adam . . . Adam Dawson, Mister Walker."

"Adam. Like the first man, huh? Well, come on, Adam." Walker started for the bat-wings and called back, "Put the bill on my account, Baldy. And don't try to pull a fast one."

Dawson maneuvered to move ahead and hold open the bat-wings but Walker elbowed him aside.

"Hey . . . I don't need any help."

And he didn't. Chad Walker crashed through the bat-wings with a vengeance.

Adam Dawson followed without looking back.

Four

The afternoon shadows cast cooling shade along the west side of Pinto's main street. A few more citizens had come out onto the boardwalk. Men and women, a few children. It looked to Dawson more like a village in Mexico instead of the United States. Anglos were outnumbered about two to one by the duskier natives.

As they passed, Anglos and Mexicans alike widened the distance between where they walked and where Chad Walker stood with Dawson beside him in front of the saloon. Nobody spoke to Walker, barely glanced at him, they also did their best to avoid stepping on the shattered glass—and spittoon—on the boardwalk.

Walker looked up and down the street, and still holding a cane in his right hand, managed to pull a gold watch attached to a thick gold chain from his vest pocket, flip the lid and check the time.

"Where the hell is she? Told her to be out here waiting by now. I'll kick her ass."

Dawson had no notion who Walker was talking about and made no comment, but did think to himself that in Walker's physical condition he was in no shape to kick anybody's ass.

Chad Walker pushed the gold watch back into his vest pocket as Baldy waddled through the bat-wings and spotted the spittoon on the boardwalk. He smiled at Walker who was in no mood to smile back and didn't.

It wasn't easy for Baldy to bend down and pick up the spittoon, but he did, and wiped some of the spittle off his hands onto the already stained apron that barely made it around his girth.

"Don't you worry, Mr. Walker, you'll get an honest count from me . . . always do . . . Brendon Alsap is as honest as the day's long . . . honester."

"Bullshit, Baldy." Walker replied as Brendon Alsap and the spittoon took up most of the space going back through the bat-wings. "Damn Rebs," Walker added, "can't trust a damn one of 'em . . . and I don't. Not barkeeps or bankers . . . say Adam, how many Rebs you reckon you killed?"

"Didn't count," Dawson said.

"Well, I did. I counted twenty-seven . . .'till Shiloh . . . goddam Rebs damn near whipped us there."

"Mostly they did."

"But not finally," Walker said with satisfaction. As he looked up the street again Sheriff Ben Vesper approached. "Going in to collect that free drink, Sheriff?"

"Going to get a haircut, Mr. Walker." Vesper intended to keep moving but Walker had more to say.

"By the way, Sheriff," Walker went on, "you two fellows haven't been introduced. This here is Captain Adam Walker, late of the Michigan Wolverines."

Neither Vesper nor Dawson said anything. Walker didn't give them much of an opportunity, he kept on talking.

"And you won't have to worry about him being a vagrant. The captain is going to work for me out at the ranch . . . but you better keep an eye on your friend Nueva, he doesn't have a job anymore . . . and I wouldn't trust that pepperbelly as far as . . ."

Sheriff Ben Vesper already was on his way toward the barber shop.

"Damn Mexes . . . they all stick together . . . Vesper, he's part Mex, his . . ." But Walker's attention was diverted by something else. So was Dawson's.

Dawson recognized the buckboard and the woman. It

was impossible not to recognize her, even at this distance.

She wore that soft, white summer dress that as she drove the wagon, cohered to every curve of her smooth, sensual body. A body that would give a priest pause, and a face each man cultivates in the garden of his dreams.

"There she is now," Walker said. "My wife."

Adam Dawson didn't know what to say . . . or do. So he said and did nothing. Just waited until the buckboard pulled close and stopped.

It was apparent to Dawson—the exact second she recognized him. For less than an instant she lost that assured composure in her azure eyes, but for only less than an instant, as their eyes met.

She stepped off the buckboard as regally as a queen might step off a carriage. Calm and cool in the vapid heat of a simmering Texas town.

"Where the hell have you been?" Walker barked.

"Where I usually am on Saturday afternoon, at the mission . . . helping Padre Ramos." She extended her slender hand to Dawson. "I'm Lorena. Chad's wife."

The man he had seen with her sure as hell wasn't any padre. But Dawson took her hand, briefly. Her fingers were long and sentient, and he was downwind of the most expensive and provocative perfume he had ever smelled in his life.

"Adam Dawson."

"Nice to meet you, Mr. Dawson."

"He's taking Nueva's place," Walker said. "That all right with you?"

"Do I have a choice?"

"No. Let's get out of this stinkhole." Walker began to clump toward the buckboard.

Lorena looked at the broken window and shattered glass in front of the saloon.

"What happened to Baldy's window?"

"It got broke," Walker said reaching for the buckboard.

"I'll drive if you want, Mr. Walker," Dawson said.

"You think I can't drive a buckboard?"

"I just . . ."

"Don't need legs to drive a goddam wagon. Hey, Lorena, Adam here was in the war with us."

"I gathered as much." She smiled, glancing at Dawson. "And from the looks of him it seems he's just been in another one."

"No contest. He whipped the hell out of Nueva. Adam fought with Custer at Gettysburg . . . and other places. He's gonna tell us all about it."

Dawson and Lorena waited while Walker hauled himself up and strapped his body into the seat of the buckboard. He stuffed his canes into a custom-made leather boot beside him and picked up the reins.

Adam Dawson watched as Lorena's graceful body glided up to the seat next to her husband. He thought to himself . . . nobody's wife should look, or move like that, or use that fragrance of perfume. He tossed the saddlebag into the bed of the wagon then placed his Winchester on top of the bag. He climbed up to the seat beside her and made sure there was some space between himself and Mrs. Walker.

Walker took the reins in both hands but paused as the rider astride the palomino approached.

Once again Adam Dawson didn't know how to react . . . so he tried not to. If Mrs. Walker was disquieted, she gave no indication. Her face and eyes remained serene. Her expression almost beatific.

"Good afternoon, Mr. Walker, Mrs. Walker." The man on the palomino tipped the gray Stetson atop his square face and smiled. If he recognized Dawson—and he must have—he made no acknowledgment. Just kept on riding. Mrs. Walker had responded with a slight nod, Chad Walker had continued to look straight ahead.

"Asshole," Walker said. Maybe the man on the palomino heard, maybe not. Walker didn't seem to care either way. But Mrs. Walker did.

"For heaven's sake, Chad. Would it kill you to be civil for once in your life?"

"Asshole is what Brad Hatcher *is*—and always will be."

"Oh, for Heaven's sake," Lorena repeated.

"Hold on," Walker said and cracked the reins over the backs of the blacks. The horses took off with the buckboard down the rutted street that led out of town.

Brad Hatcher dismounted and tied the reins to the hitching post in front of Baldy's Bar. He stood for a moment and watched the departing wagon moving away from Pinto ... the wagon carrying Chad and Lorena Walker ... and the stranger. Then Hatcher took note of the broken window and moved through the bat-wings, into the saloon.

Joe Nueva still sat in a chair by a corner table. His right hand was wrapped in a blood-stained bar towel. On his face and body other evidence of his recent encounter, cuts, bruises and discoloration in the vicinity of the left eye. Brad Hatcher walked past Nueva and headed to the bar.

"Afternoon, Mr. Hatcher," Alma greeted as he placed both hands on the counter.

"Hello, Alma, I'll have ..."

"I know, Mr. Hatcher, your bottle from the top shelf, already on the way." And it was. Alma set the quart of Tennessee Turkey bourbon on the bar, uncorked the nearly full bottle and placed a clean glass next to it.

"Thanks, Alma."

As Hatcher sipped the bourbon, Baldy, with a pad and pencil, came out of the back room, stood looking around trying to decide where to begin his assessment of the damages.

"Say, Alma, looks like there's been a little excitement around here." Hatcher smiled.

"You might say that, Mr. Hatcher. How's Mrs. Hatcher?"

"Huh? Oh, she's fine, just fine. What happened? Looks like Joe Nueva ran into a cyclone."

"You might say *that* too ... a Yankee cyclone, good looking and good with his fists."

"The sheriff been around?"

"Yeah, but it's all been settled thanks to Mr. Walker."

"Walker? What's ..."

"Good afternoon, Mr. Hatcher," Baldy said as he penciled down a number. "How you doin'?"

"I'm doing fine. Baldy, Alma says that Chad Walker . . ."

"Never seen him like he acted today, Mr. Hatcher. At first he was his usual self, you know, surly . . . and shitty . . ."

"Yeah, I know." Hatcher took another sip.

"Well sir, then this stranger come in mindin' his own beeswax and pretty soon Walker sics Nueva on to him . . . you can see the results of the ruckus." Baldy waved around at the room and then pointed at Nueva.

"Yeah, I see," Hatcher said.

"This bluebelly settled Nueva's hash, showed him how the cow ate the cabbage, he . . ."

"I get the idea."

"So did Joe . . . but the capper is, Walker fires what's left of Nueva, hires the stranger to go to work on his ranch, then they walk outta here like two long lost brothers after Walker stands up for the bluebelly in front of Vesper and tells me he'll pay for the damages . . . don't that beat all . . . ?"

"Yeah . . . what'd you say that stranger's name was?"

"Don't remember . . . do you, Alma?"

"Think he said Dawson . . . or Lawson, but whatever it is, I'll tell you one thing, Mr. Hatcher . . . he's gonna be worth watching."

Brad Hatcher poured himself another drink, wiped his mouth, which had become alkali dry, and drank the bourbon in a single swallow.

Five

With Chad Walker at the reins, Lorena and Adam Dawson beside him, the buckboard rattled along the wagon trail across land that was flat. Dawson did his best to keep his face and eyes straight ahead and to his right, with his body as close to the edge of the wagon seat and as far away from Mrs. Walker as he could get.

"How do you like my rig, Adam?" Walker asked.

"Great," Dawson answered, now looking past the perfect profile of Mrs. Walker. "Those animals know how to step."

"Yeah, I guess you'd know good horseflesh, what with being in the cavalry and all."

"I've known some . . . and lost some."

"What'd you say happened to your mount?"

"Didn't. But I was ambushed."

"Mexicans?"

"Comancheros, I think."

"Same scum."

"Chad," Lorena said, "to you everybody's scum . . . red, black or brown."

"Most whites too . . . around here."

"Then why do we stay?"

"You know why."

Maybe she does, Dawson thought, but he, himself, didn't, and since Lorena didn't pursue the topic, neither did Dawson.

Later they splashed across a stream, the same stream

Dawson had drunk from, but far from the spot where he had first seen Mrs. Walker and Mr. Hatcher.

Still later the buckboard was climbing, making its way along a narrow, winding, precipitous summit.

"Be careful, Chad, this slope's dangerous. They don't call it Devil's Drop for nothing. You're going too damn fast."

"You want to get out and walk . . . Mrs. Walker?" he snapped.

"Just be careful, will you please, Chad? *Please?!*"

"Sure, sure . . . beautiful country, isn't it, Adam?"

"Great."

"Too good for these damn foreigners that . . ."

"Oh, Chad, please don't start that again . . ."

"Okay, okay . . . *please* this and *please* that . . . just about all I do is have to *please* you . . . and speaking of foreigners why the hell does that Mex padre need your help at the mission?"

It occurred to Adam Dawson that in that clean, white, gossamer summer dress she was wearing, Lorena Walker couldn't do much work at a mission or anywhere else. He wondered if that ever occurred to Mr. Walker. If it did, he evidently hadn't mentioned it . . . or at least didn't mention it now.

"The mission and Padre Ramos need all the help they can get," Lorena replied. "So do the people who come there. Besides, I just like going there for a change."

"Change from what? From me?" He snickered.

"You ought to go there sometime, Chad. Might be good for you."

"It's only good for simple-minded greasers who need to listen to fairy tales."

"Chad, for . . ."

"Don't say 'for heaven's sake' again. Just turn it off, Lorena!" Walker snarled. "Just turn it off!"

"It's off," she said.

Adam Dawson thought to himself that, right then, he ought to grab his saddlebag and rifle, leap off that buckboard and leave the both of them. But there he sat with the taste of beer and blood in his mouth and the scent of her perfume in his brain—instead of doing something sensible—like joining up with Custer again and killing, or being killed by, Indians.

A couple of Mexican workers were boarding up the broken window of Baldy's Bar as Sheriff Vesper came out of Tony Amado's Barber Shop/Undertaking Parlor. The sheriff put on his hat which fit him looser than when he went in. And there emanated from him the sweet fragrance of lilac lotion that Tony Amado was so enamored of, enamored so much that Tony even splashed it with a lavish hand onto his customers who were corpses. Vesper looked east and west on the street, reflected a mite, then headed toward Baldy's Bar.

Inside the saloon Hatcher poured himself another Tennessee Turkey and reflected a mite on the day's turn of events and how those events could continue to turn with the advent of the stranger who had witnessed Hatcher's tryst with Mrs. Walker at the stream.

Brad Hatcher had assured Lorena that there was no need for concern. "Just a drifter," he had said. But evidently this "drifter" wasn't going to drift. Worse, it appeared that Lawson or Dawson, whatever his name was, had become part of Chad Walker's outfit, at least for the time being. Alma had said that "he's gonna be worth watching." Hatcher intended to do just that, from a distance. A safe distance. Hatcher was playing for a big stake, bigger than Lorena, or Chad Walker, or Hatcher's own wife, or anybody else, knew. He'd find out a few things the next time he met Lorena. But meeting Lorena might not be quite so easy with the drifter nosing around. And the stream was out from now on. But there was still the line shack where they had met before, and it was safer and a lot more . . . intimate. As Hatcher thought about those intimacies his thoughts were interrupted.

"Mr. Hatcher." Hatcher recognized Joe Nueva's voice even before he turned and saw that up close, Walker's former foreman was even more battered than he had appeared to be from a distance. His left eye now was swollen shut as well as discolored into a prime blue. From inside the deviated bridge of his expanded nose there was still a smear of red leakage.

"Hello, Joe. What the hell happened to you?" Hatcher said as if he didn't already know.

"Aww, some drifter jumped me."

"With an axe?" Hatcher took pleasure in rubbing it in. He had never much liked Nueva. The Mexican was too damned uppity and thought of himself as good enough for any woman, brown or white. Good enough even for his former boss's wife . . . and the thought of Nueva laying hands on Lorena infuriated Hatcher.

"He'll get his," Nueva said, and as he did, Sheriff Vesper walked by and went toward the end of the bar. "I ain't finished with that drifter yet, but Mr. Hatcher, I was wonderin' if I could ask you somethin'."

"Go ahead and ask."

"I was wonderin' if, well, if you need a good hand . . . at your ranch . . ."

"Who? You?" Hatcher poured himself another drink with no intention of asking Nueva to join him.

"Yeah. Sure." Nueva knew he had been insulted by the *gringo*, but tried his best not to let it show. "I'm a top hand. Everybody around here knows that."

"Sure they do, Joe." Hatcher sipped his whiskey, then held the half-filled glass in his hand and pointed it toward Nueva. "But I thought you had a job . . . with that cripple."

"Not anymore."

"No?"

"I quit."

Alma heard, and smiled as she reached for a bottle from the backbar then moved away toward Sheriff Vesper at the far end of the bar.

"*Quit*, did you, Joe?" Hatcher sipped again instead of answering Nueva's question.

"That's right. Well, do you, Mr. Hatcher?"

"This drifter ... who jumped you ... he the bluebelly who came into Pinto today?

"Yeah."

"Well, Joe," Hatcher paused just long enough to let Nueva dangle uncomfortably, "right now I'm full up, but ... something might just happen. I'll let you know ... if you're around."

"I'll be around. I appreciate that, Mr. Hatcher. I'm a top hand you know," Nueva repeated.

"Yeah, I know," Hatcher concluded as he turned away.

"Thanks Mr. Hatcher," Nueva said to the back of Hatcher's hat, then Nueva walked away toward his friends at the corner table.

Alma poured Sheriff Ben Vesper his second drink. "You sure do smell mighty purty, Ben. Mighty purty."

"Lilacs." Vesper nodded. "Ol' Tony must buy it by the barrel."

"I ..." Alma leaned across the bar and whispered so nobody but the sheriff could hear. "I like that ... musky, private kinda smell a lot better on you ... know what I mean, Ben?" She gave him that private kind of smile she bestowed only on a privileged few in Pinto.

Sheriff Ben Vesper cleared his throat, even though it didn't need clearing, as Brad Hatcher brought the bottle of Tennessee Turkey and himself closer to the lawman.

"Have a drink, Sheriff?"

"No, thanks. Already had my quota."

"A man of moderation, huh, Sheriff?"

"In some things. Not in others," Vesper said as Alma swayed away.

"Say, what do you make of that stranger who drifted into town today?"

"Don't make anything of him. Unless he makes trouble."

"I heard that he already has." Hatcher looked around the saloon. "Right here."

"Were you here, Mr. Hatcher?"

"No."

"Well, I was. Close after, anyhow. Anything else on your mind, Mr. Hatcher?"

"Not if you don't want to have a drink."

Sheriff Vesper walked past Brad Hatcher toward the batwings, but paused then moved closer to the corner table.

"Joe."

"Yeah, Sheriff, what now?"

"You want it private . . . or in front of your amigos?"

"Go ahead." Nueva tried to grin even though it hurt.

"I heard what you said back there to Hatcher."

"What did I say? I forget."

"About you not being through with that drifter."

"So?"

"So listen. I don't want any trouble in Pinto, not from you, or him, or anybody else. You . . . or your amigos start any, trouble, that is, and I'll come down on you hard . . . so hard you'll think what you got today was a picnic. *Comprende?*"

"Don't worry, Sheriff. There ain't gonna be any trouble . . . not in Pinto."

"Or anywhere in my jurisdiction."

"*Jurisdiction?* What's that, Sheriff?"

"It's what I want it to be." Vesper turned and walked out. Not fast. Not slow.

The buckboard with Walker, Lorena and Adam Dawson aboard turned off the trail and rolled to a stop just in front of a huge wooden gateway. There was no fence on either side. It seemed that the only purpose of the gateway was to support a large sign onto which were burned prominent letters.

WALKER'S WAY

Chad Walker snapped the reins. The team responded and the wagon passed beneath the sign and kept moving.

"This is it." Walker grinned.

"Some spread." Dawson grinned back.

"Take a man on a good horse days to cover it. Thousands of acres of the finest grazing land on this man's earth. I only keep a couple of day hands around right now for chores and repairs 'til I bring down the next herd."

"I don't see any fences."

"You won't. Don't need 'em."

"Suppose those cattle you bring down start wandering?"

"Wherever they wander they'll be on my land."

"Sounds like you're bigger than some countries."

"Nope . . . there's bigger spreads, but I got plenty of something that most of 'em lack."

Dawson couldn't help but think of Walker's wife sitting next to him but he knew the rancher wasn't talking about her.

"What's that?"

"Water. Been a drought. Not enough rain to wash the dust off a bullfrog. But I got a strong stream comes down from that high country." He nodded toward the sun hovering above a saw-tooth ridge. "Like having a flowing gold mine."

"I guess," Dawson jerked the thumb of his right hand behind him, "that sign back there says it all . . . 'Walker's Way.' "

"Yeah," Lorena Walker emphasized, "Mister Chad Walker's way."

"You're damn well told," Mister Chad Walker added.

There were long slanting shadows as the buckboard approached the ranch house. The structure was Spanish, two storied, with a porch.

In the distance Dawson could make out a large chicken coop and fenced yard with a small shack also inside the fence. Beyond was a barn and tack room and then bunkhouses.

The buckboard creaked to a halt near the porch where an old man, rope thin, sat on a rocking chair with a worn bible on his bony lap.

Adam Dawson stood, then jumped off the buckboard and turned to help Mrs. Walker while Chad struggled with his canes.

"Welcome home, Mister Chad, Miz Lorena," the old man called out. "Who's that with you?"

"This is Adam Dawson, Uriah," Walker called back. "Ex-Yankee. He's taking Joe Nueva's place."

"Welcome, brother Adam." The old man smiled as he rose holding the Bible. "Thou shalt eat the labor of thine hands. Make a joyful noise unto the Lord."

Dawson approached the porch and extended his hand. The old man ignored the gesture but continued to smile.

"Uriah's blind, Adam," Walker said. "Mexican War. Served with General Winfield Scott, your old boss . . . and mine."

Dawson withdrew his hand awkwardly.

"Pleased to meet you . . . Uriah."

"Thank you kindly, brother Adam." Uriah lifted a large basket of eggs from beside the rocker. "Sorry I missed you this morning, Mr. Chad. But the Lord has provided in abundance. The word of God grew and multiplied." He held up the largest brown egg. "And this is the gift of Vashti, the queen. She's my favorite, Mr. Adam. From the book of Esther."

Uriah replaced the egg and held out the basket. Walker motioned to Lorena who came closer and took it from the old man.

"Thanks, Uriah." She smiled.

"Thank you, Miz Lorena. Pleased to make your acquaintance, brother Adam." Uriah groped for a cane that leaned against the rocker. He grasped it and tapped his way off the porch and proceeded toward the chicken yard. "See you tomorrow," he called back and started to hum a hymn.

"Good night, Trooper." Chad Walker waved one of his canes.

Dawson watched as the old man headed directly toward the chicken coop and shack inside the yard.

"Is he . . . completely blind?" Dawson asked.

"As a bat."

"But he knew somebody was with you . . ."

"He heard you. Old Uriah could hear a flea buzzing in a herd of buffalo." Walker turned and looked around at his empire. "Well, Adam, take a good look. I'll show you around tomorrow. This might just be as far west as you ever want to go."

"I don't know about that."

"Hell, what's out West that we ain't got here? Maybe better lookin' whores in San Francisco. Couldn't say, though, never been there."

"Chad!" Lorena blurted.

"*Lorena!*" Walker mocked. "What's wrong with whores? Supposed to be the oldest profession. At least they're open and honest about it."

Dawson had been looking at a Chinese rickshaw near the front of the porch. He pointed to it as much to change the subject of whores as anything else.

"Well, now, that's something."

"Yeah, a rickshaw. Bought it from a Chinese restaurant in St. Louis. They kept it out in front as sort of advertising. Comes in handy for getting around the ranch here. One of the greasers pulls me usually."

"Or else I do," Lorena said.

"Got a target range out there too." Walker ignored his wife's remark. "Anyway, you'll sleep in the house tonight 'til Nueva comes and cleans out his junk. That okay?"

"Anything you say."

"Well, let's get inside. I'm hungry enough to eat a swamper's boot."

"I'll put away the team before it gets dark." Dawson pointed to the barn. "Get my gear and be right in."

"Good." Walker grinned. "Yeah, I got a feeling this is gonna work out all 'round, huh, Lorena?"

"Anything you say." Lorena repeated Dawson's words. "Anything you say." She moved up the porch toward the front door carrying the basket of eggs.

Adam Dawson did his best not to notice the way that

she moved. Before Lorena reached the front door it was opened from inside and a young Mexican girl stepped onto the porch. She could not have been more than sixteen, if that. She had the look of a frightened fawn with round dark eyes, high cheekbones and large, full lips unpainted but naturally red. She wore a plain brown dress that fell straight from her shoulders and unbound breasts. She was bent slightly forward in an attitude of humility or even subservience. She reached out a slender brown hand toward the basket that Lorena carried.

'I will take that, if you like, *señora*."

"Oh, thank you, Elena."

"*De nada.*" Elena took the basket and waited at the doorway for Lorena to pass. But Mrs. Walker turned back and looked past her husband who was making his way onto the porch with the help of his canes.

"Adam, I'd like you to meet someone. Elena, this is Mr. Adam Dawson, he's going to work here on the ranch. Elena helps me take care of the house."

"Nice to meet you, Elena." Adam Dawson tipped his hat and smiled.

"Yeah." Chad Walker wasn't smiling as he clomped by the girl. "He's gonna take the place of that greaser friend of yours. Hope you won't be too disappointed."

"Chad!" Lorena exclaimed.

" 'Chad' my ass." Walker stomped forward toward the entrance and spoke without even looking at the girl. "Quit blocking the door."

Dawson turned and moved toward the team as Lorena put an arm around the girl's shoulder and patted Elena's arm.

Six

The Conestoga's canvas top, ribbed with curved wooden frames, swayed gently like billowed sails, as the creaking wagon rolled southwest, pulled by a two-up team of tired horses ending a long day's journey.

The driver, a smiling, freckled, lanky Irishman, Tim O'Donnell, twenty-three years of age, held the reins and partly sang, partly hummed the words and melody of the old Irish favorite, "Wild Colonial Boy." His fairer, but alabaster smooth-faced wife Maureen, with blazing red hair beneath her bonnet sat beside him, emerald green eyes straight ahead locked onto the barren horizon. Tim glanced at his beautiful bride of less than a year and continued the tune.

> "She loved a wild colonial boy, Jack Dolan was his
> name,
> A poor but honest baby he was born in Castlemaine,
> He was his father's only hope, his mother's only joy,
> And dearly did his fairies love their wild colonial
> boy...

... what is it, Maureen? You haven't said a word in more than an hour. Is my singin' that bad? I'd've thought you'd be used to it by now..."

"I was just thinkin', Tim."

"About what?"

"Oh, about how different this . . . this place is from Limerick."

"It isn't very . . . green, is it?" O'Donnell looked around and grinned.

"Not at all." She tried to smile.

"It'll be greener where we're headed. Jamie says there's a river near the ranch, name of Rio Grande and a lovely place called Laredo, where he's made a good start and we can do the same."

"Your brother always was an optimist, and so are you, Timothy O'Donnell." This time she did smile.

"Is that why you married me? For me optimism?"

"Well, it wasn't for your looks. You couldn't hold a candle to Brian McCarty."

"And there wasn't a girl in the ol' sod who could hold a candle to your fair face and frame . . ."

"Timmy . . ."

"It's true. That's why I married you. That and your dowry." He laughed.

"Less than a fortune."

"I wouldn't care if it was less than a shilling, so long as you came with it. Did you ever notice the wart on McCarty's nose? Big as a prune, it was."

"It was not." She poked him in the ribs. Then her face became serious. "It *will* be all right, won't it, Timmy? Here in America?"

"Sure it will. It couldn't be worse than what we left behind, with people starvin' and leavin' in droves . . . another few years and there won't be enough people left in Ireland to fill a pub. And our son will be born here, an American."

"Timmy, I'm not even certain that I'm . . . well . . ."

"Pregnant? Go ahead and say it, there's nobody around. Well, I am. I can tell, and I can tell that it'll be a boy."

"Can you now?"

"Indeed. And I can tell you something else."

"What?"

"He won't have a wart on his beak and his name won't be Brian."

"Oh, go on." She poked him again and he began again to sing and hum.

"He was scarcely sixteen years of age when he left his father's home, and through Australia's sunny clime . . ."

"Tim!" she screamed.

"I see 'em!"

He lashed the reins as shots rang out and the riders, more than a dozen, swarmed down the flank of the hill, Corona in the lead, laughing and firing.

Even if the team of horses hadn't been tired there was no chance to outrun the Comancheros. They raced across the desert and closed in on the swaying wagon. Bullets tore into the canvas and wood of the Conestoga and one tore into the chest of Tim O'Donnell.

He lurched up then plunged from the moving wagon and bounced hard on the ground as Maureen kept screaming. The driverless horses plopped to a stop as the riders circled, then reined in their mounts.

Maureen jumped from the wagon and raced to her fallen husband. Corona, Diaz and Charly dismounted while the rest of the Comancheros laughed and holstered their weapons.

"You've killed him! He's dead!" she shrieked. But O'Donnell stirred slightly.

"Not yet." Corona grinned, then fired two shots into the man on the ground and holstered the gun.

Hysterical, she leaped at Corona and began to pound at his face and chest. He clubbed his fist into her face and she dropped to the earth unconscious, her bonnet falling away from her head.

Corona looked down at her as she lay next to the dead body of her husband.

"Red hair," he sniggered. "The Comanches are gonna like that . . . and so do I." Diaz and Charly nodded and laughed. "Tie her up and toss her in the wagon."

"What about him?" Diaz pointed.

"Buzzards."

Later the Conestoga, driven by Diaz and surrounded by Corona and the raiders, rolled into the *ranchería* greeted by cheers and laughs from the Comancheros who had stayed behind.

The first to greet them was Olita as Corona dismounted.

"One wagon and a couple of bony horses?" she remarked.

"There's something inside." Corona looked up at Diaz and motioned. "Bring her out."

"Sure." Diaz nodded. "Charly, give me a hand."

Olita's dark face turned even darker as the two Comancheros brought the woman, her hands still tied behind her, down from the wagon.

"She'll bring a good price ... later," Corona said, then looked at Olita. "Or maybe I decide to keep her. Red's my favorite color."

Maureen O'Donnell was still in shock as Corona grabbed hold of her long red tresses. But her eyes widened and she screamed again. Corona slapped her hard, tore off his bandana and stuffed it into her mouth. He lifted her over his right shoulder and walked toward his hut, whistling.

Everybody laughed. Everybody except Olita who stood silently watching.

"Looks like," Diaz beamed, "Corona's going to have some company tonight."

Olita slapped him across his dirty face and stalked away.

The rest of the Comancheros laughed even harder.

Seven

It was almost dark as Brad Hatcher rode his palomino past the Walker's Way gate toward his own ranch, Spanish Bit. Hatcher hadn't bought Spanish Bit, he had married it. He had married it when he wooed and wed Mary Ann Beaudine over seven years ago, shortly after her father, Jason Beaudine, conveniently cleared the path by dying.

Alive, Jason Beaudine had been an insurmountable obstruction on that path. His ranch and his daughter were the only things the roughhewn rancher loved since his wife Sarah died while delivering of a stillborn son when Mary Ann was five years of age. Sarah, Jason and the baby were buried on a hillside of Spanish Bit. Mary Ann, who was now in her mid-thirties, still visited and placed flowers on the graves every Sunday. It was her intention to be buried beside them when the time came.

It couldn't come soon enough to suit Brad Hatcher.

Mary Ann was not unpleasant to look at. Or to touch. She was comely. But cold. Brad Hatcher craved a warm woman. Women. He was voracious in his craving.

Jason Beaudine had heard rumors about Hatcher shortly after Hatcher had settled in Pinto. While Beaudine was in Mobile on business he had heard about a man named Hatcher who left town one step ahead of the law. Something to do with defrauding a woman out of her land after killing her husband in a duel. And there were stories about that same

Hatcher in connection with the importation of slaves, which had become illegal.

Beaudine didn't give a damn what Hatcher had done, or was planning on doing, until Mr. Hatcher began paying uncommon attention to Beaudine's comely daughter. To Beaudine, Mary Ann was not just comely, she was the most beautiful, the most precious, the most angelic creation in heaven and earth. She was also on the dark side of her twenties.

Beaudine figured that somewhere on earth there was a man suitable, if not quite good enough, for his daughter. But that man was not in Pinto. And it sure as hell wasn't Brad Hatcher.

It began when Hatcher started coming to church services and week after week, sitting closer, row by row, then seat by seat to Mary Ann Beaudine. Still several seats away but too damn close as far as Jason was concerned.

Hatcher always remained respectful and courtly, but Jason didn't want courtly to turn into courtship. On his business travels to the bigger towns and cities in Texas and other Southern states, Beaudine always kept his eyes and ears open on the lookout for a Southern gentleman with proper credentials, breeding and background who would be suitable as a husband to Mary Ann. Beaudine had even selected several worthy prospects and intended to take Mary Ann with him on his trips and make sure she met those he deemed worthy enough.

But events at Fort Sumter on April 12, 1861, preempted any and all such prospects when the Confederates opened fire. Texas had already seceded from the Union, so had Mississippi, Florida, Alabama, Georgia, Louisiana, all preceded by South Carolina on December 20, 1860.

The only prospect for any Southern gentleman became war.

But somehow Brad Hatcher had failed to hear, or, at least respond, to the call to arms. He made known far and wide his intention to join up and was casting about for the brigade he would lead. But that intention wasn't yet transformed into action by the time Jason Beaudine was struck down and snuffed out by a sudden heart attack.

And so, the insurmountable object in Hatcher's path turned into a mound of earth and good fortune.

Brad Hatcher joined the mourners and gave succor to Beaudine's only survivor...and heir. Spanish Bit was swarming with beef. And the Confederacy needed beef. In Hatcher's opinion more than it need him to lead a brigade. And Mary Ann needed someone to console, comfort and according to Brad Hatcher, marry and take care of her...and Spanish Bit.

Mary Ann Beaudine had never stepped inside of a bank, written a check or made a financial decision. Mary Ann Hatcher would not have to. Her husband would handle all of her affairs. And he did. For over seven years.

But there was one affair that neither one could handle. The one between them.

From their wedding night, when Brad Hatcher made the mistake of lust instead of love, their times of intimacy held nothing but terror for Mary Ann. From that time on she closed her eyes and submitted in silence. He rued his mistake of that first night and did his best to make up for it, with gentleness, tenderness, with restraint, but the response was always the same. No response.

Brad Hatcher never went to war. He never had any intention of going and would have found some excuse to avoid that hazard. But supplying beef for the cause gave him excuse enough. He stayed in Pinto and became one of its leading citizens, was even elected to the City Council, even though Pinto wasn't a city.

He continued to go to church every Sunday with Mary Ann and now, of course, to sit next to her, sing the hymns with her, smile and smile and have her from time to time sign papers that gave him complete control of Spanish Bit.

More and more Mary Ann found solace in her Bible and in cats. First it was one cat. She named him Hector. Hector needed companionship. So he wouldn't have to leave Mary Ann to seek companions, she provided him a feline friend,

Hecuba. Soon Hector and Hecuba begat a litter, then litters. Most of their progeny, much to Brad Hatcher's annoyance, resided at Spanish Bit, sometime even sleeping in Mary Ann's bedroom and bed. Hatcher found separate sleeping quarters in an adjoining room.

Their intimacies became less and less frequent and more and more silent. During the days they spoke almost formally and during the infrequent nights when he chased away the cats and came to her bed he stayed only long enough to take what he wanted and retire to the adjoining room. Leaving Mary Ann with her cats and her Bible.

It wasn't long before Brad Hatcher found what he wanted, what he needed, at other places with other women.

The less he came to her, the better the marriage, if marriage it could be called. The war ended badly for the Confederacy and Texas. To make matters worse, Texas, as well as their marriage, was hit by a drought. Brad Hatcher could live with the marriage drought. But he needed water for Spanish Bit.

What he really needed was a spread called Walker's Way.

Eight

Elena had brought a fresh pitcher of warmed water and a large bowl with soap and towels for Adam Dawson so he could wash up before supper.

He thanked her with just about all the Spanish he knew.

"*Gracias*, Elena."

She nodded and started walking toward the open door to the hallway.

"Just a minute, Elena." She turned back. There was a look of apprehension in her eyes as he spoke. "What's your last name, Elena?"

"Garcia, *señor*."

"Garcia. Elena Garcia. That's a nice name," he said as politely as he could and smiled.

"Thank you." Elena Garcia did her best to smile.

"Have you worked for ... Mrs. Walker long, Elena?"

"Almost a year now, *señor*. She is very good to me ..."

"You have a family?"

"Far away in Mexico. I came here because I thought it would be ... better."

"And is it?"

There was a moment of silence.

"In some ways, but ..."

"But what?"

Elena Garcia shrugged.

"You miss your family?"

"In some ways."

"Well, everything takes a little getting used to."

This time Elena nodded and did smile.

"I hope everything works out well for you."

"Thank you, *señor*. I have to help Mrs. Walker now for the food . . . with the food," she corrected. "I try to speak the . . . American, but I'm still . . . not so good with it, I . . ."

"You do very good . . . very *well* . . . and thanks again." Dawson pointed toward the pitcher on the dresser.

Elena Garcia nodded, bowed slightly and left the room.

Dawson untied the red scarf and let it drop gently onto the dresser beside the hat he had taken off earlier.

He looked down at the scarf and thought of some of the places where he had worn it since he and the other cavalrymen of the Michigan Brigade adopted it as part of their uniform in emulation of, and tribute to Custer. In battles, mostly won. And afterward, an emblem of victory and remembrance of comrades left behind.

He intended to wear it as long as it could be worn, then put it away with a letter saying he wished to be buried with it around his throat.

Somehow, he knew he would never write such a letter. A lot of good the letter would have done today in the desert with those Comancheros who were out to rob and kill him. Well, at least he had made it this far. As far as Walker's Way.

As Dawson wet, then washed his face with the soap, he thought again about what he had said to himself aboard the buckboard, about gathering up his possibles and riding West. But he had nothing to ride on.

Besides, he reflected on his own advice to Elena. "Everything takes a little getting used to."

Maybe. But he doubted if he could get used to Chad Walker . . . and Walker's Way.

It was the best meal that Adam Dawson had had in a long time. Better than the boyhood meals in Monroe, Michigan. Or the war. Better than those up north before the massacre at Washita. And far better than scrawny rabbits and jerky at campfires and on trail.

Maybe not quite as good as the suppers that Libbie Custer prepared for Autie and him, but a lot better than he was used to. It started with a serving of thick pea soup, so thick Dawson could have used a fork instead of a spoon. Oven-hot biscuits, dotted with raisins and something else, some kind of nuts. Boiled potatoes bathed in creamed onions. The best cut of beef Dawson had ever tasted and spiced with something Dawson had never tasted. Hot apple pie with cheese and rich, dark coffee for dessert. Coffee laced with brandy.

When Adam Dawson mentioned how good the steak was and how different it tasted, Walker interrupted.

"A little too Mex for me."

"It's basil and thyme," Lorena said. "And they're not from Mexico."

"Still tastes Mex to me. Don't use 'em anymore."

"I've been using them for years and you've never complained before . . ."

"Well, I'm complaining now so don't use 'em anymore . . . sweetheart."

"All right, Chad." This time she didn't add "anything you say." She took a deep breath instead.

A couple of times during the supper Chad Walker had asked Dawson questions about Custer. Adam answered as briefly as he could without being altogether abrupt. The questions had to do with battles and bloodletting, subjects that Lorena didn't appear too interested in, so Dawson cut the answers short.

As Walker poured a wallop of brandy into the dregs of his coffee, he brought up the subject of Custer again.

"Is he a big man?"

"Who?" Dawson said, even though he knew who Chad was asking about.

"Custer. General George Armstrong Custer."

"By 'big' if you mean size-wise . . ."

"Yeah, sure . . . I mean is he as big as you or me?"

"No, not quite. About average . . . on the outside. But I've found that that isn't the measure of a man. It's what's inside that counts and Autie is . . ."

"Hold on. How come you call him Autie?"

"That's what he called himself when he was first learning to talk . . . couldn't say Armstrong so he called himself Autie and it stuck . . . at least with his friends."

"When did you two get to be friends? During the war?"

"No. Before that. When we were kids back in Monroe."

"You two born there?"

"I was. He was born in New Rumley, Ohio. Came when he was ten to stay with his sister Lydia and go to school . . ."

"Was he a wild sonofabitch then, too?"

"Well, I wouldn't call him 'wild' . . . but he wasn't exactly . . . docile. Spirited, I guess you'd say. Very good coffee, Mrs. Walker, best I've ever tasted. Good and strong."

"Thank you. Chad, I think maybe Adam would rather talk about something else. At least tonight . . ."

"Why? I wouldn't. Hell, I'd . . ."

"More coffee, *señor*?" Elena held the pot near Walker's cup.

"No. No more, Maria." Walker waved her away.

"Thank you, *Elena*," Lorena said pointedly. "Everything was just fine."

The girl nodded and hurried toward the kitchen still carrying the pot.

"Dammit, Chad," Lorena hissed, "call her by her right name. You know that embarrasses her."

"Far as I'm concerned they're *all* Marias. All of 'em the same. Look, smell and move . . . all the same . . . and all worthless. Every damn one of 'em. Wish they'd all go back to where they came from."

"Most of them came from right here. Long before you did . . . or any of us."

"Yeah, well I'm here now whether they like it or not. All bought and paid for with good old Yankee dollars, *whether they like it or not.* Hey, let's go into my library. I want Adam to see my books." Walker grabbed his canes and rose with effort. "You got a surprise or two coming, Captain. Something you never expected to see out here. Yessireebob."

Adam Dawson had already had his fill of surprises since coming to Pinto. He braced himself for one or two more as Lorena and he rose and followed Chad Walker toward the library.

Lorena held the door open as Chad, then Dawson, made their way into the room. The library was already illuminated by three or four lamps. Lorena turned them up after they all entered.

"What do you think of this?" Walker beamed.

"Mighty fine." Dawson smiled as he looked around. "Mighty fine."

It was a man's room. With a capital M. Leather furniture. A massive oak desk backed by a rolltop desk against the wall. A built-in oak bar. An elaborate gun rack with a rifle in every slot. A pillowed window seat for reading. Walls lined with shelves filled with books. A huge fireplace framed with a thick wooden mantel.

"Every foot of it designed by and for me," Walker added.

"It's you, all right, Chad," Lorena said.

"Sure is." Dawson smiled. "You're a lucky man." Adam was sorry he said that and looked away from the man who was braced by canes.

"You believe in luck, Adam?"

"I'm not sure. But everybody's got to believe in something."

"Does Custer? Believe in luck, I mean."

There it was again. The subject of Custer. Dawson knew the answer to that, but didn't quite give it. Autie had told him a story about Napoleon once, just before he and Custer were going into battle. One of Napoleon's generals had recommended a young officer for promotion, saying that the officer was intelligent, loyal and brave. "Yes," Napoleon responded, "but is he *lucky*?" Napoleon believed in luck. So did Custer. But Dawson hedged his answer. "We never talked much about it." That was a lie, but Dawson didn't feel like pursuing the subject.

Something on the fireplace mantel caught his attention and he moved toward it. It was a good-sized ferrotype of Chad Walker in Yankee uniform, carrying a smiling Lorena up in his arms, his feet spread wide apart, lifting her like a toy.

"Met Mathew Brady just before the war. He took that picture of Lorena and me the day after our wedding. What a night that was." Walker grinned. "Right, Lorena?"

"You were married before the war?"

"In Chicago. I'd just won a small fortune in a poker game . . . come to think of it . . . not so small. More than some men make most of their lives. That night I won more than just money, didn't I, sweetheart?"

"Tell Adam about the poker game, why don't you, Chad? Just in case he ever thinks of playing cards with the boss."

"Sure, sure I will . . . but pour us a couple of drinks while I do the tellin', Adam." Walker managed to sit himself down in what was obviously his favorite chair, large, leather and made especially for him.

"I'll get them." Lorena smiled. "I've heard the story before . . . different versions of it." She moved to the bar, reached for a bottle of bourbon and glasses.

"Well, sit over there, Adam . . . there was this young college boy . . . thought he was a whiz at poker and his father happened to be the owner of a stockyard and a straight-laced Presbyterian . . ."

"And the college boy happened to be drunk." Lorena handed her husband a large glass three quarters filled with bourbon and gave the other glass to Adam Dawson. It seemed to Dawson that she made sure their hands touched during the transfer.

"We had both had a few drinks. Could I help it if the college boy couldn't hold his? Well, one thing led to another and he was holding what he thought was a winning hand, an ace-high straight, and he was hell-bent on showing off to his fraternal brothers who were all with him slumming in a South Side whore house." Walker took a deep swallow of bourbon and wiped his lips. "The college boy kept raising until the pot got up to an even dozen . . . twelve thousand dollars."

"That *is* a fortune." Dawson sipped his bourbon.

"I know what you're thinkin', Adam."

"Do you?"

"You're thinkin' . . . did I have enough to cover the bet?"

"That's what I was thinking."

"The answer is no. But I was already joined up and going to leave Chicago in a week for the coming war, so what could they have done if I lost? Throw me in jail? That might not be as bad as the army . . . and a whole lot safer. Besides, I'd caught the fourth deuce . . ."

"Caught?" Lorena emphasized.

"What's the difference? It ended up with the other three and I ended up with the college boy's signed marker which I presented to his daddy the next morning."

"And he honored it?" Dawson asked, although it wasn't actually a question.

"Daddy was an honorable man, besides he didn't want me to go waving it all around Chicago, telling everybody how and where I got it. Wouldn't look good for a straight-laced Presbyterian businessman's family. Now . . ." Walker looked at his wife and took another drink, ". . . comes the part about Lorena and me getting married."

"Chad!"

"Why not tell him? This part's very . . . romantic, a real love story. I'd seen Lorena a couple of nights before . . . on the stage . . . she was an . . . actress, with a traveling theatrical company . . . even had two lines . . . but it was her other lines I was interested in . . ."

"I think I'll . . ."

"Oh, Lorena, don't worry . . . I'm just about finished with the story . . . just relax . . . see, Adam, the first time I waited outside to see her she didn't pay any attention, but the second time, after the poker game, I got her attention and . . . we fell in love and got married . . . course I told her about my good fortune and she promised to be there waiting when I got back . . . *if* I got back. If not, she'd be a rich young widow. She promised to wait and I promised . . . what was it I promised, Lorena?"

"The world. The moon. The sun and the stars. Instead I got . . ."

"What?" Walker's voice was harsh and bitter.

"Texas," Lorena said.

A momentary silence settled on the room.

"Why Texas?" Dawson then asked his boss.

"Why? I'll tell you why, my comrade in arms. I'll tell you why. Because I had the urge to come down and get something back from the damn Rebs. And I've done it . . . with Yankee dollars. Rubbed their faces in it!"

"Walker's Way." Dawson smiled.

"Damn right. Here I am and here I'll stay just as long as I feel like staying . . . and rubbing. See what I mean, Adam?"

"We all see," Lorena said and started to move. "If you'll excuse me, I'm going to help Elena and change into something more comfortable."

Adam couldn't help looking at Lorena and what she was wearing which looked comfortable enough to him. He rose as she left.

"Fix us another drink, will you, Adam?"

Dawson took Walker's glass, went to the bar and poured out the bourbon.

"Make mine a double. Save yourself a trip."

"Sure, boss."

"First time I was ever called boss by a captain." Walker grinned.

"Like I said, the war's over."

"Yeah." Walker nodded, but didn't mean it. "Just let me tell you one more thing about that theatrical company. The leading man was a good actor and damn good looking, too. Lorena was a lousy actress, but he kept her with him because she was good . . . company. You know what I mean?"

Dawson didn't answer as he handed Chad Walker the drink.

"You know what the actor's name was, Adam?"

Dawson shook his head.

"It was Booth." Walker drank. "John Wilkes Booth . . ."

Adam Dawson almost dropped the glass he was holding as Walker concluded.

". . . the dirty, no good, murderin', Rebel sonofabitch. Now Adam, let's talk about war."

Nine

Saturday night was always the liveliest night at Baldy's Bar, except when the trail hands were in town. Then every night was Saturday.

There was another saloon on the south edge of Pinto, the Iguana. The Iguana's customers were almost exclusively Mexicans and some Indians who had left the blanket and tepee and come closer to the white man's culture, but not close enough to frequent Baldy's Bar. Baldy catered to the brown brothers of Pinto out of fiscal necessity but he drew a red line at the bat-wings. Money or no, there was no such thing as a good drunken Indian as far as Brendan Alsap, also known as Baldy, was concerned.

Occasionally some Anglos would duck into the Iguana and head straight for the cribs out back where females of color, in varying hues, would satisfy their desires.

Baldy didn't have any cribs out back. He did have some rooms upstairs which served the same purpose, but with more comfort and cleanliness. When times were better Baldy had as many as six females on the night shift working for the Texas dollar. Actually the usual fee was two dollars unless the customer negotiated for extraordinary fillips.

These nights Baldy was down to two regulars, Francine Needle and Goldie Bright. Francine Needle looked like her name and Goldie Bright was anything but. Still, they were both more than a cut above the crib girls at the Iguana, both good-natured and both good at their trade.

Alma Gorsich was not a whore. Not anymore. She had been, in other days and other places. These days and in this place she was bartender, sometime singer, and part owner. She had forked up five hundred dollars when Baldy needed it. The Bank of Pinto had turned him down because they considered the Confederate cause a better risk than Baldy's Bar. The bank had, of course, been proved wrong and Alma Gorsich got a steady job and 15 percent of Baldy's profits.

While Alma was not a saloon girl like Francine and Goldie, she was not exactly abstemious. She chose her companions for fun and for their looks, and, on some occasions, was not above accepting a gift or gratuity from a grateful recipient of favors bestowed.

That night Francine and Goldie had already made several ascents and descents to and from the second level, but were currently drifting toward the customers and card games on the main floor.

Joe Nueva, Pete Sommers, Paco and two other patrons were at their usual table playing their usual poker game, table stakes. The window was still boarded up, waiting for the glass replacement, and all the furniture and most of the customers were sitting or standing in an upright position . . . until the gunshots rang out just in front of Baldy's bar, and glass shattered.

Then everybody ducked.

Three men slammed through the bat-wings, grinning and waving pistols. The first man also held a near-empty whiskey bottle in his left hand.

"Evenin', folks, no need to be alarmed, we're peace lovin' . . . and whiskey lovin'. My name's Rip Stacey and my two *compañeros* here are Jake and Snake, the brothers Rankin. We just got paid off and got a powerful cravin' for whiskey and . . . women." Rip Stacey looked at Francine and Goldie, then his look settled on Alma. "Seems like we found both."

"Look here, Rip, or whatever your name is," Baldy bellowed, "you want to stay in here you put away them guns and settle down."

"Sure. Sure. That's what we aim to do is settle down."

He moved closer to Alma, still holding the gun and bottle. "I'll settle down on this one here." Rip Stacey licked his lips and grinned wider. He was bigger and dirtier than the other two.

"No, you won't," Alma said.

"Sure I will, Red. You know how much money I got?"

"Not enough."

"You're mighty snickity for a saloon gal. 'Pears like you figure your britches is filled with somethin' special. Well, we'll just find out about that." Stacey laughed and took another step. "You ain't all painted up like that to go to church."

Nobody had noticed Sheriff Ben Vesper come in, at least the three strangers hadn't, but he stood just inside the bat-wings.

"You," Vesper said. "Big mouth."

Now everybody noticed, including the three intruders.

"First off, put away that iron. All three of you."

"Who says?" Rip Stacey smiled.

"Sheriff Ben Vesper says . . . and he only says it once."

"Anything else on your mind, Sheriff Ben Vesper?"

"Three things. You're gonna leather that gun. Then you're gonna pay for the damage outside. Then all three of you are gonna mount up and ride in the direction of your choice out of Pinto."

Sam Mendez, the young stable boy, stepped through the bat-wings.

"Suppose we don't?" Rip Stacey looked at both his pals.

"Then I suppose you'll be buried right here."

There was a heavy silence.

"You expect to get some help from these donkeys?" Stacey glanced around the room, still holding the gun and whiskey bottle.

"Don't expect, want, or need any. Now drift."

"Sure, sure, Sheriff, just as soon as . . ."

"Now! And you lift that hand another inch and I'll kill you."

Rip Stacey's gun hand had begun to rise almost imperceptibly.

"What with?" Stacey said. The sheriff's gun was still holstered. Stacey's hand started to move up but didn't quite make it up to an inch.

Vesper drew and raked the barrel hard across Stacey's nose with a resounding crack and a blast of blood erupted across his dirty face. With a swift almost simultaneous backhand swipe of the same gun, Vesper raked the barrel just as hard across Jake's temple, grabbed him and using him as a shield, whirled with gun aimed at Snake behind him.

But Snake Rankin was no longer upright. Sam Mendez had leaped onto Snake's back, knocked him to the floor, taken away the gun and was pummeling him senseless.

"That'll do, son," Vesper said.

Sam smashed his fist once more into Snake's face, then looked up and grinned.

"Yes, sir."

Rip Stacey's gun had fallen to the floor. So had Jake's.

"Collect those pistols," Vesper said to Sam.

"Yes, sir." Sam rose, still holding Snake's gun and proceeded to pick up the other two pistols from the floor.

"Now, Mister Big Mouth, can you hear me?" Vesper asked.

Stacey managed to nod while still trying to stanch and wipe away the blood that covered his face.

"How about you?" The sheriff looked at Jake who was still on his feet but staggering.

Jake also nodded.

"Good. Now pick up your friend, mount up, and ride in the direction of your choice."

Stacey started to move.

"Just a minute," Vesper said. "You got a wallet?"

Rip Stacey shook his head no.

"Pull out your roll."

Stacey reached into his left pant pocket and lifted out a wad of bills.

"Hand it over."

Stacey did. The sheriff selected what he considered a fair amount to cover the damages, then stuffed the rest into Stacey's shirt pocket and shoved him toward the entrance.

"Good night."

Stacey and Jake managed to lift and half carry, half drag the third man to the bat-wings and onto the street.

The patrons of Baldy's Bar burst into laughter, even scattered applause. Brendon Alsap approached Vesper, took the sheriff's right hand and pumped.

"You ain't ever gonna have to buy a drink in here again, Sheriff, no siree."

"Here." Vesper handed Baldy the money he had taken from Stacey. "This ought to cover the damage."

"You bet." Baldy took the bills and stuffed them into his pocket.

Vesper moved a step toward Alma and spoke in a low voice.

"You all right, lady?"

"Thanks." Alma smiled.

Ben Vesper turned and looked at Sam Mendez who was holding the three guns.

"You," the sheriff said. "Bring them guns and come with me."

"Yes, sir." Sam Mendez nodded.

Ben Vesper walked out through the bat-wings and the armed stable boy followed.

Ten

For nearly an hour Chad Walker had been drinking bourbon and questioning Dawson about the war and mostly about Custer. Walker wanted to know how the two boys met in Monroe.

"It was at a picnic, just before school started." Dawson answered, but didn't go into details, without being curt.

"You two the same age?"

"No, he's a couple years older, but we were both about the same size."

"Did the two of you join up together?"

"No. Autie had gone to West Point and graduated. I stayed in Michigan and didn't get in until later."

"How'd you hook up again?"

"It was at Chickahominy." Again Dawson told of the event without going into too many particulars. "I was with the Fourth Michigan and Lieutenant Custer was with General McClellan who had ordered him to take over and capture a picket post on the other side of the river. There were thirty of us from Monroe when Autie rode up and recognized all of us. 'Well, boys, I'm glad to see you, but right now we're going to charge across that river. We'll talk later. All Monroe boys follow me! Let's go Monroe! Ride you Wolverines! Follow me!' And we did. After that I was with him 'til Appomattox."

"And he came out a general and you a captain."

"We were both glad to just come out. I sure as hell was."

"I want to hear about Gettysburg." Walker took another drink, then waited. Dawson remained silent. "What's a matter? You tired of talking? I guess you must be. Well, Gettysburg can wait 'til some other time."

Dawson was relieved and hoped the conversation was over for the night. But it wasn't, at least not on Chad Walker's part.

"I remember at Fisher's Hill . . . the Rebs didn't know what hit 'em . . . we wiped out the whole stinkin' lot of 'em . . . left nothing alive . . . not even a goddam dog . . . then at Goldsboro, I got mine . . . up in a barn I think he was . . . the backshooting sonofabitch. Bullet's still in there . . . be buried with it." Walker took a deep breath. "Even hurts when I . . . breathe sometimes."

Adam Dawson still said nothing.

"How about some more Tennessee bourbon?"

"Thanks, I've had enough." He had had more than enough of Chad Walker and Walker's Way and was about to rise and say good night when Walker's hand swept the room and its book shelves.

"You do much reading?"

"Sometimes. When there's a book handy."

"Plenty of *everything* handy here." Walker lifted himself from the chair with the help of his canes and hobbled toward the book shelves around the room. He was more drunk than sober, but not as drunk as he should have been considering the amount of bourbon he had consumed. "Everything I need . . . and want. Everything. My world. And people do what I tell 'em . . . what to do . . . and what not to do."

Walker made his way toward the almost empty bottle on the bar. Dawson started to rise again but stopped as Walker turned back toward him.

"The eagle . . ." Walker muttered.

"How's that?"

"I said the eagle. 'The eagle suffers little birds to sing.' Bet you don't know who wrote that, Captain Dawson."

"Shakespeare." Dawson smiled, "Wasn't it?"

"Yeah, Shakespeare. How'd you know?"

"Maybe," Dawson shrugged, "it was just a guess."

Walker stared at Adam and studied him in silence, as if taking measure of the man he had met just hours ago. Then Walker smiled.

"Maybe," he said. "And maybe... you're an educated sonofabitch."

"Not as educated," Adam Dawson looked around the room, "as you, Mr. Walker."

"Adam." Walker lifted the bourbon bottle and drank it dry. "I'm glad you came this way, Yank." He looked at the empty bottle in his hand. "Wiped out the whole stinking..." He hurled the bottle across the room. It shattered against the fireplace "...lot of 'em."

Walker staggered and almost fell. Adam took a step toward him, but Walker waved him off and regained his balance.

The door opened and Lorena stepped into the library. She wore a light, form-fitting robe over a flimsy chemise. She said nothing. She was a calm night vision of absolute beauty, but her eyes were twin spears of tempest.

"So?!" Chad looked at her and smirked.

"Are you through, Chad? Or is there anything else you want to break?"

"Whatever I break around here belongs to me. Everything and..."

"Everybody," Lorena finished.

"The eagle..." Walker looked at Adam and almost smiled. "...the eagle suffers little birds to sing."

"What the hell are you talking about, Chad?"

"You wouldn't know, but Adam does... I'm talking about... about Walker's Way."

"Well, I think you've done enough talking," she looked at the broken glass around the fireplace, "and drinking for one night. Let's leave some for tomorrow."

"Tomorrow... and tomorrow creeps... and so do I... don't we all."

"Oh..."

"*For heaven's sake!* I know, Lorena... to hell with it.

Let's get upstairs." He started toward the door. Lorena looked back at Adam Dawson as her husband walked past her and into the hallway.

Dawson wanted to avert his eyes, but didn't. He had never seen eyes like hers and in a face so beautiful, and something told Adam Dawson, so dangerous. Still, he looked at her until she turned away and followed her husband into the hallway, then Dawson followed them both.

At the foot of the staircase in the main hallway Adam and Lorena watched as Chad Walker sat, canes on his lap, in a basket-like apparatus attached to a hanging rope threaded through an overhead pulley system with counter weights. He grabbed a dangling rope and hauled it with his great arm strength. The apparatus started to move the basket and him up the stairway.

"That's quite a contraption," Adam said as Walker began his ascent.

"Rigged it up myself."

"Don't know of any army engineer who could've done better."

"Yeah," Walker called back as he continued to haul himself upward. "Necessity, they say, is the mother of invention . . . so I guess this makes me the father."

"You know where your room is," Lorena said to Dawson.

He nodded.

"Is there anything you need?"

Dawson shook his head no.

"Good night, Adam." She started to walk up the stairway.

"Good night."

But it wasn't a walk. It was persuasion. Or a pitfall.

There was a light in Sheriff Ben Vesper's office. The office was in a small fortress-like building on the north side of Main Street. Beside the office, the building consisted of three cells on one side of a short corridor, and on the other side, a storeroom and another small cell-like room, but with no bars, where the sheriff slept when he had guests across the corridor.

Tonight there were no guests, but Ben Vesper and Sam Mendez were in the office on opposite sides of the sheriff's desk. The expression on the sheriff's face was not pleasant to look upon.

"You're a damn fool, Sam."

"Yes, sir."

"An idiot."

"Yes, sir."

"You're . . ."

"Yes, sir."

"Let me finish before you agree."

"Yes, sir."

"You coulda got yourself killed."

"Yes, sir."

"And me. You say 'yes, sir' one more time and I'll crack your skull." Vesper waited a couple of seconds to see if the stable boy would say it. He didn't. But Sam Mendez kept looking straight at Vesper without averting the sheriff's eyes and what Vesper was dishing out. Sheriff Ben Vesper liked that, but didn't show it. He pointed a thumb toward the saloon, then a finger back at Mendez.

"What the hell do you think you were doing?"

"Following your advice . . ."

"What advice?"

"Well, sir. I couldn't see the look in his eyes, but I did see him start to move so that's when I took your advice and jumped the sonofabitch . . ."

"Just two things, Sam . . ."

"Yes, sir."

"Number one: I could've shot you . . ."

"I didn't think you'd do that."

"Not on purpose, but it could've happened . . . don't say it . . . number two: I'm an officer of the law and paid to take risks, you're not. And while I'm at it, number three: you heard me say I didn't expect or need any help. You could've bollixed things up."

"But I didn't." Sam smiled.

"Not this time. But there ain't gonna be any next time. Now get back to the stable."

"Can't."

"Why not?"

" 'Cause I quit."

"When?"

"Tonight."

"Why?"

" 'Cause I want to go to work for you."

"You're loco."

"Maybe. But that's what I want to do."

"You think that because of what you did back there you're fit to be a deputy?"

"No, sir. Not yet, but I could learn ... from you ..."

"You're too damn young."

"How old were you when you started?"

"Times are different now."

"They're always different. But we're the same ... sort of ..."

"What do you mean?"

"Well, part white and part Mex ..."

"You think that makes us the same?"

"Sort of ... for starters."

"Go back to the stable. Linus'll take you back. You're a good worker."

"I want to work for you, cleanin' up, runnin' errands ... anything, so's I can watch and learn. I'm gonna do it anyhow whether you want me to or not."

"What're you gonna live on?"

"I don't need much."

"Where you gonna sleep?"

"In the back room," Sam pointed.

"Got it all figured out, have you?"

"Yes, sir."

"Well . . . step back, don't say or do anything." Vesper rose and walked to the door, looked outside for just a beat, then opened it. "What the hell do you want? Didn't I tell you three . . ."

"Please, Sheriff, can we talk to you for just a minute? We don't mean no harm, honest."

"Come on in and stand against that wall and don't even blink."

"Sure." Rip Stacey, followed by the two Rankin brothers, walked in with heads bowed and absent of any arrogance. They lined up against the wall and gazed down on the floor in silence.

"What do you want?"

"Sheriff, them guns you took," Stacey pointed to the weapons on the desk, "all three of us, well, we had 'em with us all through the war . . . with the Third Texas, and . . ."

"Oh, you're sentimental, is that it?"

"No, sir. Not exactly, but, look, we're sobered up now and we know we done wrong, and we thought maybe . . . I promise you'll never see us again . . . we was wrong, Sheriff, but . . ."

"Shut up." Vesper's voice was soft. "You got rifles?"

"Yes, sir, outside."

"That's a good place for 'em. Pick up those pistols and get the hell out."

"You bet." All three retrieved their guns and headed for the door. "You're a good man, Sheriff . . . and so's he." Stacey pointed at Sam, smiled, and left followed by Jake and Snake Rankin.

Sam Mendez stood smiling at Vesper who walked back and sat on the edge of his desk after the door closed.

"Why'd you give 'em back their guns?"

"Because I felt like it. You think you can get along on two bits a day?"

"Yes, sir."

"Now don't go thinking you're a deputy or anything else but an errand boy and swamper."

"Yes, sir.

"I'm the high hickolorum around here and the law's in my holster."

"Yes, sir."

"All right then. Two bits a day, five days a week."

"Yes, sir."

"But you work seven . . . and don't say it."

Sam Mendez grinned and nodded.

The Hatcher house, formerly the Beaudine house, was located to the northwest of Pinto. It was the biggest and best dwelling in the area. Two full stories, three-quarters embraced by a filigreed porch wide enough to accommodate a two-up horse and carriage. The house had been built by Jason Beaudine for his bride from New Orleans and for the many children they had planned to have. Those plans had ended abruptly when his wife and second child died.

Jason Beaudine went on living there with Mary Ann and the ghosts and memories of his departed wife and baby.

Since Jason Beaudine fell with a heart attack, Mary Ann had gone on living there with the ghosts of her father, mother and infant brother . . . and with Brad Hatcher and her cats.

There was also Marissa, her maid—more than a maid—who stayed with her and despised Brad Hatcher, but stayed because she loved Mary Ann. Marissa kept as far away from Hatcher as she could and spoke to him only in answer to his occasional questions. Her answers were civil, but short.

Hatcher knew how Marissa felt but allowed her to stay as one of the few concessions he made to his wife.

Marissa prayed every morning and night. Foremost in her prayers was the supplication to the Mother of Mercy that Mr. Hatcher would be struck dead that morning or night. But that part of her prayers was yet to be answered. Still she did not give up hope.

Marissa was praying late that night in her quarters as Brad Hatcher knocked softly, then entered his wife's bedroom.

"Mary Ann . . ."

"Yes, Brad, what do you want?" Mary Ann's heart beat faster in dread of what might be in her husband's mind and other places.

"Oh, nothing much, my dear, just saw your lamp was still on and thought I'd come in and see how you were." His voice was soft and gentle.

Mary Ann was relieved when she saw that he was still dressed. Whenever he came in wearing his nightshirt she knew what he had in mind.

She set aside her Bible and stroked the cat that lay beside her. Hatcher came closer and sat on the edge of the bed. The cat jumped to the floor.

"I'm fine. Thank you."

"Good."

"Mary Ann, you know that I've had a lot on my mind lately . . ."

"Yes, I noticed."

"Spanish Bit . . . well, it's a big responsibility, and you know times here in Texas . . ."

"Yes, I know. The war and all. I'm glad you didn't have to go." That was a lie. She had hoped that he would go and never come back.

"And now this damn drought."

"I'll pray for rain." She lifted the Bible slightly.

"Good. I'm trying to keep our heads above water." He grinned. "If there was any . . . water, I mean."

"Yes, I know."

"Speaking of water. I saw Mrs. Walker in town today. She invited us over to supper."

"Both of us?"

"Yes, of course." Brad Hatcher wasn't too sure of the point of his wife's remark but he suspected that she suspected. "You know that I've been trying to acquire Mr. Walker's spread. I've already talked to the bank and Terrance Swerd would make the necessary loan. That's a good piece of property. Plenty of water . . ."

"But is Mr. Walker willing to sell?"

"Not yet. But Mrs. Walker is all for it."

"I'm sure. You can be very . . . persuasive, Brad."

The conversation wasn't going quite as Hatcher wanted, but he needed his wife with him in order to turn the social occasion into a business proposition.

"It'll make Spanish Bit into a well-paying proposition. They've already started driving cattle north, a half-breed named Jesse Chisholm has . . ."

"Yes, I've heard about the Chisholm Trail."

"You have? Where?"

"Some of the people in church."

"Oh, yes, of course. Then you'll come?"

"Where?"

"To the Walkers'."

"I couldn't let you go alone, could I, Brad? It wouldn't look proper, would it?"

"Good." Hatcher thought of leaning over and kissing her, but instantly thought better of it. He rose and patted her hand.

"When?" She smiled.

"How's that?"

"Supper at the Walkers'?"

"Oh, next Friday. Why don't you go into town and get yourself a new dress?"

"I think I have something that would be appropriate . . . besides we've got to save all the money we can . . . for the Walker spread."

"You'll look beautiful, as always, I'm sure."

"Thank you, Brad. Good night."

"Good night, Mary Ann."

She watched until he left the room and closed the door. So did the cat.

All these years, for Mary Ann, living with Brad Hatcher was like living with half a dozen different men, depending on what Hatcher wanted at the time. He could be charming, persuasive, thoughtful and gentle. Or he could be, if it suited his purpose, rude, mean, demanding and ruthless. She was on to him, but in all cases it was easier to acquiesce and be rid of him sooner, than to resist and face confrontation. A confrontation she just didn't have the will to face . . . at least not yet.

The cat sprang silently back onto the bed. The cat's flowing tail brushed along Mary Ann's throat as the cat settled against her shoulder. The cat purred.

"I know, Caesar. I know," Mary Ann said and stroked her companion of the night.

Eleven

Past midnight Adam Dawson lay in the unaccustomed comfort of a bed and mulled over recent events.

For the first time in weeks he was going to sleep under a roof instead of a big sky. Just a short time ago he wouldn't have given a short bit for his chances of staying alive. Not with a dead horse and Comancheros trying to kill him too. Not while he was afoot and thirsty in a blazing desert.

And now he was alive and awake, with a blanket, a bellyful of beefsteak and bourbon. And maybe a bellyful of something else he couldn't help thinking about. A beautiful woman and a bigot. A beautiful woman he first saw in the arms of a man who was not her husband. And a husband who was now his boss, a man crippled in body and mind, who cursed Rebels, redskins and greasers, and who reveled in talking about war and Custer.

When Walker had asked, Dawson told him that he'd met Autie at a picnic in Monroe. That wasn't the whole truth. And he had left out one important detail that changed the course of both their lives and more, much more, the course of many battles fought and yet to be fought while Autie was still alive.

Dawson was eight years old and living with his grandfather, both his parents had died, when ten-year-old Autie came to Monroe to live with his sister Lydia and go to a better school than they had in New Rumley, Ohio, where he was born and where his mother and father still lived.

Within days, the newcomer with the long, golden locks
and impish grin had gained a reputation as a carefree, reckless, high-spirited practical joker who was not afraid of anybody or anything. Who could be startled by nothing. Except
once, when he was skipping past the house of Monroe's leading citizen, Judge Daniel Stanton Bacon.

Libbie Bacon, age eight, the judge's only daughter, pert,
dimpled, and beautiful, was swinging on the front gate.

"Hi, you, Custer boy!" she blurted and ran into the
house, leaving him dead in his tracks and wanting to see her
again. He did, at the picnic, along with the other children,
including Adam Dawson, who were on a get-acquainted celebration along the Raisin River.

It was an ideal opportunity for Autie to show off, and
he did, winning all the athletic games and finally the pie-
eating contest, and then diving into the river after announcing
that he was going to swim across and back.

Mrs. Willow protested but Autie paid no heed. Twenty
yards out his head was swallowed by the river. He bobbed
up a few seconds later and gasped. Everybody thought it was
another one of his jokes, everybody except Libbie. She
screamed. Mrs. Willow could not swim.

But Adam Dawson could. He dove in as Autie disappeared again. Adam Dawson was big for his age, a strong
boy and a strong swimmer. Autie went down for the third
time as Adam reached the cramped and retching Custer boy
and got hold of his golden locks, then shoulders, and pulled
him back against the current toward the river bank.

None of the other student-spectators, or Mrs. Willow
moved. Only Libbie dashed into the water up to her waist
to help Dawson drag the Custer boy onto dry land, where
all three, Dawson, Custer and Libbie collapsed, spattered
with the mud and dirt of the river Raisin.

Then everyone burst into cheers and applause and rushed
to the side of the muculent trio. But it was Adam Dawson
who turned Autie over, straddled him, and pumped with
both palms hard into his ribcage. There was no breath from
the boy until Adam turned him over again onto his stomach

and whacked him as hard as he could between the shoulder blades. There was a sudden eruption of assorted pie-filling, mucky crust and indeterminate matter from Autie's stomach followed by deep, if irregular, breaths.

More cheers. More applause.

Later, when Autie was fully revived and had been apprised of what happened and properly admonished by Mrs. Willow, he sat against a tree with Adam and Libbie beside him.

"Your name's Adam Dawson, is it?"

Adam nodded.

"I'm George Armstrong Custer." He grinned and stuck out his hand.

"I know." Adam took Custer's hand and grinned back. "Everybody knows. At least everybody in Monroe."

"Someday everybody in other places'll know, too, thanks to you. You saved my bacon."

"No. Libbie Bacon did. If she hadn't yelled, well . . . everybody thought you was funning."

"Well, I thank you both. I guess that makes us . . . the three musketeers of Monroe, Michigan."

And it did.

All three were enrolled at the new Dublin School where Autie set a new record for outlandish pranks and after-school punishments. During school hours and afterward Autie and Dawson were almost inseparable. Fishing along the banks of the Raisin, hiking and riding farm horses that belonged to his sister Lydia and her husband, David Reed.

Whenever possible, Libbie joined them, but her father, the eminent citizen-judge, glowered with disfavor on both ragamuffins and admonished his beloved daughter to keep distant from such riff-raff. She did, but only when the judge was in the vicinity.

Adam lived on a hardscrabble little farm with his grandfather Jethroe Dawson, a sober, solitary man who considered it his duty to provide shelter and nourishment for young Adam, but stopped short of including companionship. But Adam found more than enough companionship with the irrepressible Autie, and whenever possible, the pert and lovely Elizabeth Clift Bacon . . . Libbie.

When he was sixteen Autie moved back to New Rumley where he obtained the unlikely position of substitute principal and teacher in a one-room schoolhouse. A position that held none of the excitement, education, and mostly the adventure that Autie craved.

On a visit back to Monroe Autie told Dawson and Libbie that he had petitioned Senator John A. Bingham, Ohio Senator, for an appointment to West Point where he was more likely to encounter excitement, education and most important, adventure.

Custer had passed the examinations, barely, and was accepted. But barely was good enough for Autie and he bid Libbie and Adam good-bye.

That was the last Adam Dawson saw of George Armstrong Custer until Chickahominy.

Lt. George Armstrong Custer had graduated last in the West Point class of 1861. Last in academic subjects and first in demerits and more important in marksmanship and horsemanship. But by then the country was at war and the army was less in need of scholars and more in demand of soldiers, leaders who could shoot straight and ride hard.

Custer fit the bill.

Lieutenant Custer was willing, able and eager, more than eager, to prove his mettle.

First attached to General MacDowell's Second Cavalry Brigade where he led a decisive charge at Bull Run, then he was assigned to General George B. McClellan who desperately needed a victory to maintain command of the Grand Army of the Potomac, since he had fallen into disfavor with President and Commander-in-Chief Abraham Lincoln.

The opportunity came at Chickahominy, for McClellan and Custer. McClellan ordered Custer to lead the attack at dawn.

"Cross that river and you'll come out a captain. Good luck, Lieutenant."

"Luck's my guiding star," Autie replied and rode off.

That's when he came across the thirty Monroe men of the Second Michigan Brigade. He instantly recognized Adam Dawson, leaped off his mount and put his arms around his boyhood friend.

"Adam! Now we'll give 'em hell! If it weren't for you I wouldn't be here. I wouldn't be anywhere. Are you ready for a ride to glory?"

"I am if you are, Autie." Dawson smiled. "But you've already had your share."

"I'm just getting started. Ride next to me, Adam. We'll scatter those Rebs."

Custer jumped on his mount, waved his hat, spurred the horse and hollered.

"Come on, Monroe. Follow me. Ride, you Wolverines! Charge!"

And charge they did, with Custer in the lead and Dawson close behind, into the eruption of Rebel rifles across the swamp, into flashes of smoke and a fusillade of bullets out of the brush.

One of the bullets crashed into Custer's horse. Animal and rider toppled into the murky water. Custer fell face first clutching his saber, as hooves thundered and splashed about him. Some of the riders turned back, or circled in confusion.

Once again Dawson reached out and down, this time from the saddle, to grab and hold the dazed and muddied Custer. Autie swung on behind Dawson, still gripping his sword, waving it and once again giving the order.

"Charge, you Wolverines!"

Out of the churning chaos and confusion the Michigan Brigade regrouped and rallied behind the hatless lieutenant, wet-haired and swinging his saber toward the retreating Rebels and close to Dawson's head.

McClellan had his victory and Custer his captaincy.

Afterward Autie obtained cigars for Dawson and himself.

"Light up, Adam. We've got a little time to smoke and celebrate. You are now looking at Captain George Armstrong Custer, late of Monroe, Michigan."

"Congratulations, Autie. You won the day."

"*We.*" Custer puffed and grinned. "Once again, Adam, you saved my bacon . . . say, uh, speaking of . . ."

"Of what?" Dawson inhaled the smoke of his strong cigar, smiled and waited.

"Of Monroe . . . how's everything back home?"

"Everything's fine."

"And everybody?"

"Everybody's just fine."

"Uh, huh."

"Anybody in particular, Autie?"

"You know damn well . . . how is she? Have you seen her lately?"

"Saw her the day I left."

"Did she say anything about . . . well, you know."

"She said, if I saw you to say . . ."

"Yeah, what? What?!"

"To say, 'Hi, you, Custer boy.' "

"Oh." Custer didn't mask his disappointment.

"And something else."

"What?!"

"That . . . she's waiting."

"For me?"

"No. For Simple Simon, you damn fool. Of course for you. Haven't you written her?"

"Yeah, but it's better hearing it from you. Nothing can stop me now, Adam. I'm going to ride to glory and you're going with me all the way. You're part of my luck. I know it and I'm going to make sure you're with me 'til it's over. 'Til we've won! Then, we'll find us . . ."

"What?"

"I don't know yet. Let's win this war first."

That was the part of the story about Custer and himself that Adam Dawson hadn't told Chad Walker earlier that night. A part that he would never tell, not to Walker, or to anybody else. It was one thing to keep Walker amused and informed regarding Custer the public figure and another to violate the confidentiality of his best friend in order to amuse and inform his current boss.

Dawson reached over to the bedstand, took and looked at the silver watch that Autie had given him. He could not see the time because of the darkness, but the watch was still running. He wound it and wondered what Autie was doing and where he was. With Libbie at his headquarters up north, or in the wilderness on some campaign, still seeking glory?

At least Autie would have his wife to go back to . . . if he survived.

Dawson had nothing and no one. Well, not quite nothing. He had a job. And not quite no one. There was Chad Walker, a Yank, twisted and tormented, a man of contrasts and contradictions, brilliant in many ways, who could quote Shakespeare and design contraptions to compensate for his feckless limbs, who showed compassion for a blind old soldier, but could be cold and cruel to everyone around him. And there was Lorena Walker, who walked in beauty and . . .

There were sounds, voices, muffled at first . . . sounds and voices that Adam Dawson didn't want to hear . . . words indistinguishable, then louder.

"No!"

"Get back here!"

"No!"

Again indistinguishable.

"Come here, dammit!"

"Chad!"

"Now!"

"Please . . ."

"Right here!"

"You're drunk."

"Drunk or sober . . . you're my wife."

"Chad, I . . ."

"It won't work, Lorena, it . . ."

"He'll hear you."

"I don't give a damn, Mrs. Walker. Do you hear that? Or do I have to . . ."

There was the sound of a slap and something breaking. A lamp. Then silence.

"That's better . . . that's it."

Adam Dawson was squeezing the watch in his hand. His hand trembled.

There was no longer any doubt in his mind as to what he was going to do, even if he had to do it afoot. He started to rise but thought better of it. Whatever was going to happen, or was happening, had happened before. What good would it do to leave tonight? He was tired. He needed to sleep, or at least to rest.

His hand still shaking, he placed the watch back on the bedstand and buried his head in the pillow.

He would strike out in the morning. Keep moving west. Early.

Twelve

In his hut Corona stood naked, swaying from the effect of the bottle of tequila he had consumed, still holding the empty bottle in his hand as he bent over the unconscious form of Maureen O'Donnell, with her hands still tied behind her on the bed.

And as he had done earlier, more than once, Corona squeezed her face in the palm of his hand and shook it, this time harder.

And as before, her emerald green eyes fluttered open for just a moment, there was a gasping sound from her throat and mouth, still stuffed with Corona's bandana, her chest heaved and pumped for air, her shoulders shuddered, but she remained unconscious.

Corona relaxed his fingers and her head plopped back onto the bed. He staggered toward the table next to a chair in the middle of the room. He let the empty bottle drop to the floor and reached for a full bottle on the table and uncorked it. Corona took a long pull and the overflow of tequila from his mouth flushed down his face, throat and onto his naked chest and belly.

He looked back at the red-haired woman on the bed, shrugged, then half-sat, half-fell into the chair. He managed to take another pull from the bottle before the bottle dropped from his hand onto the floor, and his head dropped onto the table.

The bottle did not break, but the liquid spilled from its

nape onto the stolen carpet that covered the dirt floor of the hut.

Maureen O'Donnell's eyes fluttered open once again, and this time stayed open. She had been aware of Corona and his intention for some time, but had feigned unconsciousness. In her heart she knew her inevitable fate, at least the inevitable fate that awaited her at the hand of the man who had killed her husband.

If there were some way that she could have killed herself, and God help her, her baby, she would have done it and joined Tim O'Donnell in heaven, if God would forgive her for taking her life and the baby's.

But there was no way to do that. And no way of escaping her fate when the man came to.

Olita had to wait until she was sure, until she heard the familiar sounds of his snoring. The sounds she had so often heard while they lay together in the bed and other places after he had been drinking and their naked, sweating bodies still touched.

When she *was* sure, Olita stepped through the half-open door, looked first at Corona, then with the knife in her hand walked without a sound toward Maureen O'Donnell.

Olita leaned closer, her massive breasts suspended just above the prostrate girl, the knife in her hand near Maureen's white throat.

Maureen had been watching paralyzed with fear, but strangely, at the same time, almost relieved at the prospect of death instead of . . .

Olita's left hand went to her own mouth in warning against making a struggle or causing sound that might arouse the stupored Comanchero. Olita's knife sliced through the rope that bound Maureen's wrists, and again indicating silence, pulled away the bandana and pointed toward the entrance.

The bed squeaked as Olita helped Maureen to her unsteady feet, but Corona did not hear it, or anything. The two made their way across the room and through the door.

The night was moonless and the *ranchería* quiescent, as

Olita led the way past the other huts where Comancheros slept, most of them as drunk as Corona, to a boulder where a horse was saddled.

"Can you ride?" Olita whispered.

Maureen nodded.

"Walk this horse far away, then get on and ride until he drops. If they catch you and bring you back . . ."

"I won't tell that you . . ."

"Shut up and get out."

"Thank you . . ."

"I'm not doing it for you. Get out!" she droned and handed Maureen the reins.

Olita stood and waited until the girl and horse disappeared into the darkness.

When she turned back, Diaz was standing, grinning but silent.

Olita raised the knife and took one step toward him.

"You say anything, I'll cut off your *cajones*. You don't and . . . you'll get something you want."

Diaz looked at her bare breasts, smiled. Then walked away.

For more than two hours through the dark desert night Maureen O'Donnell rode the animal like a devil wind. Unused to a western saddle though she was, she stayed on and whipped the horse with the reins, and thought only of what and who might be riding after her and what would happen if she was overtaken.

The cold night air thrashed her face and spilled her hair out into a flowing red wake until nearly dawn when the speeding animal's hoof hit a sharp rock, stumbled and the horse dropped and Maureen dropped with it. Both hit the ground hard and lay on the cold barren earth of the desert.

It took a while and considerable effort, but the horse rose to its four legs, whinnied, then slowly began to limp back in the direction from which they came.

Maureen O'Donnell did not move.

Thirteen

Even before first light Adam Dawson bolted upward from the bed, for an instant not knowing where he was.

For weeks he'd been sleeping with his clothes on, a saddle blanket for cover and saddle for pillow.

But in that instant he had relived the events of the day and night before, and reinforced his intention to get the hell away from Walker's Way while the getting was good.

The best time was now, while nobody else was awake to try to talk him out of it; now, before he saw either Chad or Lorena.

A few minutes later his saddlebag was on the kitchen floor and Dawson sat at the table writing a note addressed to Mr. and Mrs. Walker.

"You're leaving." Her voice was barely audible.

Dawson looked up at Lorena framed in the doorway, fresh as a spring garden, as if she had spent a restful night of sweet, harmonious dreams. She looked at him with those eyes and moved a step closer, and spoke softly, with resignation and without rancor.

"I don't blame you. You don't *have* to stay."

"Neither do you."

"He's not always like that."

Dawson said nothing.

"I *am* his wife."

"You're a human being...I'm sorry. I shouldn't say anything...and I'm not going to."

"I'm glad that you care and I want to thank you."

"For what?"

"For not saying anything about seeing me on the trail yesterday."

"Lady, that's between you . . . and you."

"It's not what you think."

"Never is."

She took another step as she explained.

"The man with me, Brad Hatcher, he's our neighbor."

"That makes a difference . . . I guess."

"Please . . . He wants to buy this place. We were . . . uh, conspiring how to get Chad to sell, that's all."

"Good luck." Dawson rose.

"You're leaving afoot?"

"That's the way I came."

"Adam, take a horse."

"You mean steal it?"

"I have some money. I'll tell him you left it . . . I'll . . ."

"No, ma'am. I'll be all right, hope you will be too." He set the pencil he'd been writing with on the table next to the note.

"Where will you go?"

"West."

"Another ranch?"

"I'm quitting the beef business. Might look into the saloon business . . . as a customer."

"Adam, don't waste your life."

"Good advice. Take it."

They both reacted to the sound of the carriage basket settling onto the bottom of the stairway, then of Chad Walker and his canes.

"You'd better get going," she said and pointed to the note on the table. "I'll give that to him."

But Adam Dawson just stood there until the sound of the footsteps and canes grew louder and until he and Lorena heard the sound of Walker's voice as he approached the kitchen.

"Hey! Where the hell is everybody?"

Still Adam didn't move.

"Lorena!"

"In the kitchen, Chad."

Dawson picked up the note and folded it just before Walker clumped into the room.

"I don't smell any coffee," Walker said as he came in. "Where's Maria?"

"I don't know where Maria is . . . but Elena is probably at the mission. It's Sunday, remember?"

"Oh, yeah, so it is."

"I'll put the coffee on," Lorena said and then went about doing it.

"Morning, Adam."

"Morning."

"Sleep good?"

"Bed took a little getting used to. Slept just fine."

"Good." Walker glanced at the saddlebag. "See you're getting ready."

"How's that?"

"To move into the bunkhouse."

"Oh, yeah."

"Nueva show up yet?"

"Not yet," Adam answered.

"Lazy damn greaser. I oughta toss his junk out with the garbage." Walker settled into one of the hardback chairs at the table. "Say, that was a nice little visit we had last night, wasn't it, Adam?"

"Yeah, real nice."

"Well, we're gonna have plenty more from now on. Yes, sir, 'mi casa su casa,' as those greasers say, right Lorena?"

"Right, Chad."

"Hey, come on with that coffee, will you?"

"The water's got to boil first, Chad. Before it can boil, it's got to get hot. It takes a little while for it to get hot. In the meanwhile I'm working on the eggs and bacon, as you can see. Do you think you can survive for just a few minutes, or would you like to suck a raw egg while you wait?"

"Isn't she something?" Walker laughed. "Sure, honey, I can wait. How about you, Adam?"

"I'm not too big on breakfast."

"You will be the way Lorena fixes it. A lot better than that Mex does . . ."

"She's just a child, Chad, and since she's come here she's learned . . ."

"Okay, Okay, hey! The water's boiling."

"I see it." She lifted the pot from the flames.

"Adam, after we eat, we'll give you a tour . . . if you don't mind pulling the rickshaw."

"All in a day's work, I guess." Adam smiled, folded the note again, then stuck it into his shirt pocket.

"Corona! Hey, Corona! *Arriba!* Come out here!" Charly stood just outside Corona's hut and hollered through the door.

More than half the other residents of the *ranchería* were there too.

So was the horse.

Under ordinary circumstances they all knew better than to disturb their chief when he had company inside his hut. Sometimes when the company was good Corona had stayed inside for days. As far as Charly and everybody else knew, except for Olita and Diaz, Corona was in there with the red-headed captive.

Even so, when the horse came back limping, shuddering and barely able to stand, Charly took it upon himself to violate the do not disturb order. Still, he didn't go as far as opening the door. That just might be too far.

"Corona!" He banged on the door twice and hollered again.

Inside, Corona's head finally came up from the table. He rubbed his eyes and tried to clear the haze from his throbbing head. Still naked, he managed to get to his feet, look around and see that the bed was empty.

He couldn't exactly remember what happened. But he knew what didn't happen. And now she was gone.

It wasn't easy, but he pulled on his pants, got to the door and opened it.

"What the hell's going on?" he barked at Charly. "What?!"

"It's the horse," Charly said.

"What horse?"

"Cheecho." Charly was holding on to the reins.

"What about him? Goddam it!"

"He's been gone, must've gone a long way all saddled up and he come back limping . . ."

"Shut up about the horse. Where is she?"

"Who?"

"The *gringo* girl, you idiot son of a bitch, the one we brought back yesterday."

"She's inside with you . . . isn't she?"

"No."

"No?"

"No! She musta got away after I"—Corona almost said "passed out," but caught himself—"after I got finished with her."

"How could she do that?"

"She did it."

"You untied her?"

"Shut up!" Corona didn't want to admit that he couldn't quite remember what happened. But he remembered that he hadn't untied her. Hadn't raped her. And that he had passed out. But he couldn't figure out how a woman with her hands tied behind her could get up, saddle a horse and ride away without any help. He couldn't figure it out because he knew it couldn't have happened . . . without any help. But Corona didn't want to get into that now. Not before his head cleared and he had a chance to think a little more.

"What're we gonna do?" Charly asked.

"Yes, Corona," Olita inquired, "what are you gonna do?"

"We're gonna go after her, find her, bring her back and I'm gonna take up where I left off. That's what."

The Comancheros all nodded and laughed.

"Where's John Goose?" Corona asked.

"Here." A voice responded.

"Are you drunk or sober?"

"Sober," John Goose, who resembled his name, said. "I haven't had my breakfast yet."

"Don't."

John Goose, drunk or sober, was the best tracker among the Comancheros. But sober he was even better.

"You want me to go with you?" Olita asked.

"No, you stay here. Hey, where were you last night?"

"Not with you."

"I know that."

"If I was, she'd still be here..."

"Never mind that. Where?"

"I was sleeping like everybody else... like Charly, Diaz and everybody else... haven't I told you a hundred times to post guards? Haven't..."

"Never mind that either. We've wasted enough time. She's out there, with no horse. John Goose'll follow the tracks, we'll find her. Saddle up!" The Comancheros started to disperse. Charly still held Cheecho's reins.

"Corona."

"What?"

"What about the horse? What're we gonna do about Cheecho?"

"Shoot him. Eat him. I don't give a damn." Corona had wanted to rape the redhead then sell her to the Comanches. He had done neither. He was still determined to do both—and more—to punish her for escaping and making a fool of him in front of the camp. He headed back into the hut to get dressed for the ride.

Diaz stood looking at Olita for just a beat, then walked away toward his horse.

———

"When was the last time you had a breakfast like that, Adam?" Walker asked from atop the rickshaw as Dawson pulled the rig toward the henhouse while Lorena walked alongside.

"Never."

"Didn't your mother fix ..." Lorena started to ask.

"Don't remember my mother much," Dawson interrupted. "Or my dad. Both died young and so was I, a lot younger."

"Who took care of you?" Lorena asked.

"Grandfather, if you could call it that. He believed in growing up independent and staying that way."

"That's a hard way," she said.

"Good way."

"You appear to have thrived."

"Survived. So far." He grinned and looked back at Walker. "All three of us have."

"Not good enough just to survive," Walker said. "Almost anybody can survive. The trick is to prevail."

"At any cost, huh, Chad?" Lorena didn't look back at her husband.

"That's right. There's only winners and losers and the dead in between."

"What a philosophy," Lorena murmured, but loud enough for Walker to hear.

"*My* philosophy ... hey, there's ol' Uriah lookin' after his kingdom."

A rooster, the cock of the walk, was strutting the chicken yard area among flocks of Rhode Island Red hens skeltering all over the ground and each other.

Uriah, amid flying feathers, was tossing feed and talking to himself and the chickens. He set down the pan as the reddest and plumpest of the chickens came clucking up to him like a pet puppy dog.

"Ah, there you are Vashti, my beautiful queen. 'My eyes shall be upon the faithful of the land, that they may dwell with me. That ...' " He reacted to the sound of the approaching rickshaw. "Good Sabbath, Mr. Chad ... and who else?"

Dawson stopped the rickshaw close to the fence and eased the handles to the ground.

"Morning, Uriah," Walker said. "It's good ol' Lorena and Adam, the new man."

"Morning, brother Adam." He picked up the plump red hen and stroked her back. "This is Vashti. She's the queen. Isn't she beautiful?"

"Sure is," Adam said. "They're all beautiful."

"And fruitful." Uriah nodded.

"Yeah," Walker laughed. "We had some of their fruit for breakfast."

"Thank you, kindly," Uriah said as he kept stroking.

"Over there," Walker pointed, "is the target range. Scares the hell out of the chickens, but doesn't seem to interfere with their laying, if you know what I mean."

"Yes, Chad," Lorena said. "We know what you mean."

"We'll do a little shooting, Adam. Your Winchester against my Henry."

"At twenty paces?" Lorena volunteered.

"Very funny," Walker replied.

"I'm not all that handy with a long gun," Adam said. "Didn't have much use for 'em in the cavalry."

"Well, I'll teach you. But you're probably just being modest."

"We're not used to much modesty around here," Lorena said. "Are we, Chad?"

"Hell no. Over there are the bunkhouses. We'll see you later, Uriah, and remember, this is a day of rest, so take it easy, Trooper."

"Yes, sir." Uriah nodded. He set Vashti on the ground, found the pan and picked it up.

There were two small bunkhouses, both in need of attention. One with curtains, the other without. The curtains were worn and dirty.

"We got line shacks for most of the hands during the

round-up," Chad said as the rickshaw pulled up. "Nueva's junk's in there." He motioned toward the curtained structure. "Toss it out and move in or fix up the empty one. Unless you want to sleep in the guest room for a while?"

"I'll fix up the empty one," Dawson said without hesitation.

"Okay. Lorena, get Adam some curtains and whatever stuff he'll need."

"Sure."

"You're better off out here," Walker added, "more privacy."

"What happened to your corral?" Adam pointed. Almost half of it had fallen down. The rest was in disrepair.

"Damn wind blew it down."

"When?"

"Last week."

"I'll fix it up."

"Good," Walker said. "Let's go over to the stable."

The wagon tugged by two mules clattered onto the nearly empty main street of Pinto faster than it should have. At the reins was a Mexican farmer, Pedro Rojas. Next to him was his pregnant wife, Candida, and visible in the bed of the wagon were three children, two boys and a girl, none over the age of six. There was something else in the bed of the wagon not visible.

Most of the citizens were still asleep or at the Methodist Church on First Street, or at Baldy's Bar. Young Sam Mendez was sweeping up the area in front of the sheriff's office as the wagon slammed to a stop just in front of the building.

"*Señor,*" the driver called out. "Where is the sheriff? Where's Sheriff Ben?"

"He's inside."

"Will you get him, please . . . I've got to . . ."

The door opened and Ben Vesper stepped out before Rojas could finish.

"I'm right here, Pedro," Vesper said. "*Qué pasa?*"

"I don't know, Sheriff Ben. Maybe it's too late . . ."

"Calm down, Pedro. Just take it easy and tell me what happened. Too late for what?"

"For her." Rojas pointed back as the three children stood up and looked down onto the wagon floor.

Vesper came closer and also looked. So did Sam Mendez, still holding on to the broom.

The bruised, unconscious body of Maureen O'Donnell lay inside.

"Sam, get Doc Bonner. Try the church, but find him. Get him. Bring him here. Fast!"

"Yes, sir." The young man ran toward First Street still carrying the broom with him.

"What happened? Where'd you find her?"

"On the way to the mission. Candida saw her first. We tried to help her but she wouldn't move. I think she hurt bad . . . I don't know what else to do so we brought her here . . . for the doctor . . ."

"You did good, Pedro. Probably saved her life . . . if she lives. How long ago you find her?"

"Maybe an hour . . ."

"She's lucky you came along."

Doc Bonner, Sam Mendez and half a dozen of the parishioners came running from First Street.

"In there, Doc." The sheriff pointed. Bonner was over sixty-five, but nearly sprang into the wagon and kneeled close to the woman.

"What do you think?" Vesper asked.

"Can't tell much out here. Get her over to my office and I'll do what I can. Get these kids off here."

"*Abajo! Abajo!*" Pedro hollered to the children as he climbed up and took hold of the reins.

"Get a move on!" Doc Bonner barked. "It's that green house on the next corner."

Candida and Vesper helped the three children onto the ground. Sam Mendez leaned his broom against the hitching post in front of the sheriff's office and also helped. Then the wagon took off toward the green house on the next corner.

"What do you think happened?" Sam Mendez asked the sheriff.

"I don't know. You stay here. I'll go over and find out . . . maybe."

Fourteen

Inside the stable there were half a dozen horses in the stalls.

They had left the rickshaw outside. Adam, Lorena and Walker, now using his canes, walked into the barn.

"I keep the best ones in here. Let the rest of 'em run free," Walker said. "And here's the best of the best."

He stopped in front of one of the stalls where a big pinto stallion stretched his head out to Walker. Chad stroked the animal's nose. Even in the stall the animal was fractious.

"This is Domino. He's mine. He's got power and can go the distance."

"Beautiful animal," Dawson said.

"Gets spooky and wild sometimes."

"Yeah. Looks like a lot of horse."

"I can handle anything I put my mind to."

Lorena, standing a little behind Walker, glanced at Adam, took a stalk of straw from a bale and put the end of it in her mouth. Dawson avoided her glance.

"Look here." Walker hobbled over to a saddle rested on a rack. Not an ordinary saddle. Adam and Lorena followed.

The saddle had been specially fashioned to accommodate and protect Walker. Strong straps on the skirt for binding his legs. Leather, oversized boots riveted to the stirrups.

"I designed this rig myself."

"Well." Adam regarded the saddle, impressed. "I've never seen anything like it."

"But somebody has to lift him up and strap him into it," Lorena said, taking the straw out of her mouth.

"Sure. So what?"

"So nothing." She shrugged.

"Once I'm up there, there's nothing I can't do, or no place I can't go." Walker looked at Lorena. "Yeah, that's right, until I have to get off."

"Well." Adam smiled. "I guess that's where I'll come in, once I get the hang of it."

"Nothing to it, Adam. I'll show you how it hooks on and off."

"Good."

"First thing you'll need around here is a horse for yourself."

"Guess so."

"Use the appaloosa. Over here." Walker made his way to another stall. Adam and Lorena followed. "Good animal. Nueva rode him some, but with a good scrub and curry you can get the stink off."

"Thanks," Adam said. "What do you call him?"

"Pard."

"I'll take good care of Pard."

Walked moved to yet another stall, leaned on the edge and looked at the horse inside critically, a large, strong animal.

"Just bought this roan for Lorena." He motioned back toward his wife. "Don't believe in a woman riding a stallion, but . . ."

"Just *what* do you believe in a woman doing?" she said.

"Fine animal," Dawson quickly remarked.

"Yeah, but if he gets the smell of a mare . . . or a woman at certain times of the month, he can go crazy."

"Don't worry, Chad. I know when to ride and when not to."

"Sure you do. You know everything. But Adam, I want you to go out with her. Get to know the range."

"With Lorena?"

"Why not? She likes to ride more'n I do, and I don't like her going out alone."

"That's not a good idea," Adam said. "I mean her riding out alone. What with those Comancheros on the loose."

"But they wouldn't come this close," Lorena said. "Would they, Adam?"

"No tellin'. But it's better to be cautious."

"How many hit you?" Walker asked.

"Just two. I stashed my saddle. Sure would like to get that saddle back."

"You will. But tell me something."

"What?"

"How'd you get away?"

"Winchester."

"Very good." Walker looked at Lorena, then back at Dawson and smiled. " 'Specially for somebody who's not all that handy with a long gun."

On his way to Doc Bonner's office, Sheriff Ben Vesper had to walk past Baldy's Bar. But as the sheriff approached the bat-wings a man staggered through. At first Vesper thought it was still too early on a Sunday morning for the man to be that drunk, then he realized that the man wasn't . . . drunk. His face was bruised and bleeding.

"Hey, Rico, what's wrong? What happened to you?"

"That crazy sonofabitch." Rico motioned at the bat-wings.

"What crazy sonofabitch?"

"Nueva. Joe Nueva. He's inside pickin' fights. I didn't say nothin'. Crazy sonofabitch." Rico wiped at the blood and walked away.

Inside Joe Nueva hit another man, who slammed against a table, breaking it, then crashed onto the floor.

Half a dozen customers stood in an uneven semicircle viewing the damage to man and furniture. So did Baldy and Alma.

"All right, you bastards." Nueva beckoned with both

hands. "Anybody else?" Nueva swaggered over to the biggest customer. "You."

"Joe," Baldy said. "Why don't you go outside?"

"I ain't goin' no place. I like it here."

"You been drinkin' all morning." Baldy took a step forward.

"And I'm gonna keep on drinkin'."

"I said *you*." He moved closer to the biggest customer. "You got somethin' to say about that drifter before I get his ears?"

"Not me, Joe. Hell, no!"

"Anybody else?" Nueva turned around and came face to face with Sheriff Ben Vesper.

"I got something to say, Joe." Vesper drew his gun and smashed the barrel hard across Joe Nueva's forehead.

Nueva dropped like a shot buffalo.

"A couple of you men carry him over to jail," Vesper said. " 'Til he sleeps it off."

"I'll do it." Sam Mendez spoke from near the entrance, then walked over and lifted Nueva onto his shoulder like a sack of potatoes.

"What're you doing here?" Vesper asked.

"Saw you come inside." Sam Mendez grinned. "Thought you might need some..." Sam just smiled and shrugged "...company."

"Look, son, for a good many years, man and boy, I've made my way through life without you..." the customers laughed, then Vesper added, "but thanks, I guess you do come in handy."

"Thanks, Sheriff."

"Well, don't just stand there. Take that drunk bastard and deposit him over to the jail."

"Yes, sir, Sheriff." Sam Mendez moved easily to the entrance and through the bat-wings with the drunk bastard over his shoulder.

"That your new deputy, Ben?" Alma smiled.

"Nope," Sheriff Ben Vesper replied, then added, "not yet."

When the sheriff walked back onto Main Street from Baldy's the street was much busier than just a short time ago. Church services had ended and the good Christian citizens of Pinto were on their way to diverse destinations in and around town via foot, horse and carriage.

The finest carriage in and around town was owned by Brad Hatcher. It just so happened that Mr. and Mrs. Hatcher were aboard that carriage just passing by Baldy's as the sheriff strolled out. Hatcher reined the carriage horse to a stop.

"Good morning, Sheriff."

"Morning, Mr. Hatcher, Mrs. Hatcher." Vesper tipped his hat to the lady.

She smiled in return. Brad Hatcher pointed toward the sheriff's office and jail.

"See that Joe Nueva's been at it again. Just noticed Sam toting him toward the lock-up."

"Yeah."

"What happened?"

"Nothin' unusual. Just feelin' ornery."

"Say, I also noticed that Doc Bonner left right in the middle of Reverend Groves' sermon. Somebody sick?"

Vesper thought that Hatcher was inordinately inquisitive this Sunday morning, but he didn't want to appear impolite in front of Mrs. Hatcher, so he remained pleasantly accommodating.

"Yeah. Pedro Rojas found a woman out in the desert in pretty bad shape, took her over to the Doc's place."

"How bad?"

"That's what I'm my way over to find out." If I ever get there, Vesper thought to himself, as Alma, who had been listening, stepped through the bat-wings.

"I see." Hatcher nodded. "Well, good day to you, Sheriff." Hatcher cracked the reins without acknowledgement of Alma, and the carriage moved off.

"You know who she is?" Alma asked.

"Who who is?"

"The woman in the desert."

"No. What's the matter, don't Hatcher talk to you on Sundays?"

"Not when his wife's around but I don't give a damn. Mind if I go?"

"Where?"

"With you to Doc's."

"What for?"

"Maybe I could help."

"Doing what?"

"Well, that's what I intend to find out. I used to be a nurse."

"You?"

"Me."

"When?"

"During the war."

"Well then come along." Vesper did his best to hide his amazement. They started to walk.

"I didn't know that about you," he said.

"There's a lot about me you don't know." She smiled as they walked. "But then again, there's a lot about me that you *do* know."

Vesper cleared his throat and they kept walking.

Fifteen

Lorena had fixed the Sunday noon meal for the three of them. Walker had invited Uriah, but the old trooper declined, preferring to fix his own edibles and spend the time with his chickens and Bible.

Walker drank a few drinks along with the Sunday dinner and Chad had started to pour for Dawson, but Adam demurred.

"No, thanks, boss. I got some work to do."

"What work? It's Sunday, remember?"

"Got to clean up the bunkhouse if I'm going to sleep out there tonight."

"Yeah, that's right. Well, I'm going to go up and take me a *siesta*, that's one good greaser tradition. Lorena, why don't you give Adam a hand out there?"

"No," Adam said. "I don't need any help."

"Well, you two do whatever you want. Me, I'm going up."

Corona, Diaz, Charly and the other Comancheros, still on horseback, were clustered around John Goose who had dismounted and was reading tracks and interpreting events.

"Here." John Goose pointed. "Here the horse went down. Her over there." He moved a few feet to a nearby spot, then motioned with his right hand. "Wheels. Wagon wheels. Stopped here. Mule tracks. Two mules. Boots.

Woman shoes. Must be they picked her up. Her no walk."

"Dead?" Corona asked.

"Can't tell. No way to tell. But didn't walk. Load into wagon." John Goose pointed again. "Wagon moved that way. Maybe Pinto."

"Shit," Corona muttered.

"You want to follow?" John Goose asked.

"What for?" Diaz answered quickly and looked at Corona. "Can't get her back now and she's probably dead." Diaz hoped that she was and he certainly didn't want Corona to question the woman if she wasn't. He wanted to share the secret of her escape with Olita ... and something else. "Might as well go back," he advised.

"Yeah, goddammit." Corona wheeled his horse. "We go back."

"Amazing," Doc Bonner had said. "Amazing. I never thought she'd recover so soon, if at all. This lady is made of hardy stock."

When Maureen O'Donnell had first opened her eyes she had no idea where she was, or whom she was with. But she realized that she was away from the Comancheros and that she was safe.

Doc Bonner, Vesper and Alma had watched as she came to and asked her whereabouts and how she got there.

"Maybe you better rest now," Doc said. "We can talk later, when you ..."

"No, please, I want to talk, I have to know how'd I get here?"

"I guess the sheriff can best tell you," Doc said.

And Ben Vesper did, as briefly as he could, about Pedro Rojas and his family finding her and bringing her into Pinto.

"Thank you." Maureen nodded. "Did they find ... Tim ... my husband?"

"No, ma'am," Vesper said. "There was nobody else."

"They killed him." Her eyes filled. "And took me with them."

"Who did?" Vesper asked.

"Corona . . . they called him Corona."

All three knew about Corona and his Comancheros and that he had a hideout somewhere in the desert. The wonder was that she wasn't still there or someplace worse, if there was someplace worse. But all three, especially Doc Bonner, thought it inadvisable to pursue the wonder.

"That's enough for now, ma'am. You're safe and are going to be all right, but you need to get back your strength. Just tell us your name."

"O'Donnell, Maureen O'Donnell, Tim, he . . ."

"We'll try to . . . we'll do what we can, ma'am," Vesper said.

"Please." Doc Bonner soothed her brow and adjusted the damp cloth he had placed there. "Close your eyes. We'll be close by."

"Thank . . ." She didn't finish. Maureen O'Donnell was unconscious, again.

"Christ almighty," Doc Bonner said. "She's been close enough to hell to smell smoke."

"Yeah." Vesper nodded.

"Damn." Bonner took the pocket watch out of his vest and looked at it.

"What's the matter?" Vesper asked.

"Ol' Claude Hawkins is bad off. Promised I'd look in on him before noon. I'm way late, but . . ." '

"You go on there," Alma said. "I'll stay here with her."

"You will?"

"Sure, Doc." Vesper smiled. "And don't worry about your patient here. Alma's a nurse."

"She is?"

"I am."

"Well, I'll be damned." Doc Bonner put the watch back into his vest pocket. "Will wonders never cease."

"I hope not, Doc," Sheriff Ben Vesper said. "Better get going."

Adam Dawson spent most of Sunday cleaning up his new quarters. Lorena stayed away until it was time for supper. She came out to tell him to come in.

They walked back to the house without speaking. The conversation at the supper table was sparse. Afterward in the library, Chad Walker had a few drinks, Dawson had one and Lorena had none.

A couple of times Chad asked about Custer. Dawson got away with the telling of only one incident Custer had related to him about when he was a cadet at West Point. One of Autie's superior officers took great pride in a flock of prize hens and a buff cock he had dubbed "Mr. Chanticleer" who kept Custer and the other cadets awake with his boastful crowing, until Autie took it upon himself to kidnap the cock, dispatch and pluck it, prepare the unfeathered remains in a stew pan and devour the result with the assistance of two other cadets and enjoy uninterrupted sleep of satisfaction, if not innocence, from then on. The superior officer had his suspicions as to the identity of the culprit, but lacked evidence of proof.

As Walker laughed, Dawson was quick to excuse himself, saying that he had a little more work to do in the bunkhouse.

In Pinto, Sheriff Ben Vesper unlocked the cell as Sam Mendez watched.

"Okay, Joe, you can leave now. But don't go to Baldy's. Not tonight. Or to the Iguana. Go home and think things over. You even look sideways and your next stay'll be for thirty days. Goodnight."

Maureen O'Donnell was asleep. Doc Bonner had come back to his place after Claude Hawkins died that night. Alma had sent word to Baldy that she wouldn't be in. She told Doc Bonner to go to bed. She'd stay with Maureen O'Donnell that night and sleep in the chair. Bonner was too tired to argue.

Mrs. and Mr. Hatcher in separate rooms lay in their respective beds. She with her cat, Caesar, and Bible. He with his schemes for the future.

Corona was in bed, naked. So was Olita. In the same bed.

Adam Dawson was stripped to the waist, except for the red scarf around his neck. From the scarf up, his throat and face to the top of his forehead where the rim of his hat circled, were as bronzed as a newly minted penny.

His untanned arms, long even for a man his length, were corded with well-knit sinew, leading up to hard mounds of shoulders topping a broad span of chest and tapering to a narrow circle of waist.

He moved with the silken ease of a panther as he lifted a chair to a new location in the bunkhouse, which was lit by a single kerosene lamp atop an oval table, then looked around the room.

Against the walls there were four double bunks to accommodate cowboys at other times, times of round-up and branding, bunks now empty. During those times the room would seem small and crowded. Now it appeared downright spacious. More room indoors than Adam Dawson was used to.

From the pocket of his shirt hanging on a peg, Dawson took one of the two cigars Chad Walker had given him earlier, and with a match from the same pocket, struck it across the wall and lit the stogie. He inhaled the smoke then turned toward the sound at the door he had left ajar.

Lorena Walker knocked again then stepped inside carrying folded sheets, but only a step inside so she was still silhouetted by the gleam of moonlight.

She literally stood in beauty of the night. A portrait of perfection. Her flowing flaxen hair spread gently against her shoulders, her azure eyes plumbed at Dawson's powerful body, just a little too long before she looked around at the room.

"Well, the place hasn't looked like this since . . . ever."

"Just tidied up a little."

"More than a little."

Dawson didn't know whether to go for his shirt or not. He didn't. He took another puff from the cigar.

"Thought I'd have a smoke before turning in." He smiled. "Fine cigar." He felt he had to say something as she stood there looking at him again.

"Yes. Chad has nothing but the best. Cigars. Horses. Whiskey . . ."

"Well, he's got it coming." Dawson didn't let her finish whatever she was going to say. "He's had a bad break . . ."

"It seems that you've changed your opinion of him from this morning when you were going to leave and advised me to do the same."

"No, I haven't. But like I said, I shouldn't have said anything. That's between you and you."

"You're a strange man, Adam Dawson."

"I guess everybody seems a little strange, until you get to know him, or her."

"Not everybody. Wait 'til you really get to know Chad."

"I probably won't . . . be around that long, I mean."

"Why *did* you stay this morning? Was it because of me?"

"Partly. Partly because of him. Nobody's all good or all bad."

"In his case you think the good outweighs the bad?"

"I don't know, yet. But Uriah thinks so."

"I brought you some sheets for the bunk."

"Thanks but I'm not used to 'em."

"We've all got to get used to things." She held out the sheets and he took them. As he did their hands touched.

Adam took the sheets and drew his hand away as she looked at him.

"Well . . . thanks. But I don't want to get used to 'em. The sheets, I mean."

"Why not? You might get to like 'em. The sheets, I mean."

"Yeah, but they might not be around the next place I go."

"Why go?"

"Don't . . . don't you think it's better if you go inside?"

"Not better . . . but I will. Good night, Adam Dawson."

"Good night . . . Mrs. Walker."

She turned smoothly and walked out of the door leaving it open behind her.

Dawson, holding the sheets, still breathing in the fragrance of her perfume, walked to the door and watched her moonlit silhouette move away from the bunkhouse and toward the house.

He closed the door and inhaled the smoke of Chad Walker's cigar, hoping it would dissipate the fragrance of Lorena Walker's perfume.

It didn't. Not for a long time.

Sixteen

Adam Dawson, astride the appaloosa, rode hard and fast.

But not as fast as Chad Walker, strapped into his rig, riding Domino six lengths ahead of Adam.

Dawson spurred Pard. The appaloosa responded, stretching his strides and gaining ground, but as the gap narrowed, Walker rein-whipped Domino, who bolted faster and kept the lead.

Lorena, atop her stallion, stood at what had been designated as the finish marker. Chad raced by, then reined Domino to a stop as Adam, then Lorena came up alongside on their mounts.

Dawson had been reluctant to race against Walker, but Chad Walker was the boss and had made it sound more like an order than a suggestion.

Maybe Dawson could have done better, he certainly had done better when his life had depended on it, but there was nothing at stake here, except Walker's ego. Still Adam was surprised, even astounded, at Walker's ability as a horseman, especially under the circumstances.

"You win, boss." Adam grinned as he patted the appaloosa. "You should've been in the cavalry."

"Good enough to ride with Custer?"

"Autie would've been glad to have you, anytime."

"You hear that, Lorena?"

"I heard."

"Let's head back to the stable," Walker said and moved ahead as Dawson and Lorena followed.

"I heard the sound of hoofbeats," Uriah said, standing near the stable.

"Yeah, Trooper. We gave the horses a little exercise this morning." Walker smiled from his mount.

"We had a race, Uriah," Adam added. "Mr. Walker won."

"You gave it a good ride, Adam. Came closer than anybody else has. Right, Lorena?"

"Right, *boss.*"

"How do you like Pard there? Getting used to him?"

"He's easy to take to."

"Looks like he's taken to you, too."

"I'll see you later," Uriah said. "Got to get back to my chores now." He turned and walked away toward the henhouse.

"Well, let's go inside, get me outta this rig. Say, Adam, you really think I coulda rode with Custer, wore a red scarf?"

"No doubt about it."

"Where's he now, Custer?"

"Up north."

"With his wife?"

"Yep. And they've got Cheyenne and Sioux for company."

"Sure would like to be up there with him teaching those redskins a thing or two."

"Yeah, well they can do a little teaching, too."

"Ever been up there, Adam?"

"For a while. Well, let's go inside and get you off. Then I'll give the horses a rub."

"I'm sorry, ma'am." Ben Vesper, Doc Bonner and Alma were at the bed where Maureen O'Donnell was now sitting up. "We buried him and left a marker."

What Vesper hadn't told her was how little of her husband they had found. No flesh. Bones picked clean by buzzards.

"Thank you," she said. "I'll pray for him in heaven. He was a good man."

"I'm sure of that," Vesper whispered.

"Those men who...who killed him...do you think they'll ever be caught and..."

"They're what we call Comancheros, Mrs. O'Donnell, rob and kill and take prisoners to trade with the Indians, still don't see how you got away from them..."

"Please, I'd rather not talk about it, yet, I..."

"What are you planning to do, ma'am?"

"She's got to take it easy for a while," Doc Bonner said. "Still in bad shape, she..."

"There's something else I haven't told you." Maureen spoke slowly. "We...I was going to have...a baby... Doctor...I don't know, after what happened, if..."

"Can't tell yet." Doc Bonner shook his head. "After that fall and...well, it'll take some time to be sure, one way or other."

"You have any relatives, ma'am?" Vesper asked.

"Tim's brother near Laredo..."

"There's time enough for that later," Alma said. "Meanwhile, you're gonna stay with me 'til you get well."

"No..."

"Yes, and don't argue. I'm all alone and I've got plenty of room and could use company. Ain't that so, Ben?"

"That's so."

"Then that settles that," Doc Bonner said. "You know, Alma here used to be a nurse."

As Sheriff Ben Vesper walked up the street toward his office he saw Sam Mendez standing in front of Baldy's Bar.

"What're you doing out here, Sam?"

"Nothin'."

"Nothin'? Must be doing somethin' beside standing like a cigar-store Indian."

"Well..."

"Well what?"

"I saw Joe Nueva goin' in and I thought I'd stand here 'til you came by and tell you, in case . . ."

"All right, you told me. Now get back to the office and I mean get back. Don't hang around. Folks'll think I can't get along without you."

"Yes, sir."

"What're you doing in here, Joe?" Nueva was playing poker with three of his amigos.

"Looking for a job," he said.

"Think you'll find it in that deck of cards?"

"People come in."

"Yeah."

"Look, Sheriff, you told me not to come in last night. You didn't say anything about today."

"Guess not. By the way, Joe, ain't you acquainted with them Comancheros? Got a cousin or something riding with 'em?"

"No."

"No, huh?"

"Well, I ain't seen him in a long time."

"Good. Keep it that way. And good luck, finding a job." Ben Vesper turned and walked out.

Sam Mendez was standing in front of the sheriff's office looking back toward Baldy's Bar.

Inside, Brad Hatcher was at the bar having his one or two, three at the most, drinks whenever he came into Pinto, and had been watching and listening to the exchange between Nueva and the sheriff.

"You can put the bottle away, Baldy, I've had my quota. Got to get over to the bank."

"Yes, sir, Mr. Hatcher."

"Where's Alma?"

"Said she was takin' a few days off."

"That so." Hatcher smiled. "Place isn't nearly the same without her."

"Yeah, and I don't get my afternoon snooze." As Baldy

took the bottle and walked away, Joe Nueva got up from the card game and approached Hatcher.

"Mr. Hatcher..."

"How you doing, Joe?" Hatcher noticed the latest bruise on Nueva's forehead, but made no mention.

"Remember what you said the other day?"

"About what?"

"When I asked you for a job and you said somethin' might happen and..."

"Oh, yeah, I remember. Well, nothing's happened, Joe. Everything's still the same. But I'll let you know if it does."

"I'll be here, Mr. Hatcher... and thanks."

"Sure, Joe. *Adiós*."

Brad Hatcher walked past Joe Nueva, out into the street and headed toward the Bank of Pinto.

"Sheriff?" Sam Mendez asked as he mopped the office while Ben Vesper was rifling through wanted dodgers. "What prompted you into being a lawman?"

"Part of my inheritance, I guess."

"How's that?"

"My old man, the white part of the family, was a lawman."

"A sheriff?"

"Worse. By that I mean a lot more dangerous. A Texas Ranger."

"I guess that is a lot more dangerous."

"Sure. Sheriff sits and waits for trouble to come to town. Ranger has to go lookin' for it at times. They don't call 'em 'rangers' for nothin'. There was a time when nothin' stood between law and disorder in Texas but the Rangers."

"So I heard tell."

"You heard it right and Bill Vesper was among 'em at that time. Was with 'em when Captain Jack Hays and his rangers rode south and helped the U.S. Army win the Mexican Campaign, from Monterrey to Buena Vista. That's where he fell in love with my mother and brought her back to Texas. And I think that's enough biography. How about getting back to mopping?"

Sam did. But not for long. After a few strokes he leaned against the mop handle and looked over at Vesper.

"Sheriff?"

"What?"

"How's she doin'? The woman Rojas brought in?"

"Well, considering what she's come through ... losing her husband, being taken by them Comancheros, getting away and falling off a horse, I'd say better than could be expected."

"What's gonna happen to her?"

"Well, for the time, she's going to move in with Alma."

"Alma?"

"Alma. Used to be a nurse."

"I didn't know that."

"Nobody did, and now just about everybody does."

"Sheriff ..."

"What?"

"You think them Comancheros, well, you think that they ..."

"I think ..."

"Yes, sir?"

"I think you ought to do more mopping and ask less questions. That's what I think."

"Yes, sir." Sam started mopping, but before he did, asked one more question. "Ever see hair so red?"

"No," Sheriff Ben Vesper replied. "Nor a face so ... lovely."

He went back to the dodgers, looking at faces that weren't at all lovely. Just dangerous.

"Sheriff ..." Sam looked up again.

"Mop!"

"Yes, sir."

———

At dusk Brad Hatcher was riding the palomino toward Spanish Bit. Once again, not far from the entrance to Walker's Way he reined in the animal and gazed toward what he coveted. Land. Water. And . . .

One way or another Brad Hatcher would have all three.

Seventeen

The sun cast its long, last shadows of the day and disappeared behind the Texas horizon.

Texas. Beautiful. Bountiful. A battlefield since time remembered. Rich plains. Thick forests. Deep natural harbors curving along the Gulf of Mexico. Flowing rivers replenishing the land.

But much of the land was hard and hostile, as hard and hostile as those who dwelled and fought on it and for it; the tribes who fought each other, at first on foot with arrows and tomahawks: Comanche, Kiowa, Cherokee, Apache.

Then the conquerors. From this and other continents. Mexicans. Spaniards. Bringing horses. And gunpowder.

And finally those who came to stay. Americans. Maybe the most civilized. But certainly the most determined. Lusty. Land hungry. Unyielding. Undaunted. A perpetual procession of seekers. Cattlemen. Entrepreneurs. Farmers. Runaways. Outlaws and lawmen. The women who would bear a new breed called Texans.

Among them a giant, Sam Houston. When Texas declared its independence from Mexico it was Houston, the Commander-in-Chief of the Revolutionary Forces, who led the Texans against the army of Santa Ana, defeated the Mexicans at San Jacinto and became the first president of the new Republic of Texas.

It was Houston who led the movement for Texas to join the United States and later opposed the secession from the

Union. It was Houston who had warned his fellow Texans—
a warning that went unheeded:

"Your fathers and husbands, your sons and brothers, will
be herded at the point of bayonets . . . while I believe with
you in the doctrine of states' rights, the North is determined
to move with the steady momentum and perseverance of a
mighty avalanche: and what I fear is, they will overwhelm
the South."

Sam Houston's warning, fear, and prediction came to
pass.

And with it the black shadow of defeat and drought that
now choked the lifeblood and spirit of what once was a
proud land.

Still, most of the Texans stayed. And others came, in the
hope that out of defeat, destruction and desolation the black
shadow would lift, the drought would end and the lone star
of Texas would once again shine bright and proud.

And among those who had come was Chad Walker,
bringing with him his wife. Walker didn't give a hoot in hell
for Texas or Texans, nor for its past glory or future prospects. Only for his own . . . and for the chance to take back
something from the Rebel bastards who took away his free-
dom to move and walk and lay with his wife . . . like the
enemies who could still move and walk and cause their wives
to bring forth sons and daughters that he, Chad Walker,
could never have.

Instead, he had a slug in his back and hate in his heart.

That night at the supper table with Lorena and Dawson,
Walker was expansive, smiling and gesturing. For two days
in a row he had been of almost cheerful aspect, at least for
Chad Walker.

He had even been almost civil to Elena who was serving
supper. In contrast she appeared more apprehensive than
ever, hunched over in an odd manner and wearing an even
looser fitting garment.

Walker held out his empty wine glass toward his wife.

"Hey, honey, pour me another dollop of that stuff, will
you? It's settling in there pretty damn good."

"Sure, *honey*," Lorena replied and poured.

"How about you, Adam?" Walker asked.

"Can't you see his glass is still full?" Lorena said and put the bottle back on the table.

"So it is," Walker noted. "Say, Adam, your friend, 'Autie,' is he a drinking man?"

"Not anymore."

"That mean he used to be?"

"Some. 'Til we were home on leave once after Chickahominy."

"What happened?"

"Went to a saloon together. By that time he was quite the local hero and everybody insisted on buying him drinks and Autie didn't want to insult 'em by refusing. So they kept buying and he kept drinking until I managed to get him back to his sister's house."

"So?"

"So on the way we happened to meet up with Judge Bacon, Autie's prospective father-in-law. The next day Autie couldn't remember a thing about the night before except the hangover and running into, actually stumbling, into the judge."

"That did it?"

"That and the lecture his sister delivered on the evils and stupidity of drinking. Autie impulsively grabbed hold of a Bible and swore to her that he'd never take another drink as long as he lived. And he hasn't."

"As far as you know."

"I'd stake my life on Custer's word. He's never broken it and never will. That's his way."

"I'd bet it's your way, too," Lorena said.

Walker drank his wine and Dawson didn't answer.

"Hey, Adam." Chad smiled. "Lorena says that you cleaned up the bunkhouse real good. Not like that pesthole that greaser lived in, damn scum."

Elena didn't react to the epithet.

"And I see you started to fix up the corral."

"Yep. Ought to have it all straightened up in a couple of days. After that, if you don't mind, thought I'd do a little repairing on Uriah's place."

"Place? If the termites ever quit holding hands, that shack'd fall apart. But go ahead do what you want."

"Fine."

Walker eyed Elena as she came out of the kitchen holding a pot of coffee.

"Hey, you." Walker scowled as she placed the pot on the table. "Why you hunched over like that?"

A look of fear bolted into Elena's dark eyes and she drew back a step.

"You hurt your back? Something happened while you were away?"

Elena shook her head no.

"Then straighten up!"

Reluctantly, the girl stood straighter and the incriminating bulge in her middle became evident.

"I'll be damned!" Walker's fist pounded on the table. "You knocked up?"

There was no answer from the quaking girl.

"Pregnant! Pregnant!" Walker slapped his belly. "Knocked up!"

"Chad!" Lorena exclaimed.

"Answer me." Walker demanded. "Are you?"

"*Sí, señor*," Elena barely whispered.

"*Sí, señor*, my ass. You're all alike. You stinking greasers multiply like rabbits. Who was it? Who? Nueva? Yeah, Nueva, the sonofabitch, that's who it was, wasn't it?"

"Chad, it's none of your business," Lorena said.

"What am I doing here? Running a whorehouse?"

"Elena." Lorena tried to comfort the girl who had begun to sob.

"They go around wearing crosses and beads and humping everybody in sight!"

"Elena, please leave now." Lorena rose. "I'll talk to you later."

Elena Garcia left, walking as quickly as she could.

"Chad. What good does screaming at her do? The poor girl..."

"Poor girl, hell. Probably got some kind of a disease... most of 'em do." Walker managed to get to his feet with the help of his canes. "Aw, shit. Let's go into the library, Adam, have some bourbon... damn pepperbellies," he muttered. "Makin' a whorehouse outta my place..."

Chad Walker hobbled off on his canes. Lorena looked at Adam for a moment, then went after Elena in the kitchen.

Dawson followed Walker toward the library.

Sheriff Ben Vesper and Sam Mendez walked into the sheriff's office.

"She looked a whole lot better tonight," Sam said as he hung his hat on a peg, "than when she come into town, huh, Sheriff?"

"Whole lot."

"I'd judge she's the best lookin' girl around here, except maybe Mrs. Walker, but then Mrs. Walker is..."

"Is what?"

"Oh, you know... more big-city like. Mrs. O'Donnell, she's country folk. I sure do admire the way she talks with that... that waddya call it?"

"Brogue."

"That's it. Say, Sheriff, ought we to go on our rounds about now?"

"Still early, Sam. Another hour or so, and when we go, I'm going alone and you're staying here."

"Yes, sir."

They had just come back from taking Maureen O'Donnell from Doc Bonner's house to Alma's cottage, using Doc's buggy. Vesper had carried her from Doc's house to the buggy, then from the buggy into Alma's cottage, where Alma had an extra room and bed all made up for her guest-patient.

Never had anyone except her husband held Maureen in

his arms and with such strength, yet gentleness.

After the sheriff and Sam left Alma's cottage Alma fixed some tea and the two women talked. First about Pinto and Doc Bonner, then Alma mentioned Sheriff Ben Vesper.

"He seems like a very nice man," Maureen said.

"He's better than that and he's made a big difference in Pinto since he took over as sheriff."

"How's that?"

"Well, have some more tea and I'll tell you, if you'd care to hear it."

"I would."

"It was right after the war . . ."

Ben Vesper had come back to Pinto after three years of fighting and losing. He had a small ranch where his mother had stayed until she died of fever in '64.

One Saturday afternoon he rode into Pinto, tied his horse to the rail outside Baldy's and went in for a drink. Alma had only been in Pinto a short time herself.

After his drink he walked across the street to the bank to talk to Terrance Swerd who held a mortgage on the Vesper ranch and also was the mayor of Pinto.

"Can't loan you any more on it, Ben. You know how things are in Texas."

"I know. Thanks anyhow, Mr. Swerd."

"But I will cut the payments in half. 'Til you get on your feet."

"I thank you. That'll help."

"You know, Ben, we don't need any more ranchers around here. Got too damn many as it is. What we do need is a sheriff. I knew your dad and . . ."

"You already got a sheriff, Mr. Swerd."

"Mike Hotchkiss is old. 'Fraid of his own shadow. He lets himself be hurrahed by snot-nosed kids and any-body . . ."

"Sorry, Mr. Swerd, not my business . . ."

"Your father . . ."

"Got a bullet in the back and a cheap funeral. Sorry, I . . ."

Gunshots. Two, three, four. From the street.

"Goddammit!" Terrance Swerd rose from his desk and looked out the window. "The Plummers again, shooting up the town."

"Yeah, well, I got to be gettin'."

"Just a minute. Maybe this is your business. Take a look."

Luke and LeRoy Plummer had ridden into town, reined up in front of Baldy's and dismounted. There were already three horses tied to the hitching post including Ben Vesper's and no room for any more.

Luke had pulled out a knife and instead of untying the three horses' reins, cut them close to the bit, drew his pistol and fired, spooking the animals. LeRoy also got off a couple shots. The last one shattered a second-story window.

When Terrance Swerd and Vesper came outside from the bank, Sheriff Hotchkiss was standing there watching. He started to move away toward the sheriff's office.

"Just a minute, Mike," Swerd said. "Aren't you going to do something about that?"

"Them Plummer boys is crazy," Hotchkiss answered.

"And you're the sheriff. That's what you get paid for."

Brad Hatcher came up the boardwalk and stood next to the banker/mayor.

"What about this?" he said to the men.

"That's just what I was asking the sheriff." Swerd looked at Hotchkiss.

"Fellas, I'll be sixty-three tomorrow. I don't intend to be buried on my birthday." He took off the badge, handed it to Terrance Swerd, and walked in the opposite direction of the sheriff's office.

Both the Plummers had just finished tying up their horses to the recently vacated hitching post and were heading for the bat-wings of Baldy's.

"Assholes! Both of you!"

Both of the assholes turned and saw Ben Vesper standing close to the hitching post.

"What did you say?" Luke Plummer's eyes narrowed and the fingers of his right hand flexed.

"I wasn't talking to your horses."

"Who the hell do you think you are?"

"I'm the owner of that rein you cut and you're going to pay for it." Vesper pointed to one of the sliced reins still dangling from the post.

"Try to collect, I'll pay you with this." Plummer's hand inched toward his holster.

Ben Vesper's hand streaked, his gun flashed twice and Luke and LeRoy's hats flew off their owners heads, a hole in the center of each crown. Both men's guns were still leathered.

"That'll be five dollars," Ben said.

The Plummers paid, picked up their ventilated hats, mounted and rode out of Pinto respectful-like.

Both Swerd and Hatcher walked up to Ben Vesper. So did a lot of other citizens.

"Ben," Swerd said. "You just elected yourself sheriff. Fifty a month and whatever bounties you collect ... and I'll make you a further accommodation on that mortgage. Deal?" he held out the badge.

"Deal," Sheriff Ben Vesper said and pinned on the badge.

"That," Alma told Maureen O'Donnell, "is how Ben Vesper came to be sheriff of Pinto and it's made a big difference."

It had been more than two hours since Adam had followed Walker into the library as Walker continued his discourse on morals and Mexicans. Adam said nothing, just let Walker blow off sanctimonious steam for a few minutes until Chad finally looked at him and said, "What do you think, Adam?"

"I ... thought you wanted to come in here and drink a little bourbon."

"Hell, yes!" Walker's face brightened and his demeanor changed as if he had forgotten all about Elena's pending motherhood, at least for the time being. "Pour me a double."

"With pleasure." Dawson went straight to the bar while Walker made his way to the round table in the middle of the room and settled into a chair.

"You much of a card player, Adam?"

"Played some." Dawson's grandfather seldom took his grandson fishing, hiking or even spent much time talking to the boy. Two things the old man enjoyed doing was shooting and playing cards. And those were the two things he spent time doing with his grandson. The old man was good at both. And so was Adam Dawson. By the time Adam was thirteen he could count the cards at blackjack; by fifteen, he was a poker master.

"Tell you what, Adam." Walker opened the drawer of the table and scooped out a pile of silver dollars. "Just to make it interesting . . . instead of playing for matches or mar-bles . . . suppose I hand you an advance of your wages, say ten dollars, make it fifteen, and we'll play a little blackjack. That suit you?"

"Why not? As the saying goes, I'm playing with house money . . . sort of."

"Blackjack?"

"Blackjack." Dawson handed Walker the drink and hold-ing his own glass, took a seat across the table.

"Good." Walker smiled. "I'll bank."

During the first hour they played the two gamblers won and lost almost alternately. Sometimes twice in a row for Walker then twice, maybe three times successively for Daw-son.

But in the second hour a pattern began to emerge. One win for Walker, then two or three wins for Dawson.

Adam had already brought the bourbon bottle from the bar to the table to save trips. Walker drank, but not nearly as much as the other night. But his losses grew and so did the stacks of silver dollars in front of Adam. Each hand Daw-son won was never any more than by one or two points. When Chad won it was always by two or three.

A good gambler never counted his winnings while the

game was in progress, but by estimating the heights of the silver stacks and the smaller rick of Double Eagles on his side of the table, Dawson knew that he had won close to one hundred fifty dollars.

The bet was Walker's Double Eagle against Dawson's two stacks of ten silver dollars in the center of the table.

Walker showed a black queen and Adam figured him for another face card. Dawson had a red king and an eight of spades face down.

"Hit me," Adam said. "Easy."

Walker flipped out a three of diamonds and Dawson turned over his other card.

"Damn! You sonofabitch!"

"*Lucky* sonofabitch."

Walker swallowed his drink, grabbed the bottle and started to pour into Adam's glass. Dawson slapped his hand over the rim.

"Had enough, boss."

"Me, too ... of blackjack. But I'll have just one more of Tennessee. Well, Adam, I enjoyed the company. Can't say the same for the game. I'll get it back."

Adam started to push the piles of money back toward Walker.

"No. I mean I'd win it back some other time. You won it fair and square ... didn't you?"

"You were dealing."

"So I was. Then why're you pushing money at me?"

"I want to buy something."

Lorena walked into the library as Dawson said it. She had heard.

"What do you want to buy?" Walker asked.

"The appaloosa."

"Not for sale," Walker said, then smiled. "Except to you."

"How much?"

"Just what I paid. One hundred."

"Man's entitled to a fair profit. Make it a hundred ... and a Double Eagle."

"Done." Walker looked at the money still in front of Adam. "What about a saddle?"

"I'll borrow one of yours, if you don't mind, 'til I find my own."

"Lorena," Chad Walker laughed. "I can't refuse this man anything tonight."

"It's just your good nature, Chad." Lorena smiled a cold smile.

"I'll make you out a bill of sale, Adam, for the appaloosa," Chad said.

"Don't need one."

"Yes, you do. This is business." Then Walker turned toward Lorena. "What're you gonna do about her? The Mex whore?"

"Chad, what do you expect me to do? Turn her out? Where would she go?"

"Maybe over to the Iguana for a while. They ain't fussy."

"That is a despicable thing to say."

"And what she did? That's not . . . despicable?"

"Boss," Adam said. "You don't know the circumstances."

"No, you're right, Adam, I don't, and I wouldn't put anything past that greaseball Nueva. Well, I guess she can stay until you figure something out, Lorena."

"Thank you, Chad." This time her smile was not cold. "We all thank you."

"Don't mention it. It's just my good nature." He turned toward Dawson. "Adam, I want to hear about Custer and Gettysburg and how he got that general's star . . ."

"It happened in reverse order." Dawson smiled. "But I'll tell you about both sometime."

"Yeah, I guess it is getting late." He rose with the canes and made his way toward the door. "You coming, Lorena?"

"Be right up."

"Good night, boss."

When Walker was gone, Lorena moved close to Dawson, very close. Close enough so he moved back slightly.

"I want to thank you for what you said . . . on Elena's behalf. You were very . . . decent."

Dawson said nothing.

Lorena reached with her right hand and let her fluent fingers touch, then slide down the side of his cheek.

"Goodnight, Gallant Man." She turned and walked slowly out of the door.

Eighteen

Maureen O'Donnell shuddered. The bed was soaked in her sweat where she lay, her hands tied behind her back, Corona's filthy bandana stuffed into her mouth.

Naked, his smelly body and face bent close. His left hand held a bottle and with his right, he reached down and tore away her blouse exposing her creamy white shoulders and breasts.

She bolted upright, awake and screaming, her trembling hands covering her eyes and mouth.

Alma rushed through the doorway, hurried to the bed, sat and held the sobbing girl close and stroked the back of her head.

"It's all right . . . it's all right, Maureen . . . you've had a bad dream. You're here with me, Alma . . . you're here and safe . . . you understand?

Maureen O'Donnell nodded.

How many times had Alma rushed to the bedside of wounded Rebs, some without an arm or leg, some without both, who screamed in pain or in the agony of reliving the impact of body ripped by blade or bullet? More times than she could remember . . . or wanted to remember. In hospitals set up too close to battlefields where doctors, nurses and medication were in short supply and where most of those young soldier boys who woke up screaming in the night did not survive.

But Alma was there with them and tonight she was here

with the young widow who would survive, but with the
memory of seeing her husband killed and with the horror of
the Comanchero camp burned into her brain.

Corona lay awake in the bed with Olita next to him asleep
and snoring. They were both uncovered. His face turned and
he looked at her, at the brown flesh outlined in the dark, the
mounds and dips, bountiful and voluptuous.

As always, that night she had been wild and willing,
bending to his every want and still a wild animal with wants
of her own.

But lately, Corona's times with her had changed. Corona
had never felt love for her, or anybody, or anything. But for
a long time there was something, maybe it was just satisfaction at what she did and how she did it. He had always had
other women, many other women, older and younger, willing and unwilling and always he would have Olita come back
to him. And she would, even more wild and willing.

But lately he thought of her and wanted her less and less,
and the more she tried to pleasure him the less pleasure he
took in having her.

More and more he took other women, from the camp
and captives. And more and more he knew, and Olita was
beginning to realize, that her time with him was running out.

Tonight, as she lay snoring beside him he thought of the
red-headed woman who had been in that same bed and what
he should have done, but didn't.

He would have to find another red-headed woman, or
maybe one with yellow hair.

Corona's elbow poked into Olita's shoulder blade. Once.
Then once again.

Olita stopped snoring.

Adam Dawson had been asleep almost three hours when he
awoke looking at the bunkhouse ceiling instead of the dark
sky he was used to.

He couldn't help but smile. He was glad that he had stayed . . . so far.

The last couple of days with Chad Walker hadn't been so bad. Walker had flared up about Elena's condition and unleashed his usual litany of slurs, but once he got it out of his system he did calm down and while he didn't exactly exhibit compassion, he did let her stay.

And Dawson was no longer afoot. If and when he decided to leave, he could ride instead of walk west. But there was no "if" about it. This was no place to plant roots. "When." Not "if." He knew that this was temporary. Maybe a month or two, then *adiós* Walker's Way.

"You did win fair and square, didn't you?"

He recalled Chad Walker's words. Yes and no. He knew the three of diamonds was due. Walker should have known too. But Walker wasn't counting cards. Walker was counting on luck. Like Custer.

Adam didn't look forward to talking about Autie with Chad. Adam was trying not to think about Autie up north looking for glory, and how his friend and even Libbie had pleaded with him to stay. But after Washita, Dawson couldn't stay even though he felt that Custer's luck was running out.

From Libbie, Adam's thoughts went to Lorena. He rubbed his cheek where her fingers had touched.

"Gallant Man" she had called him. He couldn't help it, but his thoughts about her weren't exactly gallant.

But "Gallant Man" closed his eyes and went back to sleep.

Nineteen

Breakfast with Chad and Lorena was pleasant enough, even though Walker didn't say a word to Elena as she served it.

Adam was glad that Chad hadn't brought up the subject of Custer's star or Gettysburg and he wanted to get back to fixing up the corral before Chad did get around to asking. Dawson took the last sip from his coffee mug and started to rise.

"Well, I'd better get to work on that corral . . ."

"Don't be in such a hurry," Walker said. "I got plans for us this morning."

"All three of us?" Lorena asked.

"Sure. You can watch."

"Watch what?"

"Adam and me having some target practice."

"*That* sounds like fun," she said.

"You got anything better to do?" Walker asked.

"I could probably think of something."

"Don't. You got cartridges, Adam?"

"Some."

"Well, I got plenty. Get out your Winchester and I'll grab my Henry."

"Any instructions for me, sir?" Lorena rose.

"Just stay as sweet as you are." Walker grinned.

"I'll bring the rickshaw from 'round front." Adam walked past Elena toward the door, and smiled at her as he passed.

"Thanks, Adam." Walker elbowed his way up from the table.

Adam had taken his Winchester from the bunkhouse, walked back to where the rickshaw had been and brought the rig to the rear porch where Chad and Lorena were waiting. He placed his and Chad's rifle in the rickshaw and watched while Walker got aboard.

Uriah came out of his shack as the rickshaw approached. He carried Vashti under his left arm.

"Morning, Mr. Walker, and that must be brother Adam with you . . . and Miz Lorena?"

"That's right, Trooper." Walker said and motioned for Adam to stop. "All three of us. How's everything?"

"The Lord has lifted up the light of his countenance upon us."

"You bet he has," Chad said.

"I've been hearing brother Adam working on that fallen-down corral."

"Yes, he has, Trooper, and I'll tell you something else brother Adam wants to do when he's done with that. He wants to do a little repair work on your sh . . . on your dwelling. Discourage the wind and the rain from coming through."

"Thank you, thank you kindly, but we're happy as we are . . . aren't we, Vashti?"

"Yeah, well you and Vashti are going to be a lot happier. Nothing's too good for the hero of Chapultepec. Adam did you know that Uriah here served with U. S. Grant in Mexico?"

"No, I didn't."

"Well, he did. Didn't you, Trooper?"

"It was my great privilege and honor to serve." Uriah nodded.

"From Monterrey to San Cosme and to Chapultepec where those greasers blinded him. Came out a corporal, didn't you, trooper?"

"Two stripes."

"Yeah," Walker said softly, but Uriah heard. "Two stripes for two eyes," then louder, "well, we're going to get in a little target practice, Trooper, so you'd better warn the chickens. See you later."

"Windage and elevation, our sergeant used to teach us, windage and elevation," Uriah called out as the rickshaw pulled away.

The six-up stagecoach, on its way to Houston, had pulled up on Pinto's main street, where the passengers had debarked for a rest stop and meal at Reighnhold's, the only restaurant in town. But four of the five passengers made their way to Baldy's Bar instead, while the driver, Shorty, handed over the mailbag to Ed Rusky the nominal postmaster.

"Howdy, Shorty." Sheriff Ben Vesper had walked from across the street.

"Sheriff."

Ed Rusky, who never said much, said nothing as he walked past Vesper with the mailbag for Pinto in his arms.

"Got anything for me, Shorty?" the sheriff asked.

"Yes and no."

"What the hell does that mean?"

"It means no, nothing personal. But yes something official."

"Let's have it."

"Bundle of dodgers." Shorty tossed down the dodgers, which were tied together by heavy string, at Vesper who caught them before they hit the ground.

"Much obliged," the sheriff said, but Shorty had disappeared off the top of the stagecoach from the other side and was making toward Baldy's.

Sheriff Ben Vesper entered his office where Sam was washing the inside of the windows.

"What's that?" Sam asked as Ben walked to his desk.

"Dodgers."

"Huh?"

"Wanted posters."

"Bad men?"

"They ain't running for governor."

"Could I look?"

"Mind if I look first?"

"Oh, no, sir."

"Railroad's still after Frank and Jesse . . . but I'm not." Vesper was sorting the dodgers in stacks on his desk. "Bill Longly, the Tall Texan . . . the Daltons . . . here's something close to home . . ."

"What?"

"Corona." Sam came closer as the sheriff went on. "It's a drawing of him. 'Corona, leader of Comanchero band. Approximately six feet tall. Weight approximately two hundred. Swarthy. Beady eyes. Large nose and mustache. Wanted. Robbery. Rape. Murder. Six hundred dollars reward. Dead or alive.' "

"Hey! Ain't he the one killed that lady's husband and . . ."

"He's the one."

"You figure he's still close by?"

"I hope so."

"You do?"

"I do. That's one sonofabitch I'd like to meet."

"Six hundred dollars. There ain't that much money in Texas. Boy, I sure could . . ."

"You sure could finish washing those windows."

"Yes, sir."

"Corona," Sheriff Ben Vesper whispered, looking down at the dodger. "You dirty bastard." Then the sheriff looked up and spoke up. "And Sam . . ."

"Yes, sir."

"When you're through with those windows take some of these dodgers and post them around. Make this official."

"Yes, sir."

"Dirty bastard."

"How's that, Sheriff?"

"Not you." Vesper held up the dodger. "Him."

Dozens of spent cartridge shells were scattered around the boots of Adam Dawson and Chad Walker who had propped himself against a post while they had been firing the Winchester and Henry, and while Lorena stood by watching, most of the time with her fingers in her ears.

The targets were side by side twenty-five yards away and already riddled with holes attesting to the excellent marksmanship of the shooters.

Five more shots rang out and all five hit pretty close to, or in the bull's-eye of the target on the right.

Five more shots, fired in even more rapid succession, hit even closer to the center of the bull's-eye of the target on the left.

Chad Walker, the second shooter, lowered his rifle, aglow with satisfaction at his superior marksmanship. Lorena unplugged her fingers from her ears.

"Can we call it quits, boys? I'm going deaf."

"Good shooting, Adam," Walker said.

"Not as good as you. Let's do call it quits. I surrender."

"Maybe next time." Walker grinned.

"Maybe never . . . say, boss, look there. Seems we got company."

Two men on horseback were approaching at a leisurely pace just past the main house.

"Oh, yeah. That's Rico and Juan, a couple of day hands I hired to seal up the roof of the stable. It leaks some."

"Hell, I can do that."

"Well, I already committed so let 'em go ahead and do it. Nueva kept saying he was busy doing something else, the lazy bum."

"In that case I wonder if you'd mind if I did something else?"

"Sure, what?"

"Mind if I take the appaloosa and . . ."

"It's your horse."

"And go look for my saddle. Might take awhile."

"Go ahead. Lorena, why don't you go with him?"

"What?"

"I said why don't you go with him? Give you a chance to work out that new stallion."

"You mean it?"

"Why not? Better than going to that mission, isn't it?"

"Well, it's different," she said and glanced at Dawson.

"Why don't we all go?" Adam quickly suggested.

"Nope. Got some accounting to take care of. Might catch up to you later."

"But . . ." Adam looked at Walker who was now standing with the aid of a cane ". . . how you going to . . ."

"Saddle up?" Walker pointed to the two day hands who were dismounting near the stable. "They'll get me up." He smiled pleasantly, probably still the effect of his superior shooting. "You two go ahead."

"Okay," Dawson said. "I'll get you back on the rickshaw while Lorena gets ready."

By the look on Lorena Walker's face she was already ready.

With a hammer and small nails, Sam Mendez had been putting up a few dodgers on Corona at strategic spots in Pinto.

He was hammering one into the post in front of Baldy's Bar as Joe Nueva and three of his compadres, Paco, Jake and Jaime came up the boardwalk.

Paco, Jake and Jaime kept walking and went into the bar. Nueva stood next to Sam and watched.

"What you got there, Sam?"

"Dodger. That's what they call a wanted poster."

"Yeah, I know."

"You ought to tell your cousin about it." It was Sheriff Ben Vesper's voice. He was now standing behind Nueva.

"What?"

"Your cousin, or whatever he is, the one who rides with Corona."

"I don't know what you're talking about."

"You don't, huh? Well, he might want to turn Corona in. Pick up six hundred bucks. He just might even split it with you, Joe."

"That's a lie. I don't know anybody who knows Corona and you better..."

"You better watch who you call a liar, Joe. I'll overlook it this time."

"You think that badge..."

"I said *this time*, Joe. Now your friends inside are waiting."

"Yeah, *Sheriff*." Nueva turned and walked through the bat-wings.

"Is that true?" Sam asked. "About his cousin, I mean?"

"Maybe we'll find out, Sam. Maybe we'll find out. I'm going to look in on Mrs. O'Donnell, see how she's doing. See you at the office later."

"Yes, sir, Sheriff."

After the sheriff walked away, Linus McCloud, the owner of the stable where Sam Mendez had been employed tapped his former employee on the shoulder.

"Morning, Sam."

"Oh, morning, Mr. McCloud."

"Nice day, huh, Sam?"

"Yes, sir."

"Say, Sam, I was just wondering if maybe you changed your mind?"

"About what, Mr. McCloud?"

"Oh, about working at the... working for me."

"No, sir. I'm still of the same mind."

"How much you getting paid?"

"Nuff to get by, sir."

"Well, I might see my way clear to up you a dollar. That'd make it four dollars a week, plus sleeping quarters. Good pay in these hard times."

"Yes, sir, and I sure do like you and the stable, but I'm in the law business now... sort of. Why don't you talk to Mr. Tucker's boy, Ned?"

"Too damn skinny."

"Well, sir, I'll let you know if I think of anybody." Sam pointed to the dodgers with the hammer in his hand. "Got to get back to work now."

"Yeah." Linus McCloud turned and started to walk away then turned back. "Say, what kind of a lawman are you anyhow . . . without a gun?"

"You know, sir," Sam said, "that's just what I been thinking."

They had been riding, Dawson on his appaloosa and Lorena on her stallion, for half an hour cantering across the flatland of open prairie, then cautiously along the narrow precipitous ledge of Devil's Drop and later trotting near the more verdant bank of the stream.

Neither had said a word as they approached the willow grove area where they had first met.

More than once they had glanced at each other, but kept riding silently until now. She was beautiful astride the stallion, her golden hair loosely floating onto her shoulders under the brown brimmed hat she now wore instead of the white bonnet. Adam Dawson was tall in the saddle with the easy cradle of a cavalryman, his long legs turned slightly forward, his large hands with strong fingers on the ribbons of the reins.

Dawson tugged lightly on the reins and the appaloosa eased to a stop in response. Lorena Walker's hands pulled back on her reins and the stallion came to a standstill next to Pard.

"Why'd you stop here?" she asked, looking at him, and this time without glancing away.

"Don't you know, Mrs. Walker?"

"I've asked you to call me Lorena."

"Don't you know, Lorena?"

"I think so."

"This is where I first met you . . . and Mr. What's-his-name?"

"Hatcher. Brad Hatcher."

"That's right. Good neighbor Brad Hatcher."

"Please, Adam. Let's get something straight..."

"I'm sorry, Lorena..." He smiled. "You know something? I've never said 'I'm sorry' three times to anybody else in my life that I can remember."

"I told you, I was inviting him..."

"That was some invitation."

"...inviting him—and his wife—to the ranch so he could talk to Chad about buying the place."

"Does Chad know?"

"About the invitation? No, not yet."

"I want to be somewhere else when he does."

"No, Adam, please. I wish you would be there."

"Why?"

"Well, you seem to have, well, a calming effect on him..."

"You call that calm?"

"He's much better in the last few days, since you came, than he has been. You must've noticed..."

"I don't know whether it's me or Custer, but it appears that he's a mite...mellower."

"That's what I mean. You do understand, don't you, Adam?"

"I guess so." He looked away from her and toward a scandent stretch of boulders far in the distance. "My gear's up there in those boulders somewhere."

"Let's get off and rest for a minute. Do you mind?"

"No, ma'am, I don't mind and neither will the horses."

Sheriff Ben Vesper had seen Doc Bonner's carriage outside Alma's place as he walked toward the cottage.

He was surprised, almost amazed, to find all three, Alma, Doc Bonner and Maureen O'Donnell in the small parlor. Maureen was sitting in an overstuffed chair with one of Alma's shawls over her shoulders and wearing a robe that also belonged to Alma.

"Don't blame you," Doc said when he saw the look on Vesper's face. "I couldn't believe it either, but I did tell you she came from hardy stock. Never had such an improved patient in so short a time."

"I am a bit . . . wobbly yet, but I just didn't want to stay in bed any longer." Maureen O'Donnell's face was still a little pale and still bruised, but her eyes were clear and green as gems of emerald.

"You look just fine, Mrs. O'Donnell."

"And you, sir, Sheriff Vesper, isn't it?"

"Yes, ma'am. Ben Vesper."

"So Miss Alma told me. I want to thank you for all you've done . . . I can't thank all of you enough."

"Just seeing you up and about is thanks enough," Alma said. "Isn't it, Ben?"

"You bet." Vesper smiled.

"But you've all got work to do . . . you . . ."

"This is my work." Doc Bonner smiled.

"I'm afraid I haven't any money to . . ."

"Don't you worry about that," Doc said.

"Mrs. O'Donnell." Vesper took a step closer. "You mentioned some relatives. Is there someone we can . . ."

"Tim's brother. I'll write him a letter and tell him about . . . what happened . . . then I don't know what . . ."

"Don't even think about that now," Alma said. "You're more than welcome to stay here until you get all your strength back and then . . . when you decide what you want to do, we'll see that it gets done, won't we Ben?"

"We sure will, and ma'am, you write that letter when you're ready and I'll get it mailed for you."

"You're all so kind."

"Kind," Ben thought to himself when he left. After what that poor beautiful woman had been through she deserved all the kindness that could be bestowed on her.

And Corona deserved something too.

———

Adam Dawson was stretched out in the lush grass, propped against the bole of a tree. Lorena sat close by, arms hugging her drawn-up knees and staring at the lines of his lean, firm face.

"Who are you, Adam Dawson?"

"What?"

"A soldier? A gambler? A hero? Who are you, stranger?"

"Just a drifter. Heading West."

"I don't believe that. Why did you leave Custer?"

"It was time to leave. There's a time for everything."

"To be born . . . and to . . ."

"Doesn't much matter where you're born. It's where you die that counts. Where and when . . . and how."

"Are you talking about the war? That's over."

"Wars never end. It's a warring world. Ask your husband."

"Never mind him."

"Then ask yourself. What about your war, Mrs. Walker? How did it start? With John Wilkes Booth?"

"So Chad told you about that. I might've expected he would."

"He didn't say much."

"He wouldn't have to. No, Adam. It wasn't John Wilkes Booth. It started with a minister. That's right. A man respected and admired, who loved his congregation . . . the men and women and little children who sat on his lap . . . especially his little daughter who grew too old to sit on his lap . . . but he didn't think so . . . but she did . . . and so she ran away . . . I guess she's still running."

"I'm sorry . . . well, that makes four times I've said it."

"Quit counting. And quit being sorry. I'm all grown up now."

"I can see that."

"Can you?"

"Anybody could."

"Don't you like what you see?'

"Anybody would. Even a drifter."

"I'd like to think you're a knight in shining armor off on a quest."

"Not likely."

"And I'd like to go off with you . . ."

"You're a married woman, Mrs. Walker. Your husband . . ."

"Having a husband and being married aren't always the same. Do you know why Chad was so mad about Elena being pregnant? Not because she isn't married. It's because his wife can't ever be pregnant . . . not by him . . . that part of him is . . . well. . . ."

"I think," Adam got to his feet, "I think we better start looking for my gear." He began to walk toward the horses.

Lorena watched him walk.

Joe Nueva led the horse and buckboard out through the red double doors of Linus McCloud's Livery and Stable where Linus stood in the street biting into a plug of tobacco.

"See you got her all hitched up, Joe."

"Yeah. I appreciate you lettin' me borrow the rig."

"That's all right, you threw some business my way when you was foreman at Walker's."

"Yeah, I sure did. Say, I like the looks of that chestnut in there."

"Fine animal."

"And I'll be needin' a horse of my own now that I'm not . . . with Walker anymore."

"Sure, Joe. Just let me know when you're ready to talk business. I'll give you a good price."

"Well, not right now. I'm working on a couple of deals and . . ."

"Hell, maybe you'd want to come to work for me . . ."

"Doin' what?"

"Well . . . be my . . . assistant. Look after the place. I could pay three fifty a week to start and . . ."

"Look here, Linus, I draw foreman wages. I ain't no damn stable boy!"

"Hell, nobody said you was. Don't have to get your hackles up for chrissakes, I just thought that . . ."

"Well, think some more and if that changes your mind about loanin' me this rig, then . . ."

"Joe! Joe! Calm down, dammit! And go ahead and use the rig."

"All right then." Nueva started to climb aboard. "I'll have it back before dark."

"Sure, sure." Linus McCloud walked through the double doors and into the stable muttering. "Never saw anybody so damn touchy, thinks he's the damn Duke of Edinburgh . . ."

As Joe Nueva settled into the driver's side of the buckboard, Brad Hatcher on horseback slowed then stopped in front of the stable.

"Hello, Joe."

"Mr. Hatcher."

"Well, congratulations. Looks like you found yourself a job." Hatcher nodded toward the stable.

"No, Mr. Hatcher, just turned one down. Still wide open to go to work for you."

"All right. I'll keep it in mind."

"Headin' out to pick up my stuff at Walker's."

"Say hello to him for me . . . and to Mrs. Walker."

"I'll do that."

Hatcher nudged his animal and rode down the main street of Pinto.

As the buckboard reached the edge of town, Nueva spotted something on a tree. He drew the buckboard to a stop, looked around and made sure nobody was in sight, then climbed down, walked to the tree, pulled down the dodger on Corona, folded it and tucked it inside his shirt.

Dawson and Lorena rode side by side through the scrub grass and mesquite then the clusters of rocks, upward toward the convention of boulders.

It had been some time, more than a month, since he had been with a woman. The last time was with a saloon girl in

Wichita. The first time was when he was fourteen and Autie introduced him to one of his many lady friends in Monroe and she introduced him to the pleasures all boys his age wanted to make the acquaintance of. In-between there had been more women than Adam Dawson could count or remember. But he could not remember any woman who looked and had the fragrance of the one who rode beside him now. He tried his best not to look at her. Not to inhale the fragrance. Not to think of her and the man she married. The man who could not . . .

"That stallion's behaving well," he said.

"I knew he would." She smiled.

"Did you think of a name for him?"

"Yes. I named him after you . . . Gallant Man."

"Mamacita."

Joe Nueva had stopped the buckboard in front of the one room cabana, little more than a hovel, where his aunt lived alone.

"*Hola*, Joe," she said as she stood in the doorway, a thin woman of sixty years whose Indian lineage was evident in her umber face and sooty hair now streaked with gray.

"How are you, Mamacita?"

"The same. Waiting for whatever will come."

"Has he come by lately?"

"No. But any time now. He promised. He always promises. Sometimes Jorge keeps his promises. Brings money, enough to keep his mother alive until the next time."

"When he comes, give him this." Nueva took the folded dodger from inside his shirt and stretched out his hand.

Mamacita came close enough to the buckboard to take the paper. She unfolded and looked at it.

"What does it say? You know I can't read."

"But he can. Probably the only one among 'em who can."

"What does it say?" she repeated.

"It's about his boss. Just give it to him and tell him I gave it to you. Will you do that, Mamacita?"

"I will. Anything else?"

"Yes." Nueva reached into his vest and pulled out a coin. "Put this in your pocket."

"You're very good to me, Joe."

"You been good to me, Mamacita." He snapped the reins and the buckboard moved ahead.

Jorge Diaz was Joe Nueva's cousin. Their mothers were sisters. There were times when Diaz had tried to talk him into joining up with Corona.

But Joe Nueva told his cousin that he wasn't cut out to be a Comanchero.

Still, Joe Nueva thought it was a good idea, from time to time, to cast a little bread upon the waters.

It didn't take long. Adam had located his gear and was examining the saddle.

Lorena stood watching, her body moving ever so slightly. As Adam lifted the saddle and turned toward her, a soft breeze sailed across her blouse and glided through the flaxen hair dancing on her shoulders.

She stood outlined against the azure sky with eyes that matched its purple hue.

"Well," he said. "We got what we came for."

"Did we?" She moved close. Too close. "Did we, Adam?"

Lorena touched his face then put her arms around him.

He stood rigid as she kissed him. Soft. Tender at first. Then fierce and passionate.

He dropped the saddle. Adam Dawson put his arms around her and drew her body into his. He kissed her the way she wanted him to kiss her. The way that he had thought about . . . and fought against as he was fighting now . . . and then he started to pull away.

"Lorena . . . Chad . . . he . . ."

"He's not the man I married. He's warped . . . bitter . . . crazy . . . Adam, you don't know . . ." Her face was still close to his, her arms tightened around him and he could feel her tremble.

Locked together they began to slither down against a boulder.

But suddenly he snapped upright, still holding her, but now holding her away from him, and she knew that this was as far as it would go . . . this time.

"All right, Gallant Man. But will you please do just one thing?"

"What?"

"Let's not find the saddle . . . not yet."

Twenty

"Are you sure you don't want to go back to your room and rest, Maureen?"

"No thanks, if you don't mind I'll just sit here in this grand ol' chair for a bit."

"Would you like a little more tea?"

"No, Alma, thank you. I've been such a bother to you. I don't want to keep you from your work. Doctor Bonner did mention that you had a business to take care of."

"Oh, that? Did he mention what kind of business?"

"No, I don't believe he did, or I don't remember."

"Well, Maureen, my little colleen, you're lookin' at a saloon gal."

"Doctor Bonner said something about you being a nurse . . ."

"I got outta the nursin' business and into the barkeep business a few years ago."

"You mean you work in a pub?"

"I guess you'd call it that in Ireland, in Pinto we call it Baldy's Bar and Alma Gorsich is bartender, part-time singer and junior partner."

"That sounds . . . exciting."

"Too damn exciting sometimes but it beats choppin' cotton and I've done some of that, too."

"My Tim was a farmer . . ."

"Honey, I can't say I know how you feel and how you

must've felt about him, but you've got to think of yourself now . . . and think ahead."

"I've been doin' just that."

"Good. And you know that we meant what we said about helping you . . ."

"Tim did send some money, what little we had, ahead to his brother for the land he was to acquire."

"Well, that's a start."

"But I don't know yet whether I'll want to go on to Laredo . . . or back to Ireland."

"Why don't you think about staying here?"

"And what would I do here?"

"*Not* work in a saloon. What did you do in Ireland before you were married?"

"I taught school for two years."

"Well, Pinto could probably use a schoolteacher. We'll talk to the mayor, Terrance Swerd, and Brad Hatcher, he's on the city council, and Doc and Ben Vesper, they'll put in a good word if you decide to stay and I wish you would."

"Ben Vesper . . . oh, yes, the sheriff."

"You bet he is. And you can stay right here with me while you teach until you find . . . whatever it is a beautiful lady like you should find. Will you think about it?"

"I will." She smiled. "On one condition?"

"What's that?"

"That you go back to Baldy's Bar and yours, and take care of business. I'm well enough to fend for m'self around here."

"Colleen Maureen, you've struck a bargain!"

Brad Hatcher was about to mount his palomino in front of Baldy's Bar as Sheriff Ben Vesper walked by on his way to his office.

"Hello, Sheriff."

"Howdy."

Hatcher stayed on the ground and pointed to the dodger nailed to the post.

"See they got out a reward for that Comanchero."

"Yep."

"He's a bad one."

"That's why there's a reward."

"You intend to go after him?"

"I intend to bring him to his milk if I get the chance."

"I hear he's got plenty with him."

"Yep."

"How come the Rangers or the Yankee army haven't gone after him?"

"I guess they got bigger fish to fry."

"I guess."

"But I haven't."

"Good luck. You'll need it." Hatcher started to mount again.

"You know that bunch has been known to hit a ranch or two around here from time to time. I'd have your boys keep a lookout, Mr. Hatcher, for any suspicious strangers."

"Yeah, but those were scrag outfits. I don't think they'd hit Spanish Bit. But we'll be ready." This time Hatcher mounted.

"It's good to be ready," the sheriff said and started across the street.

Twenty-one

The prancing shadows of the two horses and riders moved almost directly beneath them as Adam and Lorena rode through the gate of Walker's Way.

Adam Dawson had not brought back his saddle.

Spider-fly. Moth-flame. Delilah-Samson. Dawson didn't want to think about them, the magnets of doom. And he wouldn't let himself be magnetized or doomed. He felt he was a long way from that. He could ride away anytime from Walker's Way and from her.

Still, when he had felt himself stiffen with the feel of the pulsing curves of her breasts against his chest, the soft sweet taste of her lips and her slender, coiling arms around him, and knew that she was his for the taking, he had come close, too close, to the spider. The flame. Delilah.

But he would not let himself be snared. He would not allow himself to be burned. And he would not permit himself to be consumed.

When he saw the look in her eyes . . . declaration, desire, then disappointment, almost betrayal, he had succumbed to her one last request of Gallant Man and placed the saddle back between the boulders.

Even then he knew it was a mistake. But he had made mistakes before, mistakes that might have proved fatal. This was one mistake that he might regret, but a mistake that wouldn't prove fatal, a mistake that Adam Dawson could rectify by riding away from the gate that they had just passed through.

As they came within sight of the ranch house they saw him.

Chad Walker astride Domino, strapped into his saddle rig, rode closer and Adam waved.

Walker waved back and pulled up alongside.

"Have a good ride?" Chad asked.

"Pretty good," Adam said.

"How'd she do with the stallion?"

"She can handle him."

"Figured she could."

"Thank you, Chad." Lorena smiled. "Did I tell you that I thought of a name for him, the horse I mean?"

"Not that I remember."

"Gallant Man."

"He's your horse. You can name him what you want. Let's head back."

Chad wheeled Domino around and the three of them started to ride back with Lorena between the two men.

"No luck with the saddle?" Chad asked.

"Not yet," Dawson replied and made sure not to look at Lorena.

"We'll find it," she said.

"Sure you will." Walker glanced at Adam. "Nothing like putting your legs astride a saddle you're used to . . . well, almost nothing." Walker's smile turned into something else as he looked in the direction of the bunkhouses. "Goddammit!"

Chad Walker slapped the reins across both sides of Domino and galloped toward the two structures.

Joe Nueva was loading the last of his possessions onto Linus McCloud's buckboard. Clothes, pots, pans, a couple of scarred satchels. Nueva started to climb aboard the wagon.

"Hey, you! Greaseball!" Walker hollered and rode closer.

Nueva settled into the seat and took up the reins in both hands, but said nothing as Walker pulled up in front of the buckboard, blocking its way and glaring at the driver.

"Snuck back here like some thief, huh?"

"You said to pick up my stuff. That's what I did."

"Yeah? What else you got in there?"

"Want to take a look, Mr. Walker?"

"I wouldn't touch any of that shit."

"Then get outta the way . . ."

"You shut your goddam greasy mouth. I don't take orders from any stinking pepperbelly."

Nueva snapped the reins but the buckboard horse stood fast with Walker still blocking the way.

"Can't keep it in your pants, huh? Why don't you pack *her* in with all your junk and take her with you?"

Nueva stared straight ahead.

"Look at me when I talk to you, you goddam greaser! You knocked her up didn't you?"

"Which one?" Nueva looked at Walker for the first time and smiled a crooked smile.

"Which one?" Chad Walker was outraged by the implication. He lashed his horse and rode up to the side of the wagon. "Why you dirty, lying bastard!"

Instinctively, Walker reached to his side before realizing that he wore no gun belt and that his rifle boot was empty of the Henry.

"I ever see your greasy face around here again, I'll put a bullet up your ass!" he raged. "You got that? Answer me you sonofabitch!"

"When the time's right," Nueva spoke evenly. "You'll get your answer, *Mister* Walker." He flapped the reins again and this time the buckboard moved forward.

"Heah! Heah!" Nueva hollered and whacked the reins again.

The buckboard rumbled ahead churning dust as Walker charged his stallion after, then close, dangerously close alongside, yelling above the bouncing wagon and pounding hooves.

"How about right now, you dirty sonofabitch! Come on, get down now, you yellow-belly bastard! Come on, get down!"

Chad Walker's stallion, close to crazed, fought to stay away from the wagon spewing dirt and gravel. Nueva, in a swift, sudden move, swerved the wagon toward the stallion. Walker reined away with a sharp jerk but was almost hit broadside. The stallion whinnied, shuddered and reared to a dead stop as the buckboard rolled ahead.

Adam started to ride out after Nueva, but looked back at Walker whose upper body swayed and slumped forward on the stallion as it stomped the ground. He turned and rode fast toward Chad Walker. Lorena was close behind.

When they got to him, Walker was visibly exhausted and still shaking on the fractious stallion. Adam extended a soothing hand and stroked Domino's mane to calm the animal, then spoke.

"You all right?"

"I'll kill that dirty bastard." Walker snarled. "Adam . . . get me off this thing."

Twenty-two

Sheriff Ben Vesper sat at his desk. He had spent the last couple of hours cleaning and oiling the three rifles that normally rested in the gun rack on the wall. When he finished he replaced the rifles, slipped the chain through their trigger loops and locked the chain.

He was working on his .44 when Sam came in through the back entrance toting a mop and an empty bucket.

"Outhouse is all cleaned up, Sheriff." Sam set the mop and bucket in a corner. "Clean enough to eat out there."

"No thanks."

"See you finished cleaning up them rifles, too." Sam pointed at the gun rack.

"Yep."

"Mr. Reardon said he'd have a new batch of dodgers printed up on that Comanchero this afternoon . . . about four-thirty."

"Good."

"How far out you want me to go post 'em?"

"You got a horse, Sam?"

"Sure, over at the stable."

"Well, wait 'til morning and go out a few miles, six or seven, and tack 'em up."

"Sure thing. Think it'll do any good?"

"Can't do any harm, Sam. By the way I saw ol' Linus McCloud talking to you this morning."

"Yes, sir."

"He offer you your old job back?"

"Yes, sir."

"With a raise?"

"How'd you know that?"

"I know Linus. You been underpaid over there for quite some time, but not as underpaid as you are now. You know that don't you, Sam?"

"The way I figure it, Sheriff, I'm learnin' a new trade."

"Cleaning outhouses?"

"If that's what it takes to get started."

"Started at what?"

"Being a lawman."

"That again, huh?"

"Yes, sir."

"How old are you son?"

"Seventeen . . . in a couple weeks."

"Too damn young to even think about it."

"How old were you, Sheriff, when you went off to fight Yankees?"

Ben Vesper spun the cylinder of the .44 and didn't answer the question.

"I been wonderin', Sheriff . . ."

"What now?"

"You think it'd be all right if I carried a gun?"

"Carried it where?" Vesper smiled.

"You know what I mean, Sheriff . . . in a holster on my hip like you."

"You own a gun, Sam?"

"No, sir."

"Ever fire a gun?"

"Yes, sir. Squirrel gun. Pretty good with it too."

"Well, these guns aren't for squirrels." He held up the .44 and pointed it toward the rifle rack. "They're for rats. Two legged rats with no tail and no conscience . . . like Corona."

"Could we go out back or someplace sometime and see what I could do with one?"

"Right now you can go out front with a broom and see what you can do with *it*."

"Yes, sir."

Joe Nueva, aboard the empty buckboard, was going through the double doors of Linus McCloud's livery.

On his way back from Walker's ranch he had passed by Mamacita's just in time to see his cousin mounting up as Mamacita stood by the side of her son making the sign of the cross.

"Hello, Jorge."

"Joe, *qué pasa?*" Diaz asked as his right boot slipped into the stirrup. "What're you haulin'?"

"My possibles. I quit Walker."

"Want me to talk to Corona about you?"

"Are you *loco*? Did Mamacita give you that dodger?"

"So?"

"So they'll be lookin' for you . . . for all of you."

"They been lookin' for a long time." Diaz grinned. "They'll never find us and if they did we could hold off an army up there. But there ain't no army around here."

"There's a sheriff in Pinto thinks he's a one-man army."

"He better think different."

"Even said you might want to turn Corona in for that six hundred."

"Now *you're loco*. So's anybody who tried. I can think of better ways to die."

"Jorge, please," Mamacita said. "Don't talk about dying."

"Don't worry, Mamacita, I'm gonna live forever." Diaz spurred his horse, waved with his hat and rode north.

Mamacita made the sign of the cross again.

After that Nueva had unloaded his gear at Paco's shack where he was sleeping and drove the wagon into Pinto and through the double doors of the stable.

Linus McCloud was already hurrying up close to the horse pulling the buckboard.

"What the hell's amatter with you, Nueva?"

"What're your hackles up for?"

"Look at the condition of that animal!"

"What about it?"

"He's been abused, that's what about it! All sweaty and foamed up for chrissake. What've you been doin' to him?"

"Nothin', he's just old . . . damn bag of bones, useless as a three-legged mule."

"Get off that wagon! And don't you ever set foot in my place again . . ."

"All right, all right, take it easy." Nueva jumped off the wagon.

"Never mind the easy, just get the hell outta here and keep on goin' . . ."

Nueva was already through the doors.

". . . Damn fool!" Linus McCloud hollered after him, "abusing an animal like that!"

The sheriff had seen Alma on the boardwalk through the window of his office as she went into Baldy's across the street.

He waited a few minutes, told Sam he'd be back shortly, and made his way across Main Street.

Alma was behind the bar when he came in.

"What'll you have, Ben?"

"Beer." The sheriff reached for a piece of cheese on the free lunch plate while Alma drew the beer. "Is Doc with her?"

"Nope."

"Well, then . . ."

"Look, I wouldn't've left her alone unless I thought it was all right, you know that."

"Sure, I do." He took a bite of the cheese.

"Well, it is all right. Doin' real good. Doesn't want to think that I'm neglecting my . . . business, so I thought I'd come over for an hour or so and let Baldy take a snooze. Which is what he's doin' now."

"If you say so, Alma." He chased the cheese with a swallow of beer.

"You know something, Ben? I think there's a chance she'll stay here in Pinto."

"You do?"

"If we can get her a job teaching school. That's what she did in the old country before she got married."

"She did?"

"What would you say to that?"

"I'd say fine if she'd do it."

"Well, maybe we can do something about that. Talk to Swerd and Hatcher and the rest." Alma smiled. "Want another beer?"

"No, thanks. Put that on my tab, will you, Alma?"

"Sure thing, Sheriff."

Vesper turned and walked toward the bat wings as Nueva came through and stood just inside. Nueva smiled and moved away, but only slightly.

"Howdy, Sheriff. You think you're gonna find Corona in Baldy's Bar?"

"Step aside," Vesper said and brushed past Joe Nueva.

Twenty-three

That afternoon and early evening after Nueva left Walker's Way, if Chad Walker had been a kettle of water he would have boiled over; a container of nitro, he would have exploded; as it was, for a long time it appeared that he might explode anyhow . . . or at least suffer a stroke.

The veins in his temple visibly throbbed. His lips reshaped into a knife-blade line and his hands still trembled.

For a time Dawson thought Walker might even take a gun and go into Pinto and carry out his threat to kill Nueva. Dawson and Lorena did everything they could to placate and calm him. But both Dawson and Lorena knew that the most effective thing they could do was nothing. Let the kettle cool. Don't agitate the container.

All through supper Walker spoke not a word. A couple of times he glanced at Elena, and the way he did, both Dawson and Lorena glanced at each other and thought the lid was going to blow off. But it didn't.

When they were finished eating Adam rose and smiled.

"Well, I think I'll go to the bunkhouse and . . ."

"No!" Walker exclaimed, then took a deep breath. "Adam, stay here." His voice softened, almost in supplication. "Please, I'd like to have a drink or two and smoke a good cigar in the library. You said you'd tell me about Custer's star and Gettysburg, and how you were with him, remember?"

"So I did."

Lorena's look pleaded with Dawson to stay. Not to leave her alone with her husband. Not yet. Not until he stopped brooding about Nueva.

"Sure. I wouldn't be averse to a good cigar myself."

It was the least Adam Dawson could do under the circumstances, for Walker and for Mrs. Walker.

For the next two hours Walker smoked, sipped bourbon and occasionally asked a question or made a comment, and Lorena listened too as Adam Dawson told them about Custer and himself . . . but not all about himself and his part in the most spectacular career of any West Pointer who climbed from cadet to "Boy General" as Custer was dubbed . . . how, in the meantime the Union Army's command had gone from General Winfield Scott to General George McClellan to General Ambrose E. Burnside to General Joseph Hooker to General George Gordon Meade and how they all suffered defeat after defeat against Lee and Lee's right hand, General James Ewell Brown Stuart—"Jeb" Stuart, the South's charismatic cavalier. Stuart was their boldest, most beloved cavalry commander, whose Black Horse Raiders hit like bolts of lightning into the blue ranks of Northern infantry and horsemen alike. For nearly two years Stuart's "Invincibles" had consistently conquered the Yankee cavalry . . . until the battle of Brandy Station where the reckless twenty-two-year-old Captain Custer led the First Michigan on what everybody thought was a suicide charge.

"Come on, you Wolverines!" he screamed charging into Stuart's gray mass until Stuart's Invincibles fell back in defeat for the first time and Custer became the first officer to jump from captain to brigadier general and become the youngest general in the U.S. Army.

What Dawson didn't tell them was that once again, this time at Brandy Station, he had saved Autie's life as a Confederate lieutenant drew a bead on Custer and Dawson's shot hit its mark between the lieutenant's eyes.

And so Custer lived to get his star and fight at Gettysburg just two weeks later. And in that time he had a new uniform tailored for himself and from then on there could be no mistaking the boy general at the head of his brigade with the broad collar of blue sailor's shirt rolled into a black velveteen jacket adorned by rows of brass buttons and gleaming braid. His legs were covered by britches of the same material seamed by twin gold stripes and tucked into top boots cupped by silver spurs. A heavy sword with Toledo blade, captured from the enemy, hung from his black belt. And, of course, the scarlet scarf flowed from his throat.

It was at Gettysburg that Custer charged again into Stuart's Invincibles as they tried to outflank the Yankees and hook up with Pickett in that valiant charge that would have sealed the doom of the North if it had succeeded. But it did not succeed because Custer and his Michiganders prevented Stuart from joining Pickett. It seemed there were a hundred red-scarfed Custers in the field that day with a hundred bloody blades striking—in and from—all directions.

And once again Custer had ridden to glory.

But the third and final campaign between Stuart and Custer sealed the doom, not of the North, but of the Confederacy at Yellow Tavern where one of Custer's officers brought down Stuart himself.

It was said that after Jeb Stuart died, the South never smiled again.

What Adam Dawson didn't say to Walker and Lorena that night was that the gun he still carried was the weapon that fired the shot that killed General Jeb Stuart.

Still, Walker and Lorena had listened with fascination as Dawson spoke.

"After that," Adam said, "the road led to Appomattox."

"And Custer was there too, wasn't he?" Walker puffed on his cigar.

"He was."

"And you too, weren't you, Adam?" Lorena spoke for the first time.

"Well, Curly was inside with Grant and Lee." Dawson smiled. "I was outside with the horses."

" 'Curly,' " Chad puffed again and grinned as if he had forgotten that Joe Nueva even existed. "Your pal's got a lot of nicknames, hasn't he?"

"Just a few. Crazy Curly. Suicide Custer. Cinnamon. Goldie Locks. Up North the Sioux call him Yellow Hair."

"That'll be something to see," Walker said. "When Yellow Hair whips their ass!"

"Well." Dawson figured he had done all he could for Walker and Lorena that night. "I'd say it's time to turn in. Thanks for the drinks and the smokes." He laid the butt of his cigar in the ashtray and rose.

"I'm gonna finish this stogie," Walker said.

Lorena picked up the ashtray and followed Dawson.

"Be right back, Chad." She smiled. "I'm going to get a breath of fresh air for a minute."

"Thanks again," she said when they were both outside. "I don't know what I would have done if you weren't here tonight."

"When are you going to tell him about Mr. and Mrs. Hatcher coming to visit?"

"Tomorrow morning at breakfast after I make sure he gets a good night's sleep. You'll be there, won't you, Adam? Please."

"Good night, Mrs. Walker."

"Dirty bastards! A lousy six hundred dollars! I'll show 'em . . ." Corona roared and swallowed more whiskey from the bottle when Diaz read the dodger to the Comancheros and their chief.

But Diaz, who was the only one in the camp who could read, was careful to omit part of the printed description of Corona. Diaz deemed it wise to skip "beady eyes" and "large nose" in deference to Corona's vanity . . . and temper.

"Robbery! Rape! Murder! What about what else I did? Setting fires. Kidnapping. Trading whiskey to the Comanches . . . and everything else! What about all that? That ought to be worth more than that stinking six hundred dollars! I'll show 'em how much I'm worth! Not that anybody's ever gonna collect . . . Olita!"

"I know," she said. "Get a bottle . . . and come with you."

"Damn right!"

Later that night as Adam Dawson lay in his bed he thought about Lorena making sure that her husband got a good night's sleep.

And he also thought about how after Jeb Stuart fell the South never smiled again. And how it was that every time he thought about having fired that shot, Adam Dawson didn't smile either.

Twenty-four

"Goddammit, Lorena!" Walker exploded. "Why the hell did you invite them over without telling me? Why the hell did you invite them over at all?"

The first part of the breakfast had gone according to plan. Lorena's plan.

Chad had been all smiles and pleasantries after the night's respite and through the morning's meal. Then after Elena left the room Lorena glanced at Adam, took a breath and as calmly as possible mentioned her dinner invitation to the Hatchers.

Chad's reaction was anything but calm. His fist banged onto the table, rattled crockery and silverware and slopped coffee onto the tablecloth.

"Chad." Lorena tried to restore some semblance of calm and reason. "They're our neighbors."

"Well, I don't have to be neighborly." He looked at Dawson. "Do I, Adam?"

Dawson shrugged and did his best to avoid Lorena's eyes that were hoping he would intercede. Even if Dawson had intended to help her cause, Walker didn't give him the chance.

"I don't like that Reb son of a bitch!"

"He didn't even fight in the war," Lorena said. "He stayed right here in Texas."

"That's even worse. The conniving, no good bastard, he's yellow to boot."

"No matter what anybody does around here, according to you, it's wrong."

"Adam hasn't done anything wrong."

"Not yet." Dawson smiled, trying to lighten things up. He started to rise. "I better leave before I do."

"Sit down, Adam." Walker's voice was not harsh. "Hell, you're practically part of the family."

"It's only for one evening," Lorena went on. "Just supper and drinks . . . a couple of hours for God's sake. I can't ask them not to come now."

"Why not?"

"Chad, be human. I never go anywhere or see any-body . . ."

"You see me, don't you?"

"And I love you, but Chad . . ."

"But Chad, what?"

"Is it asking too much to see other people once in a while? Mrs. Hatcher seems very nice. I'd like to get to know her better."

"Then go over there."

"I will, but first I've asked her to come over here."

"Ask her to come alone."

"Chad, please . . ."

"Every time I see that bastard he starts to push me into selling this place."

"Maybe you ought to just listen to what he has to say."

"*You* listen. I'll be talking to Adam." Walker looked at Dawson. "You be here."

"Boss . . ."

"What?"

"I accept your gracious invitation." Adam smiled.

So did Walker.

It wasn't exactly according to plan, but this time Lorena got her way.

The rest of the morning and afternoon Adam did his best to avoid both Walker and Lorena. He got a lot done on the corral, measuring, sawing, hammering and sinking new post holes.

"Good day, brother Adam. You see, Vashti, brother Adam is carrying out the word of the Lord. 'Neither did we eat any man's bread for naught: but wrought with labor and travail. For this he commanded you, that if any would not work, neither should he eat.' And I can tell, tell by the sound of the hammer and the saw that you've been laboring long and hard this day, brother Adam."

"Just an honest day's work for an honest day's pay, Uriah. And it won't be long 'til I get around to your place . . . couple of days and . . ."

"I'm fine, brother Adam, just as I am and just as things are."

"Things'll be even better, but if it's going to be done I'll need some help from you. Will you give me a hand, Uriah, fixing up your place, I mean?"

"In that case . . . 'let us rise up and build: so we will strengthen our hands for this good work.' You let me know when you're ready, brother Adam."

"That I will."

"Come on, Vashti, let's get back to our chores and let brother Adam go on with his good work. See you later, brother Adam." Uriah started toward the chicken coop.

"You bet."

Dawson took off his shirt, but not the scarf, and put it over a post, then went back to work. He hadn't seen her coming.

"Aren't you going to come in and have some dinner?" Lorena's eyes seemed to be devouring him as she spoke.

"No." Adam tried not to look at her while he kept working. "Think I'll skip it and save my appetite . . . for supper with the Hatchers."

"If you weren't here," she said, "I don't think Chad would have agreed to their coming over."

"You think he'd ever agree to sell, to Hatcher, or anybody else?"

"I take it you don't."

"Well, he seems to me to be pretty set in his ways, but I guess that sometimes strange things do happen."

"Yes. Like you coming here . . . and staying."

"You call that strange?" By now Adam had stopped working and no longer tried to avoid looking at her.

" 'Strange.' Fate. Destiny. Luck."

"Luck? Whose?"

"That depends. You know, Adam, you never really answered Chad's question. Do you believe in luck?"

"I've had my share . . . so far."

"Maybe you'll have more. Maybe we both will."

"You mean all three, don't you . . . you and me and Chad?"

"Would you," she nodded toward the post, "like me to wash your shirt?"

"No thanks. I'll do it myself when I'm through here."

"See you at six." She took one last look, turned slowly and walked away.

"Yes, ma'am."

Before and during supper everyone was polite. Too polite. Everyone except Chad Walker. Walker was just there. Silent. Looking no one in the eye. Absent, except in body. Uninvolved in chumship or conversation.

If anyone asked him a direct question, he or she got back a nod or grunt for an answer. During the first hour of the Hatcher visit Walker pulled out his pocket watch three times and checked the time.

Chad Walker had made one concession. He was dressed in his new tailor-made Western-cut suit. Adam had on his alternate shirt, the one he carried in his bedroll. Brad Hatcher wore an expensive gray suit that perfectly matched the color of his temple hair. Mrs. Hatcher was in black, expensive but antebellum. Lorena, more alluring than ever, filled out a clinging blue dress, very décolleté.

When the Hatchers had arrived, precisely at six, Lorena did the introductions, including Brad Hatcher to Adam Dawson. They shook hands politely like complete strangers.

A couple of times Dawson noticed that Hatcher tried his best to maneuver Lorena into a spot where he might manage even the briefest of private conversation, but Lorena had either been unaware of the maneuver or had outmaneuvered her guest. Dawson figured it was the latter, that Lorena wanted to avoid any chance of appearing conspiratorial in front of her husband.

After supper, while still at the table, Walker pulled out his pocket watch again and addressed his guests directly for the first time.

"All right, cigars and drinks in the library . . . unless you have to leave. I'm going in." He struggled to rise then plodded away on his canes as the others also rose.

"Mrs. Walker, you have a lovely home," Mary Ann Hatcher said.

"Thank you."

"I'd very much like you . . . and Mr. Walker to come visit us sometime."

"We'd like that very much. I've heard that Spanish Bit is the most elegant ranch in this part of Texas."

"Well, it used to be but we haven't made many improvements in a long, long time."

"Mary Ann insists on clinging to things as they used to be before . . . the war," Hatcher said. "But I'm hoping . . ."

"What, Brad?" Mary Ann asked.

"To make a few changes for the better." Hatcher smiled.

"Shall we join Chad in the library?" Lorena started to move.

Adam noticed that the palm of Hatcher's left hand touched Lorena's elbow as if she needed guidance or maybe as if he just needed to touch her.

On the way to the library Hatcher turned to Dawson and asked, politely, "You intend to settle in Pinto, Mr. Dawson?"

"Not sure, Mr. Hatcher. Depends."

"On what?"

"Fate. Destiny. Luck. I don't know, yet."

"I see. Well, good luck."

"Thanks."

A few minutes later, drinks had been poured, cigars lit, the ladies chatted politely on the sofa and the men had settled into an uncomfortable silence on the other side of the library.

A couple of times Brad Hatcher had tried to make conversation. The weather. The coming election. Back to the drought. Still, nothing brought more than a nod or a grunt from the host between sips from his glass and spews of smoke from his cigar. Finally Hatcher tried a less subtle and more blunt approach.

"I wonder, Chad, if you've thought any more about my proposition . . ."

"What proposition is that, Hatcher?"

"I've talked to Terrance Swerd about it . . ."

"About what?"

"A loan. Enough to set you for life."

"I'm already set for life without any help from you or Terrance Swerd or any other Southern sonofa . . ."

"Chad!" Lorena interrupted. "It won't hurt to listen to what Mr. Hatcher wants to say."

"All right, I'll listen," Walker said to everyone's surprise, then added, "for twenty seconds, then that's it!"

"Well, Chad, I just want to run a big herd of beef . . . like you."

"Then run one. You picked up plenty when you married Mary Ann."

"Chad, I haven't got enough water to . . ."

"Your time's up! Look, Hatcher, you can eat my food, drink my booze and smoke my cigars but I don't want to listen to any more shit tonight or ever about buying this place. Can you get that through your Confederate skull?"

Hatcher rose, looking apoplectic, but he restrained himself from saying anything. Lorena bolted from the sofa and took a step forward.

"Chad! For heaven's sake!" She moved closer to Hatcher,

took his arm and led him past Dawson and away from her husband. "I'm sorry, Brad. He hasn't been feeling well lately and . . ."

"I feel fine," Walker said. "I'll feel even better when they leave."

"Come on, Mary Ann," Hatcher indicated to his wife who rose.

It looked to Dawson as if there were just the slightest trace of a smile of satisfaction on Mrs. Hatcher's face. Satisfaction at witnessing her husband receiving comeuppance.

But what Dawson detected was only the surface of the contentment and elation that Mary Ann Hatcher kept hidden within her. For once Brad Hatcher's plot would not hatch. For once there was somebody, since her father died, who saw through his polite posturing, his unctuous, self-serving duplicity. Since Jason Beaudine died no one, including Mary Ann Beaudine Hatcher herself, had slammed the door in Brad Hatcher's face. It took a cripple to do it and Mary Ann was in no hurry to leave the scene of her husband's humiliation.

"Thank you, Mrs. Walker." Mary Ann smiled demurely. "It was a lovely dinner and I do hope we meet again."

"So do I, Mrs. Hatcher." Lorena was taken aback by Mary Ann Hatcher's sangfroid reaction to what had transpired. "I'll see you to the door."

"No thanks." Hatcher almost pushed his wife through the library door. "We're all right."

Chad Walker managed to rise, cigar in his mouth, with the aid of both canes and clomp toward the window.

"Fix me another drink, will you, Adam?"

Dawson moved to the bar. Lorena stood frozen for a moment then took a step forward.

"Miserable bastard!"

"He sure is." Walker turned smiling and faced his wife.

"I'm talking about you and you know it!"

"Do I?"

"You do . . . miserable bastard."

"Yeah? Well, I'll tell you what else I know. I know why you set this up . . . you want me to sell. Well, it won't work,

Lorena. This is my land . . . and I intend to keep it and be buried on it. You can damn well stay or leave. That's up to you. So what're you going to do about it? What can you do about it? Kill me?"

Walker took a step closer to the desk, jerked open a drawer and pulled out a service revolver, then tossed it on top of the desk.

"Go ahead," he said. "It's loaded."

Lorena stared at him then looked down at the gun.

"Well, go ahead! Either pick it up, take aim and squeeze the goddam trigger . . . or shut up about selling my ranch!"

Lorena's storm-fierce eyes went from the gun back to Chad. Slowly the storm subsided. She became serene, almost beatific. She turned and strolled out of the room, just as if it had been a successful supper party or as if she were on stage displaying her glimmering body as she exited in one of John Wilkes Booth's productions.

Adam Dawson came over and handed Walker the glass. Walker took it, smiled then laughed.

"You know, Adam, she's got a lot of her old man in her." He took a sip.

"Lorena?"

"Yeah."

"You knew her father?"

"Sure. He was a carny man."

"A what?"

"Barker. Snake oil salesman. You name it. Lorena used to shill for him. 'Course I didn't meet him 'til after we were married, but she'd told me all about him."

"What do you mean?"

"She was part of the act . . . to take the money from the suckers. They worked together for years 'til she joined up with Booth."

"Then how did you meet him?"

"Easy. When he heard I won his daughter and a pot of money he came to see me about bankrolling some wild ass scheme."

"What happened?"

"I gave him a hundred bucks—that's a hundred more than Booth did—and told him to go back to his snake oil."

"Where's he now?"

"Dead. Some disgruntled rube shot him in the vitals. Ain't that a hoot?"

"Yeah. A hoot. Say." Dawson pointed at the gun on the desk. "Speaking of shooting, is that thing really loaded?"

Chad Walker looked at him for a moment. He started to laugh. Louder. An impulsive, infecund laugh.

Adam figured that that was all the answer he was going to get.

"Well, boss. Thanks for the food, the drinks and the cigar. I've learned one thing tonight."

"What?"

"Never." Dawson smiled. "Never try to talk you into anything you don't want to do."

"Maybe Lorena has too."

"Good night, boss."

"Adam."

"Yeah?"

"You've spent a lot of time with Custer and his wife, haven't you?"

"Some."

"They ever fight?"

"Fight?"

"Argue . . . like Lorena and me? Ever see 'em blow up at each other, like tonight?"

"Truth is." Adam glanced back at the gun on the desk. "I've never seen *anything* like tonight." He smiled again. "Good night, boss."

"Mary Ann, I'm sorry."

"About what, Brad?"

She was in her nightclothes and in bed when Hatcher came into the room still dressed and carrying a tumbler of whiskey in his hand.

"About what happened tonight, about how that rude, insufferable fool insulted you."

"He didn't insult me, Brad. He didn't say anything at all to me."

"You know what I mean."

"I'm not sure I do."

"He'll find out."

"What'll he find out, Brad?"

"That he can't come down here with his damn Yankee dollars and lord it over his . . ."

"His what, Brad? His betters?"

"Yes, that's right, his betters. He'll regret this. I'll see that he does."

"How? The man doesn't want to sell his property and there's not a thing that you or anybody else can do about it."

"Isn't there?"

"Well, is there?"

"We'll see about that. You just don't understand, Mary Ann."

"Understand about what?"

"About . . . business."

"No, I guess I don't. That's what you've always said, Brad. That I should be glad that you're here to take care of business . . . and me. To take care of Spanish Bit, like you always have."

"And I always will, Mary Ann. You can be sure of that."

"Oh, I am, Brad. I am. But right now I'm very tired, dear. Do you mind . . ."

"Of course not. You get a good night's rest. Everything will come right." This time he leaned close and touched her forehead with his whiskey lips and she closed her eyes at their touch.

After he left and went into his room, Marissa entered with a glass of warm milk and set it on the night table beside the bed then walked silently toward the door to the hall.

"Thank you, Marissa," Mrs. Hatcher said with her eyes still closed.

"*De nada, señora.*"

As was his custom every night, Adam Dawson wound his silver watch and looked at the inscription " . . . *Come on, you Wolverine! . . .* "

It had been a present given him on February 9, 1864, by Autie in Monroe, Michigan on the occasion of the marriage of Elizabeth Clift Bacon to General George Armstrong Custer as Dawson served as Custer's best man.

After the ceremony at the First Presbyterian Church when Dawson kissed the bride, Libbie whispered: "Thank you, Adam, for saving my husband's life. Not just the first time, but all those other times since. If it weren't for you we wouldn't be here today. Please take care of him. You *are* Custer's luck."

And as he lay in the bunk, Dawson thought about what had happened earlier that evening and about Chad Walker's remarks after Lorena left the room . . .

"You've spent a lot of time with Custer and his wife, haven't you . . . they ever fight . . . argue . . . like Lorena and me . . ."

Asking to compare Chad and Lorena to Custer and Libbie was like comparing cinders to stars.

No man that Dawson had ever known was more in love with a woman than Custer and no woman so completely dedicated to her husband than Libbie to Autie.

Autie had already given up drinking and when Libbie agreed to marry him he told her he was going to give up smoking because it affected her breathing and also give up gambling because it might affect their future. He had forsworn every vice but one. Cursing. That vice proved too effective in combat for him to forswear. But his language was always comparatively temperate when she was present or in hearing distance.

And she in turn left Monroe after the ceremony and became not a camp follower, but certainly a Custer follower . . . to Washington and then as close as possible in the ensuing campaigns under U. S. Grant and Philip Sheridan at Petersburg, Fisher's Hill, Winchester, Cedar Creek, through the Shenandoah Valley which Custer and Sheridan so devastated that Sheridan's report to Grant said "a crow flying overhead would have to carry its own provisions."

Libbie was nearby at Sayler's Creek when a third of what was left of the Confederate Army surrendered to Custer ... and Adam Dawson was at his side.

At Appomattox Custer stood by Grant and Sheridan when General Robert E. Lee signed the terms of Confederate surrender on a small writing table inside McLean's house.

Afterward Sheridan paid McLean twenty dollars for that same table and presented it as a gift to Libbie along with a note he wrote to her.

> *"I respectfully present to you the small writing table on which the Conditions of Surrender of the Army of Northern Virginia were written by Lt. General Grant—and permit me to say, madam, that there is scarcely an individual in our service who has contributed more to bring about this desirable result than your gallant husband."*

Libbie took that table back to Monroe and with them after the war when her gallant husband—and she along with him—were stationed in Texas, Mississippi and later on the Western frontier.

It was with them when Autie took over the Seventh Cavalry at Forts Hays, Harker, Wallace, Dodge and Riley and so was Captain Adam Dawson after Red Cloud's Sioux massacred Captain William J. Fetterman and his company near Fort Phil Kearny.

Custer, still leading the charges with Dawson at his side, quickly mastered the art of Indian fighting in successful campaigns against the Cheyennes, Arapahos, Kiowas and Comanches ... campaigns against great Indian chiefs including Black Kettle, Pawnee Killer, Satanta and many more.

And as he lay in his bunk, still holding that watch ticking

in the darkness, Adam Dawson remembered the time when, against Dawson's advice, and in defiance of an order, Custer faced a court martial and suffered loss of a year's pay, when he made a mad dash to join Libbie at Fort Riley and escort her safely through Indian Territory to Fort Wallace.

It was only because of Sheridan's intervention that Custer's army career was suspended, not ended.

All that and more Custer did for the love of Libbie, so the two of them could be together.

How could Adam Dawson answer Chad Walker's questions about Libbie and Autie? He couldn't. Walker could never understand that kind of love between husband and wife. Few could.

But Adam did as he lay in that darkened bunkhouse at Walker's Way. He understood and remembered everything right up to Washita.

Dawson didn't want to think about Washita, not tonight or ever.

Still he couldn't help thinking about Autie and Libbie somewhere this same night.

Were they together in each other's arms, safe behind guarded walls of a fort? Or was he away, sleeping in a tent or on ground soaked in blood of Indian warriors and uniformed troopers, thinking of yesterday's victories and tomorrow's perils when he would once again lead the Seventh to the tune of Gary Owen into uncertain battle?

To glory?

What was in store?

Fate. Destiny. Luck.

And what was in store for Adam Dawson? Here, in this nowhere place called Pinto, Texas. On a ranch called Walker's Way. On a bunk holding a watch that seemed to tick with the rhythm of his own heartbeat.

Fate. Destiny. Luck . . . the ticking of the watch seemed to repeat over and over again . . . Fate. Destiny. Luck.

Dawson placed the watch on the small table next to the

bunk, closed his eyes and did his best not to think of George and Elizabeth Custer.

The trouble was that he couldn't stop thinking about Lorena and her stage-like exit from that room.

Twenty-five

Sheriff Ben Vesper entered the office carrying a bag from Reighnhold's restaurant where he had had his usual breakfast of ham, eggs, toast and three cups of coffee.

"Morning, Sheriff," Sam said from behind the swinging mop.

"Sam, you're gonna wear out that damn mop before the end of the month if you keep up at this rate. Give it a rest."

"Yes, sir." Sam kept on mopping toward the far corner.

"Well?"

"I was just finishing up . . ."

"You're finished. Put the damn thing away, now."

"Yes, sir." Sam stood the mop against the corner and turned smiling. "What's next, Sheriff?"

"Next, I see and smell that you made a fresh pot of coffee this morning." Vesper pointed at the pot atop the stove.

"Yes, sir."

"Well, have yourself a cup or two and here's a couple hot biscuits from Reighnhold's to go with it."

"Thanks, Sheriff. How much I owe you?"

"Just quit mopping for a while, that's all."

"Yes, sir."

"I'm going out."

"Yes, sir."

"Visit Alma and Mrs. O'Donnell for a while."

"Yes, sir."

"Then I got something for both of us to do so don't go wandering away."

"No, sir."

As Sheriff Ben Vesper crossed the street and started to walk toward Alma's house, he noticed Brad Hatcher dismounting from his palomino and heading into Baldy's Bar. Vesper thought to himself that it was pretty early for Hatcher to have a drink but that maybe Mr. Hatcher was going to while away the half hour or so before the bank opened.

Brad Hatcher had spent a restive night. He even got out of bed three times and poured generously from the bourbon bottle into the tumbler then walked in his bare feet around the bedroom, sipping and thinking.

Years ago it had been Jason Beaudine who stood between him and his goal . . . Spanish Bit via Mary Ann Beaudine. At that time while Hatcher was scheming schemes as how to circumvent or eliminate the old hardass—one of his schemes included seducing and impregnating the virgin daughter, thus forcing nuptials and inheritance—fate dealt him a felicitous shortcut in the form of a fatal heart attack visited upon hardass himself. That was indeed fortunate, particularly since Hatcher and the formerly virgin daughter discovered that the heir to Spanish Bit had proved infertile.

But, since then Hatcher had another goal . . . Walker's Way via Lorena Walker who was many men away from virginity. Hatcher's approach to Lorena, at first, had been exploratory, cautious, consisting of conversation . . . how she might feel about her husband selling the water-rich land.

It didn't take long for Hatcher to find out that Lorena was agreeable in more ways than one. She agreed to help him while he helped himself to her. Lorena was the warm woman that Hatcher had sought to make up for the cold fish at Spanish Bit.

She was not only warm, she was volcanic, erupting with a passion that challenged even Hatcher's zeal. But after last night and the confrontation with the cripple, Hatcher realized that the path to Walker's Way was not through Lorena.

That wasn't to say he still wouldn't take pleasure in traveling that path whenever the opportunity arose. But there now appeared to be less of such opportunities particularly since the intrusion of the stranger who had appeared in such untimely fashion and had shown himself in no hurry to drift on.

Last night Brad Hatcher had made up his mind that this time he could not wait around for fate to deal any shortcut in the form of a heart attack, stroke, fatal disease or falling timber to cancel out the crippled Yankee that blocked his path.

This time he would have to take direct action but without appearing culpable.

The link between Hatcher and his objective just might be in Baldy's Bar, if not right now, then soon. Brad Hatcher meant to connect with that link as soon as possible.

"Morning, Baldy," Hatcher said. "What the hell's the matter with you?"

Baldy had a damp bar towel circling from his chins up to, and tied at the top of his hairless dome. He was pouring whiskey from the bottle into his mouth, sloshing it around and spitting it out onto the floor.

"Toothache," Baldy muttered. "Been up all night. Sent word for Alma to come over so I can go over and have Tony pull the sonofabitch. Waitin' for her."

"Well, hand me my bottle while we both wait, will you?"

"Sure thing."

"Seen Joe Nueva around?"

"Not yet. He'll be in."

Brad Hatcher took the bottle and glass that Baldy had set on the bar and walked toward a corner table.

The door opened just as Sheriff Vesper was about to knock.

"Morning, Ben."

"Morning, Alma. You see me coming?"

"Nope. Just got word Baldy's got a toothache, gonna spell him so he can get it pulled."

"Oh, well then, I'll be on my way..."

"No, no. come in." Alma turned her head toward the parlor. "Maureen, Ben's come to visit..."

"No, it's all right, I'll come back another time, I just..."

"Please come in, Mr. Vesper," Maureen said. "Have a cup of tea."

"Go ahead, Ben. She could use some company. Just finished writing that letter ... I got to get." Alma pushed him inside and closed the door.

"How do you like your tea, Mr. Vesper?"

"No tea, ma'am, thanks and please call me Ben."

"I will if you don't call me ma'am. Maureen will do nicely and won't you sit down, Ben?"

"Thank you ... Maureen." Ben sat. "Alma said you've written a letter to ..."

"Yes. To Tim's brother in Laredo, explaining what happened..."

"That couldn't have been very easy..."

"No, Ben, but it had to be done."

"And have you decided what you're going to do?"

"Not yet. But Doctor Bonner thinks it advisable that I don't travel..."

"Good."

"How's that?"

"I mean that's good advice..."

"I think so too ... until we find out about ... the baby."

"Yes, ma'am ... Maureen. Would you like me to see that the letter goes out on the next stage?"

"Would you do that for me?"

"I would, and anything else ... that is, whatever I can do to help..."

There was a knock on the door and Maureen opened it for Doc Bonner.

"Hello, you two." Bonner came in carrying his black medical satchel. "Ran into that damn fool Baldy—told him I'd pull that molar but he prefers Tony Amado, that combination barber/undertaker who'll probably pull the wrong one. Serves the fat bastard right, pardon me, ma'am."

Both Vesper and Maureen laughed.

"Well, let's have a look, Maureen, I've got to make some rounds."

"So do I," said Vesper.

Maureen O'Donnell picked up an envelope from the parlor table and handed it to the sheriff.

"Thanks, Ben."

"You're welcome . . . Maureen. So long, Doc."

"Yeah. So long . . . Ben."

At Baldy's Bar Hatcher, still at the far table, was wiping the inner band of his Stetson as Alma came out of the back room carrying a plate of free lunch and placed it on the bar. On second thought she lifted the plate and took a couple of steps toward Hatcher.

"Care for a nibble of something, Mr. Hatcher?"

"No, thanks, Alma. Had breakfast at home."

"I've never seen you," she pointed to the bottle on the table, "chase it down so early."

"Have you seen Joe Nueva lately?" he asked, ignoring Alma's observation.

"No, but I haven't been around much lately, I'm happy to say."

"How's your patient coming along?"

"She's Doc's patient, just my friend, and God knows she needs all the friends she can get."

"Very attractive lady, I'm told."

"Who told you?"

"Well . . . I honestly don't remember."

"She *is* attractive, specially for a lady in mourning. By the way, Mr. Hatcher, there's something I want to talk to you and Mr. Swerd about. It concerns Mrs. O'Donnell, she . . ."

But Brad Hatcher's attention was somewhere else.

Joe Nueva had just come through the bat-wings followed by his friends Paco, Jake and Jaime.

———

Sheriff Ben Vesper walked along Main Street with the envelope still in his hand. He noticed Nueva and company going into Baldy's and kept walking toward Ed Rusky and the Stage Depot as Sam Mendez hurried out of the sheriff's office and caught up with him.

"Hi there, Sheriff."

"What is it now, Sam?"

"Nothin', sir. I'm just bone idle 'til you tell me what to do next."

"Eat both them biscuits?"

"Just one."

"Go back and eat the other one."

"Yes, sir. You said you had something for both of us to do and . . ."

"If we don't do it today we'll do it tomorrow."

"Yes, sir." Sam pointed to the envelope in Vesper's hand. "What you got there, Sheriff?"

"What's it look like?"

"A . . . letter, maybe."

"That's what it is, Sam, a letter, and no maybes about it. Now you go back and polish your boots or something. I'll see you later."

"Yes, sir . . . but Sheriff . . ."

"What?"

"Haven't got any polish."

"Use saddle soap. There's some in the bottom drawer next to the Uncle Henry knife."

"Yes, sir." Sam Mendez peeled off, turned around and headed back toward the office.

Joe Nueva and his friends started toward their usual table but Nueva noticed Hatcher motioning with a slight wave of his hand, motioning for Nueva to come over. Nueva smiled and walked with long, strong strides closing the distance between them.

"Morning, Mr. Hatcher."

"Morning, Joe. Sit down."

Joe Nueva was surprised by the warmth of Hatcher's greeting and even more surprised at the invitation.

"Sure thing, Mr. Hatcher."

"Alma," Hatcher called out. "Bring over another glass."

Alma was just as surprised as Nueva. Never before had Hatcher spoken to the Mexican except in reply, much less asked for his company. She delivered the glass then went back to the bar.

"Have a drink, Joe. Top shelf."

"You bet, Mr. Hatcher." Nueva nodded and poured. "You got a job for me at the ranch, Mr. Hatcher?"

"Lower your voice, Joe. This is private. Could lead to a job and more . . . much more. First of all, how soon could you get in touch with your relative?"

"Huh?"

"That cousin of yours," Hatcher whispered. "The one that the sheriff spoke about the other day."

"Well, I don't know . . ."

"Joe. I don't have time or patience for games. Now listen . . ."

Alma went about her business behind the bar and with the other customers who were drifting in for their early boosters. But every now and then she glanced at the far table.

The whispering stopped when Sheriff Ben Vesper walked in. He went straight to the bar and Alma, but took note of Nueva who rose and moved toward his friends at the table on the other corner of the saloon. Nueva passed Vesper without greeting or acknowledgement.

"What's that all about?" Vesper nodded toward Hatcher and the empty glass Nueva left behind.

"Search me." Alma shrugged. "Doc show up?"

"Yep."

"Did you mail the letter?"

"Yep."

"Think she'll stay?"

"For a while."

"That's a start."

"Yep."

"Care for a drink?"

"Nope."

"Damn him to hell! That bloody butcher!" Baldy banged through the bat-wings spitting blood onto the stained bar towel that was formerly wrapped around his face and head. "The sonofabitch liked to kill me! I'm bleeding to death! Alma!"

"What?"

"Bar towel!"

"Coming up." Alma threw him a damp towel from the bar. Baldy caught it and shoved it close to his face spitting and cursing.

"I'll poison that little rat if he ever comes in here. Poison's too good for him. I'll peel the skin off his back with a shovel. He liked to kill me! I need a doctor. Alma!"

"What?"

"If Doc Bonner comes in here tell him . . ."

"Tell him what?"

"Never mind. I'm going to lay down. Give me another towel."

Alma handed Baldy another damp towel as he passed by the bar and headed toward the back room still cursing and spitting.

"Alma." Vesper smiled. "Looks like you're gonna be here for a while."

"Looks like."

Vesper looked toward Brad Hatcher who was purposely looking in another direction.

Then Sheriff Ben Vesper walked out.

Once again, all through the day, Adam Dawson played "keep away." He tried to keep as far away from Lorena and Chad as he could.

He left the breakfast table fast and headed for the corral and the hammer, saw and nails. At breakfast Lorena had been serene and silent. It didn't seem to bother Chad a bit. He actually seemed to savor the silence. A couple of times he asked for more coffee and Lorena obliged.

Adam had said that he hoped to finish work on the corral today and wanted to get off to an early start.

A short time later the two day laborers showed up and continued their repair of the barn roof.

Around noon Lorena came out to the corral to see if Adam was ready to come in for the noon meal.

"Thanks, but I'll skip it again."

"You can't be saving your appetite for the Hatchers. They sure as hell aren't coming over tonight or any other night."

"Guess not. Well, you tried."

"Not hard enough."

"You know, I asked him if it was loaded. All he did was laugh."

"Oh, it was loaded all right."

"You think it was?"

"I know it was. And he knew I wouldn't kill him, not in his own house, with a witness . . . or any other way," she added.

Adam thought to himself that the "or any other way" came just a little late . . . and a little lame.

"Adam, can't you see how it is . . . being stuck out here in this hellspeck away from civilization . . . I just want what's best . . ."

"Best for who, Lorena?"

"All right, best for me, but for him too. I tell you, Adam, before you came he was growing worse every day, lording it over everybody and everything like some madman . . . and you watch . . . anything can set him off and something will and he'll do something crazy and hurt somebody or himself like throwing that loaded gun on the table last night . . . it could've gone off . . ."

"After you left, Lorena, he told me he met your father . . . the carny man . . . 'snake oil salesman' he called him."

That storm-fierce look came into her eyes again. Her lips

almost disappeared and her jaw clamped tight. She started to turn away but swiveled back, her flaxen hair twisting above her shoulders.

"You think I lied to you about his being a minister, well, he was a minister until his congregation caught up with him and unfrocked him literally. So instead of saving souls, he started selling snake oil and me along with it whenever he got the chance. You can believe me or not. I don't give a damn!"

This time she did turn and walk away . . . and if it was a stage exit, it was a good one.

All through the afternoon Adam Dawson worked and sweated and wondered what and whom to believe and whether he should waste time wondering . . . or caring.

Spider. Flame. Delilah.

The hell with it. Tomorrow he would start work on Uriah's shack and when that was finished he'd find some good reason to ride away. He already had a lot of good reasons. What he'd have to find was a good excuse.

Late that afternoon the two Mexican day workers finished the barn roof. They stopped by the house and Walker paid them off.

Dawson didn't look forward to dining with the Walkers that evening or any other evening until he left. He thought of going into Pinto and having a few drinks at Baldy's and eating at the restaurant in town.

But Chad Walker stood on the back porch braced by his canes, smiling and waving for Adam to come inside and eat, so Dawson braced himself and went in.

Again Lorena absented herself from much of the conversation which was mostly on Walker's part. What rotten workers the Mexican day hands were and how the stable would probably leak like a sieve if it ever did rain again in this part of the world.

When Walker took a breath from drinking, eating and talking Adam did say that he was going into town soon to pick up a coffee pot, skillet and a few other items so he could fix his own meals.

"What's the matter, Adam? Don't you favor our company?"

"No, that's not it, but . . ."

"But what?"

"Well, a hired hand ought not to impose himself on his boss and the boss lady all the time . . ."

"Hell, I told you before, you're practically a part of the family. But if you want to do a little cooking out there we got extra pots and pans . . . even a couple of coffee pots, haven't we Lorena?"

"I'm sure we could accommodate Mr. Dawson," Lorena said evenly.

" 'Mr. Dawson,' " Walker grunted, "I thought we'd come a long way from that."

"You're right, Chad. The 'boss lady' shouldn't have been so formal. Adam is practically a part of the family. I'll see that he gets what he needs."

"Right now." Adam rose. "I could use a little shut-eye . . ."

"You did a hell of a job on that corral, Adam."

"One door closes another opens. Tomorrow . . ."

"Tomorrow I want to get in a little more target practice . . . then you can start on Uriah's shack, if that's what you were going to say."

"That," Dawson smiled, "is what I was going to say."

Twenty-six

Six shots from the .44 Winchester carbine shattered six bottles atop the boulder.

"Damn good, Sam," Sheriff Vesper commented. "Now how good are you at wing shooting?"

"Don't rightly know, sir."

"Well, let's find out." Vesper picked up a tin can and hurled it on a low arc away from where the two men stood.

First one then another shot hit the can before it fell to the ground.

"I guess we found out. Gimme that carbine and strap on this rig."

"Yes, sir."

Vesper took the rifle and handed Sam a belt and holster bearing a .44 Colt Revolver.

"I wore that rig until a short time ago when I picked up this newer model. But it's a fine weapon."

"Beautiful."

"And deadly . . . one way or another."

"What's that mean, sir?"

"It means somebody else or you could end up dead. That's what it means."

"I get it," Sam said as he buckled the rig and grinned.

"Don't laugh, son. This ain't funny."

"Yes, sir."

Early that morning Sheriff Vesper had brought Sam to an isolated area just outside of Pinto. The ex–stable boy had been talking about carrying a gun ever since he came to work with the sheriff. Vesper figured it was time to find out what the youngster did or didn't know about the use of rifles and revolvers. So far the sheriff stood astounded at the boy's ability with a long gun, although a carbine wasn't exactly a long gun, measuring four inches shorter than a regular Winchester and holding thirteen rounds instead of seventeen.

"Son," Ben said, "you're a natural born rifleman. Some things can't be taught. You got the rifleman's instinct and you didn't get it shooting squirrels."

"Shot me a panther once."

"On the move?"

"We was both moving, sir, 'til I fired."

"I see. Now let me tell you a little about a hand gun . . ."

"I sure would like to hear."

"You're going to. There's them who keep the hammer on an empty chamber. I'm not one of 'em. Might need that extra bullet. Now the most important thing is this. And never . . . never squeeze the trigger unless you're willing to kill. Hear that?"

"Yes, sir."

"Because if you're not . . . willing to kill in that instant without any hesitation . . . it could cost you your life because the other fellow probably won't hesitate and that's the difference between the quick and the dead. That one split second of hesitation."

"Yes, sir."

"And don't do anything dumb like aim to wound. That lets him get off a shot. Aim to kill."

"Yes, sir."

"Don't go aiming for the head."

"No, sir. Why not?"

"Too small a target and moves quicker than the rest of the body. Got that?"

"Yes, sir."

"The chest, boy, that's the place . . . broader and slower . . . and that's where the most vital target is . . . the heart."

"Yes, sir."

"Now speaking of that, don't give him a broad target by standing square on. The less he has to aim at the better your odds of coming out alive. Got that?"

"Yes, sir."

"And forget that crap about watching his eyes. He don't shoot with his eyes. He shoots with his thumb and trigger finger. When that hand starts to move, you move . . . unless you want to move first."

"Is that fair?"

"It's necessary sometimes, when you know he's faster and deadlier. Don't worry so much about being fair . . . worry about being alive."

"Yes, sir."

"That's why I say don't squeeze unless you're willing to kill . . . and have a damn good reason or you might hang."

"Yes, sir."

"Hook. Draw. Fire."

"Yes, sir."

"See that tree over there with that small branch hanging down in front?"

"Yes, sir."

"That's a man you're willing to kill . . . and the leaf on that branch is that sonofabitch's heart. When I say 'now' his hand is starting to move. You move too. Hook. Draw. Fire. Fast but not too fast or the barrel won't be level. You ready?"

"Yes, sir."

"So's he. *Now!*"

Hook, draw, fire was what Sam Mendez did. The leaf blew away and Sam fired again tearing apart the branch.

"How was that, Sheriff?"

"That's a good start." The sheriff cleared his throat. "But it's a little different with a man and gun. Let's hope you never get around to that."

"Yes, sir."

"Unless it's absolutely necessary."

"Yes, sir."

"Now give me back that rig."

"Yes, sir."

"Until it's absolutely necessary."

Five fast shots. All dead center on the target. Adam Dawson lowered his rifle.

Lorena stood nearby watching as her husband took aim at his target.

That morning things had been different. Adam had not hesitated to do his best and so far his best had been better than Chad Walker who was propped against a bale of hay and firing within the bull's-eye but not quite dead center. The repeated gunfire had set the hens scurrying and cackling. Walker, determined to win this time, lifted his Henry to aim and fire. Dawson looked down at the ground, not at the target and already regretted his accuracy. He hoped that Walker would fire fast and true. As Walker took aim the cacophony of the chickens grew perceptively louder and more agitated.

Walker cocked and fired three times, all three shots just outside the circumference of the bull's-eye while the chickens fluttered and pothered with accelerated frenzy. Walker's eyes maddened and blazed with fury. He whirled, almost falling, and shot off a stream of lead at the cackling chickens as they raced wildly, colliding into each other.

More shots, feathers and blood commingled with the sharp reports of the rifle as bullets tore off heads and flung mangled chicken parts into the air and against the coop and fence . . . until Walker stopped firing. Slowly, with a vacant hollow gaze, he stared off at the slaughter, shuddered, then turned finally and looked at Adam and Lorena.

"Vashti . . . Vashti . . ." It was Uriah's voice as he emerged from the shack and almost stumbled into the chicken yard. He groped his way through the carnage, puzzled, bewildered.

"Vashti . . ." Uriah fell to his knees. His hands reached out and searched for what his eyes could not see.

The chickens, those who were still able, scrambled away

from him, from the man who had nurtured and protected them.

"Vashti . . ." His hands were smeared with blood and feathers as he sought the familiar form, hoping not to find it.

He found it. With trembling fingers he lifted the limp and lifeless red hen, now drenched a brighter red.

"No," he sobbed. "Vashti . . ."

Adam and Lorena had not moved, their eyes locked at Walker who stood with the empty rifle still in his hands.

"What are you looking at?" Walker growled.

There was no answer. Only human silence except for the sobbing of the blind old soldier on his knees in the chicken yard and the shrill cackle of the scurrying hens.

"You think I'm going to bust down and cry for some dead chicken? Well, I'm not. You hear me?!"

"Yes, Chad," Lorena whispered. "We hear."

"Then get out! Both of you. Get out of here!"

Nobody moved.

"Go on! I want to be by myself!" Walker raised the rifle and gripped it hard.

"Boss . . ." Dawson took a step forward.

"That's right, I'm the boss. Do what I tell you. I can take care of myself. Now ride out, both of you, and leave me alone!" Walker lowered his eyes, then his head. "Get out!"

Twenty-seven

They rode. Silent. Aimless. Away from Walker's Way. Away
from rage and madness. Away from hate and fury. But they
both knew that they would have to ride back. In an hour or
two, maybe more, but before dark.

Chad Walker had said that he could take care of himself.
In many ways he could. He had an inner strength in spite of
his handicap. He had a will of steel. Unbending. Unbroken,
like his body was broken. He had survived a sniper's bullet.
He sat on a throne in a kingdom of his own making. But like
any king he had to have subjects, those who would bend to
his will and carry out his commands.

Right now his subjects consisted of a wife seething with
inner revolt, even revulsion and of a hired hand, a comrade
in arms in a war fought but not forgotten ... a hired hand
who was bound to leave him just as sure as the turning of
the earth and a wife whom he could not satisfy as a husband.

These were Chad Walker's subjects, these two and an old
soldier sobbing on his knees in a chicken yard.

And within Chad Walker another war still raged. A
ghastly war even harder to win. A war of physical and mental
torment. A war with endless battles against the world and
within himself. A war that left him bitter and unpredictable.

Both Adam and Lorena knew that Chad would get over
what happened today. He would pull himself together and
go on in his own way, Walker's way ... until something else
blew him apart again.

Lorena adjusted the brim of her hat to better shade her sensitive eyes and delicate eggshell skin from the radiant sun still rising toward its western arc.

As she did she looked just a little too long at the man on her left astride the appaloosa. His long legs, forked into the stirrups, led up to the narrow band of waist that broadened into abundant shoulders, a thick throat circled by the scarlet scarf and a face carved like an image on a freshly minted coin. His eyes were wire-drawn but all-seeing, of indeterminate color changing with the sun. He was quiet, casual and calm but with a coil wound and set to spring. She could feel that whipcord strength when his arms and body tightened around her that day at the boulders after they found the saddle. She wanted to feel it again, that and more. Even now she wanted to leap on him and trigger that coiled strength she felt when her body had pressed against him and her lips felt his quiver against hers.

Lorena had known more men than she could, or wanted to remember. The curse and benefit of beauty. She couldn't remember the change from childhood to carnality, from innocence to indulgence. Maybe she had blotted the moment from her mind as she had tried to a blot out other things, places and people. If she remembered it all she would go crazy, as crazy as Chad.

It had started with her father who had the face of a saint and the venery of a goat. "Reverend" everybody had called him. "Reverend" Douglas. He was no more a reverend than was Cagliostro. But he could charm the fur off of a polecat. He could sell the butcher his own meat and when it came to women, young or old, hoi polloi or hoitytoity, Reverend Douglas knew the territory and how to exploit it, including but not starting or ending with his own daughter.

Lorena Douglas had never known her mother, or whether the reverend had ever married her. But he would never let Lorena forget that he had done the "right thing" by their offspring, that he had not abandoned her while he was abusing her, even though at first she was too young to understand.

When she did understand the way of the reverend and other men, she put her knowledge to use in order to get away from him. Not that the other men were much better, but her future prospect with them couldn't be worse and might lead . . . anywhere.

It led to John Wilkes Booth, who fancied himself a great leading man on and off the stage. Lorena couldn't tell when he was, or wasn't, acting. She believed that Booth, himself, couldn't tell. All the world *was* a stage and he finally got to play a part that the world would never forget.

She thought that she would have it all with Chad Walker, and for a short time she did . . . until he came back a cripple, wounded in body and soul.

And she learned a new meaning of abuse. At least that was her excuse, if she needed one, for all the other men since then.

But somehow this man riding beside her, this stranger, was different from all the rest. There was no doubt about his physical attraction. But there was more.

He was clean and uncorrupt. Honest and innocent. Honorable and untarnished. Here was a man she wanted to be with, to live with, to stay with.

The trouble was, in order to do any of that, she would have to make him corrupt.

"Adam," she whispered as they rode.

"What?"

"What are you thinking?"

"Nothing."

"Please tell me. Just now, with me here next to you, what were you thinking?"

"I was thinking . . . that I never should have hit that bull's-eye."

"That you should have let him win?"

"It wouldn't have made any difference to me."

"But it did to him. That's the way he is, the way he'll always be."

Dawson said nothing. He looked straight ahead.

"We're lucky, Adam, that he didn't kill *us*. Someday he might."

"Not if I leave."

"Then he'll kill me."

"Not if you left too."

"With you?"

"I didn't say that."

"But you thought it. Didn't you, Adam? Look at me and tell me the truth. Haven't you thought about the two of us away from here and together?"

He still did not look at her, or answer.

"I have," she said. "Almost since the day you came . . . since the day up there on those boulders, and since that day I could tell that you have too, whether you'll say it or not . . . I know and so do you. But I know him too. He'd find us. He's used to me . . . like a saddle. God, I feel dirty. Adam?"

"What?"

"There's a place near here where I go. I want you to come with me."

Five Double Eagles dropped from Corona's right hand into the palm of his left and then back into his right hand which he doubled into a fist as he grinned.

"One hundred dollars just to listen to what you have to say . . . so I'm listening."

Brad Hatcher looked around Mamacita's shack. Mamacita sat in a chair staring out of the dirty window. Diaz and Charly stood behind Corona sitting at the table across from Hatcher. Olita, her breasts plunging almost to her waist, was near the door. Joe Nueva was next to her trying to keep his eyes straight ahead.

"Look, Mr. Corona, for one hundred dollars I thought we could talk in private, not in front of your friends."

"They're not friends and for a hundred dollars," Corona stacked the coins on the table, "I'll talk in private with the devil. All of you get out."

Olita opened the door. Nueva, Charley and Diaz started to move. Mamacita did not.

"Mamacita," Diaz beckoned. "Come with me." He reached into his pocket and took out a coin. Mamacita moved.

When the door closed Corona nodded.

"Talk." Corona put an unlit cigar into his mouth.

"You know the ranch close to mine? It's owned by a man named Walker."

"I know everything. What about it?"

"I want it hit . . . hard."

"How hard?"

Hatcher pulled out a roll of bills from his coat pocket, counted out two hundred dollars and placed the bills on the table next to the Double Eagles.

"Three hundred dollars hard?" Corona smiled with the cigar under his mustache.

"I want it destroyed. Burned to the ground."

"Not enough pay for such a hard job."

"That's half the pay. You get the other half when the job's done."

"Six hundred dollars." Corona took the dodger from his shirt pocket and unfolded it. "Seems like everybody's got six hundred dollars to spend."

"Yeah." Hatcher nodded. "But this way *you'll* get to spend it."

"What's your name again?" Corona already knew but he was enjoying the conversation.

"Hatcher. Brad Hatcher. But for the six hundred dollars I want you to forget it."

"It's forgotten . . . Mr. Blanco. But tell me, Mr. Blanco, why do you want this done?"

"Does it matter?"

"Nothing matters . . . except the six hundred."

"Then we got a deal?"

"This Walker, the one who owns the ranch, he's crippled. No?"

"Yes."

"Suppose he dies in the fire?"

"Suppose he does." Hatcher put the rest of the bills back into his pocket.

Corona lifted a match from his shirt, struck it across the table, lit the cigar and took a deep, satisfying puff.

"We got a deal . . . Mr. Blanco."

Her clothes were in a pile at her feet. Naked, Lorena stood on the shore of the stream, sunlight highlighting the buttery gold of her hair and every curve and plane from the gleaming spread of her shoulders and ample circles of breasts to tapered waist, blossoming again down to the long lovely legs spread just wide enough apart.

She stood unashamed, a living monument to beauty and splendor, facing Adam Dawson, then turned with a graceful, flawless motion and slowly walked. The gently flowing green stream received and enveloped her step by step, her legs, the undulating curves of her lower body, water flowed around her waist, then her breasts, until only her shoulders, face and hair were above the sunlit stream.

She turned toward Dawson and brought her dripping hands up to her cheeks and mouth and throat.

And just as gracefully as she had entered, Lorena walked out of the stream, glistening, and came to Dawson.

Her wet hands took off his hat and let it drop beside them. And with those hands she touched his face then kissed him. It was more than a kiss and both of them knew it. An invitation. A prelude to the inevitable.

She began to unbutton Dawson's shirt.

Behind the flowering bush they lay. Clouds gathered, swept by an impatient wind. Their bodies shaking and seething, meeting and melding, strong and hard, soft and pliant. Sweet and savage. Without words and for the time without regret. How much time, neither knew nor cared.

Twenty-eight

The last mystic rays of the sun glimmered and bowed behind the purple sawtooth mountain range.

Adam Dawson and Lorena rode slowly toward the gate of Walker's Way not knowing exactly how they would find its owner.

Which Chad Walker would be there?

And how could they explain so long an absence? He had told them to get out, that he had wanted to be by himself. And by himself he had been through the day and into the night. By himself except for Uriah.

Would the madness still blaze from his eyes ... or had the fury subsided? Would he be able to tell by looking at the two of them that they had violated his trust? That he had been cuckolded by a comrade?

"Adam," Lorena said. "We could tell him that the stallion ran away and that we couldn't find him until now."

"We could."

"Is that it, then? Is that ..."

"I don't know."

"We've got to tell him something, we ..."

They both noticed the familiar figure on the palomino just as they approached the gate. Brad Hatcher was riding from Pinto to Spanish Bit, but angled his horse toward them as they reached the gate. The smile on his face was more than an implication. It was an accusation.

"Good evening," he said.

"Hello, Brad," Lorena answered. "I'm sorry about what happened . . ."

"I'm sure you are, Lorena. Things just didn't work out the way we hoped."

"Please tell Mary Ann I'm sorry and . . ."

"She understands." Hatcher looked at Dawson then back to Lorena. "We both do. I see you've been out . . . for a ride."

Lorena nodded slightly.

"Well." Hatcher touched the brim of his hat. "I've got to get home. It's getting late. Good night." He rode off still smiling.

They had looked through the house. Dark. Empty. Except for Elena.

"Elena," Lorena asked, "where's Mr. Walker?"

"I don't know, *señora*. He came in then left again."

"How long ago?"

"An hour . . . two maybe."

"He couldn't've got on his horse," Adam said. "He must be out back. I'll go look."

"I'm coming with you."

In the darkness, Chad Walker sat huddled on a feedback box, canes between his legs and staring straight ahead.

"Chad!" Lorena called from a distance.

"Boss! Hey, boss . . . you out there?"

They saw him and hurried toward him.

"We've been looking all over for you, Chad. What're you doing out here?"

"Boss, are you all right?"

Chad Walker's head turned slowly without emotion. Then his eyes looked upward. Adam and Lorena followed his gaze.

Uriah's lifeless body hung at the end of a rope from a branch of a tree.

Lorena shielded her eyes with both of her hands and shuddered.

"Oh, God . . ."

"Get inside Lorena," Adam said. "I'll cut him down and get Chad back into the house."

"God," she repeated, still trembling.

It took Adam Walker almost an hour to do what he had to do. Uriah's body, covered by a blanket, lay on the cot inside his shack.

Walker didn't say a word as Adam helped him into the house. Lorena asked if he wanted something to eat. Walker just barely shook his head. Adam helped him into the basket at the bottom of the stairway and pulled at the overhead rope hauling Chad to the second floor where Lorena had walked up and was waiting.

Chad fell into bed with his clothes on and waved the two of them away.

"Adam," she whispered. "Maybe you'd better stay in the guest room."

"No," he said quickly. "He'll be all right. He'll be out 'til morning."

Chad Walker was already unconscious.

"I'll come in early," Dawson added.

"Chad . . . thanks."

"Sure."

At supper as Mary Ann sat across the table and Marissa served, Brad Hatcher again lifted his watch from his vest by the heavy gold chain, thumbed open the lid, cast his eyes toward the face of the timepiece, snapped shut the lid and returned the watch into his vest pocket.

"What is it, Brad?"

"What?"

"Can you tell me what time it is, please?"

He reached once more for the watch.

"That's what I mean. You've looked at that watch three

times in the last few minutes and you still don't know what time it is. Your mind's someplace else."

"Mary Ann . . ."

"Ever since you came home tonight your mind's been someplace else . . . just picking at your food . . ."

"Dammit, Mary Ann, my mind is right here inside my head right where it always is . . . and I'll thank you to . . ."

"All right, Brad! You don't have to snap *my* head off. I guess it's my fault for being concerned. I just . . ."

"No, I'm sorry for snapping at you, my dear, and I do appreciate your concern. It's . . . well, it's just a business matter I didn't want to trouble you about."

"Are you still upset with Mr. Walker and his not wanting to sell his ranch?"

"No, no. That's not it at all." Hatcher had regained his composure, even his confidence. Strangely enough, just talking seemed to take away some of the inner pressure that had been building up as the time approached for Corona to hit Walker's ranch. "I'm sure," he smiled now, "that Mr. Walker will get what's coming to him and smother in his own greed. As a matter of fact, I'm feeling much better now. Mary Ann, would you kindly pass the salt?"

"Yes, of course."

Brad Hatcher did, in fact, feel much better. Corona would see to it that Walker got what was coming to him and if, in the bargain anything happened to Lorena Walker, so be it. Hatcher had recognized the look in her eyes when he saw her coming back with the drifter. He had seen that look when they had finished with their lovemaking, if it could be called that, in the line shack and other places. Of course, if she did survive, the widow Walker could still be of service to him . . . and then he thought of the drifter. If he survived . . . but Brad Hatcher was getting too many jumps ahead in the game. He would take it one move at a time.

The next move was up to Corona and the Comancheros.

———

It was a slow and quiet night at Baldy's Bar. Except for Joe Nueva. He had plunked down a Double Eagle on the bar, picked up a good bottle of whiskey and the change in bills and coins and joined the poker game already in progress.

"Bring over some fresh glasses for my friends, Baldy. Tonight they ain't drinkin' beer."

"Have one of your friends pick 'em up from the bar. I ain't making any glass deliveries."

"I'll deliver." Francine Needle rose from the table where she sat with Goldie Bright. She stuck the thumb and four fingers of her left hand into the row of whiskey glasses on the bar, turned her hand palm up and sashayed to the poker table where the players relieved her of the glassware. She leaned close to Nueva who was stuffing most of the bills into his shirt pocket.

"Joe, you wanna go upstairs?" she whispered. "I'll show you somethin' special tonight."

"Stick around, Francine. I'll show you somethin' special later."

She patted Nueva's cheek, winked and walked away.

"I'll deal, amigos," Nueva said. "This is my lucky night."

Sheriff Ben Vesper came through the bat-wings and walked straight to the bar.

"Beer."

"You bet, Sheriff."

"I see Joe and the boys are still at it."

"Yeah, and Joe's gonna be at it for quite a while. Just broke a Double Eagle."

"Joe did?"

"Uh-huh and I think it's got company."

"Say how he got it?"

"Nope."

"Keep listenin', will you, Baldy?"

"Sure will."

"Alma home?"

"Right."

"Well," Vesper drained the beer from the glass. "Good night, Baldy. Put that on my tab."

"Good night, Sheriff."

"I open," Nueva said as Vesper walked past the poker table and through the bat-wings.

This *was* Joe Nueva's lucky night. He had another Double Eagle in his pocket and a promise from Brad Hatcher of more to come, depending on how things turned out. But he figured that he had something else, maybe even Brad Hatcher in his pocket.

Lorena lay awake in her night clothes on the bed next to her husband who was sleeping still fully dressed except for his boots which she had removed from his invalid legs.

She stared through the window at the darkness of the night and thought of Adam Dawson in the bunkhouse. She thought of going to him but knew that would be a mistake. Would he be gone in the morning? She didn't think so. Not after this afternoon. He might not love her but she was sure he wanted her. If she had corrupted him he took his pleasure in being corrupted. Besides, Adam Dawson was still honorable in other ways. Lorena knew that he wouldn't leave until he knew about Chad Walker's condition after what had happened to Uriah.

Maybe Walker's mind had snapped altogether. Maybe he would never recover from the shock of what happened. Maybe his mind was as paralyzed as his body.

Lorena had never seen her husband like he was tonight. In all the times before, drunk or sober, no matter how much the pain, she had never seen him sapped of strength as he was tonight. Drained of energy and will.

Still, he might recover and be even worse, even more warped than before, if that was possible. With Chad Walker anything was possible. Anything except using his legs to walk as other men walked and to . . .

At that time, in that bed, Lorena regretted only one thing.

Lorena regretted that it was Uriah and not Chad Walker hanging from the end of the rope.

"There is no art to find the mind's construction in the face"
... or body, Shakespeare might well have added, Adam Dawson thought in the midnight darkness of his bunk.

The construction of Lorena's face and body was like
nothing Adam Dawson had ever seen or felt or even imag-
ined before that afternoon. And he could still see and feel
and even inhale the fragrance of her body, face and hair as
he had that afternoon.

The face of an angel, symmetrical, flawless in construction; and the smooth, supple construction of her body, the
body of a biblical temptress with the certain knowledge of
how to use that body. With gentle rhythm and clawing passion, with tenderness and furor. A tenderness and furor that
Adam Dawson had never felt before and as he lay there he
couldn't deny to himself that he wanted to feel again.

But what about Chad Walker? There was within Dawson
an innate code that had always censored his conscience and
conduct, always, except that afternoon. Could he ... would
he let it happen again? Adam Dawson knew of only one sure
way to prevent it.

The Comancheros dismounted three hundred yards from the
Walker ranch house.

Twenty-nine

Corona had gone over the plan half a dozen times at the *ranchería*. After they dismounted he motioned for the fourteen of them to come closer and went over it again.

"Olita, you, Diaz and John Goose stay here with the horses. String 'em up together, four or five in a bunch. No matter what happens, stay here until you see the fire then ride in. We'll mount up and get the hell out fast. Got it?"

"Don't worry." Olita nodded.

"Who's worried? Come on." Corona waved to the other Comancheros, some of whom carried long, oil-soaked, but unlit torches. They followed Corona toward the ranch house, dim stealthy shadows moving through the dark, sinking night. Only a crescent moon glimmered through the blue bowl of sky.

Closer they crouched and moved, slow and quiet, until Corona spread his arms to hold his men back. He peered into the night at the back of the house and outbuildings. Not one light shone out of the silhouetted structures. He turned and spoke in a guarded voice.

"Get close to the house . . . don't light the torches 'til you're out front."

They nodded and moved following Corona toward the rear of the house. Nothing punctured the silence. Not an owl. Not a night bird. Not even a silken wind in the hot, dry night. A night made for burning.

Charly handed Corona one of the two unlit torches he

was carrying. Corona nodded and crept closer to the house.

As Charly moved to follow, his boot stepped onto the upturned prongs of a fallen rake. The handle of the rake sprang like the arm of a catapult and cracked against the side of the rickshaw. Corona and Charly froze.

The sound reverberated through the dark night like the report of a rifle shot.

Still awake, Adam Dawson bolted from his bunk and made for the window.

Corona cursed under his breath and looked toward Charly who still stood statue-like beside the rickshaw, then shrugged almost imperceptibly.

Corona motioned for him and the rest of the Comancheros to spread out and around to the front of the house.

Dawson had no notion of who or how many were out there, but whatever and however many they were, the odds were that they were not friendly. He had pulled on his pants and boots, picked up the Winchester and a box of cartridges that he stuffed into his pocket.

From the window he could make out the shadowy movement of figures circling around the side of the ranch house. He kicked open the bunkhouse door and fired a warning shot into the black sky.

Corona whirled, drew his gun and fired twice toward the bunkhouse. Charly and three or four other Comancheros also blasted away.

Snipers! Chad Walker was back at war again, but only for an instant as he jerked to his elbow on the bed.

"What the goddam . . ." he cried out.

Lorena, sleepy and bewildered came up next to him.

"Chad! What is it?!"

Walker struggled to get out of bed, finding and grabbing both canes in the darkness. He managed to hobble toward the window.

"I don't know. Get my rifle! Quick!"

Lorena scrambled from the bed and ran out of the room toward the hallway and stairs.

Corona flattened himself against the house and fired again at the bunkhouse. He hit the ground as accurate shots tore close to him into the building.

"Get to the front!" he screamed at his men. "Light the torches!" He stayed close to the side of the house and ran toward the front porch. Dawson's gunshots followed his wake.

Corona stopped to reload as Charly ran by, torch already lit, a blazing fireball.

"Burn it! Burn it!" Corona screamed. "Burn the sonofabitch down!"

Dawson sprang across the backyard, hit the ground and started reloading the Winchester.

Walker propped himself against the second story window as Lorena ran in with the rifle.

"Gimme that." He grabbed the Henry and broke the window with the barrel. "Get down on the floor."

Olita grabbed the pommel with both hands and swung onto the saddle without touching the stirrups.

"Come on." She waved to Diaz and John Goose. "Let's get these horses over there."

"There's no fire!" Diaz yelled. "He said to wait . . . wait for the fire!"

"The hell with that. There's a war going on. Something's gone wrong!" Olita rode toward the ranch holding a lead rope tied to Corona's horse and two other horses.

Diaz shrugged toward John Goose, jumped into his saddle and loosed the lead rope from his pommel.

More gunshots.

"Come on! Let's go, John Goose!" Diaz took off leading four horses and John Goose mounted and followed with the rest of the animals.

The porch extended a good ten feet from the front door of the house. The Comancheros, a half-dozen of them with lit torches tried to get to that door and the windows.

They made brilliant targets for Dawson who had worked his way to the cover of a watering trough. The Winchester blasted three times. Three Comancheros and their torches toppled to the ground, the Comancheros dead, the torches burning, harmless.

Olita, then Diaz and John Goose, rode up leading the riderless horses. Some of the raiders already had had enough and raced toward their mounts.

"Bastards!" Walker swore, sighted and fired three shots.

Two Comancheros collapsed before reaching the animals. Another buckled and fell from Dawson's crossfire.

Olita, Diaz and John Goose had all let go of the lead ropes. They drew their guns and streaked bullets toward the upper window.

Dawson fired again and John Goose grabbed at his blood-spewing throat and fell dead on the ground.

Horses whinnied, reared and scattered in different directions.

Both Corona and Charly dashed with flaming torches toward the porch. Charly was shot through the top of the head by Walker from above. He fell on the torch that ignited first his clothes then his body, pyramiding into a pyre.

Dawson's shot ripped into Corona's ribs. He dropped the torch, stumbled, fell, then staggered to his feet. Before Dawson could get off another shot Olita rode between them and reached down for Corona. He took her hand and she yanked as he half-leaped, half-climbed onto the horse behind her.

Three of the other Comancheros made it to their horses and fired back toward the trough and upper window as they rode away. A couple more ran and disappeared into the darkness.

Walker, with the rifle through the window, kept shooting until his Henry was empty.

Dawson took another shot at the horse racing away with the two riders but it was too dark and the horse was too far away.

There were nine, maybe ten bodies scattered around the ranch house, including cremated Charly. Dawson hurried across the yard, up the porch and through the front door.

Still carrying the Winchester, he took the stairs three at a time up to the hall and doorway of Walker's bedroom.

"Chad! Lorena! It's Adam! Are you okay?"

"Come on in, Adam." It was Walker's voice from inside.

Dawson opened the door and stepped into the dark room that still smelled of gunfire.

Chad was silhouetted against the broken window and Lorena was getting up from the floor.

"Lorena," Chad said. "Light that lamp, will you?"

Lorena went to the lamp on the nightstand, struck a match and set the lamp aglow.

"Who were they, Adam?" Walker asked.

"Not sure. Comancheros probably."

"How many?"

"Dozen or more. Most won't make it back to where they came from. One of 'em's hit pretty bad. Don't know how far he'll get."

"Doesn't matter," Chad said.

"I'll ride out early to Pinto. Tell the sheriff what happened."

"Good."

"Lorena." Dawson took a step toward her. "Are you all right?"

She nodded.

"What about you, boss?" Adam turned and looked at Walker. The lamp cast an eerie light across his face, but he was smiling.

"Me? Hell, I haven't felt this good in years."

There was no doubt about it. Chad Walker had recovered.

Olita reined the horse up close to a tree. Her naked back was smeared with Corona's blood. He was breathing heavy and wobbling behind her with both arms around her belly. Diaz pulled his horse to a stop close by.

"Goddammit!" Corona croaked. "I told you not to come . . . until the fire."

"We heard gunshots," she said. "Didn't know what happened. Thought you needed help . . . horses."

"Those sonsofbitches all ran away. I'll kill every damn one of 'em."

"There's not many left," Diaz said.

"There won't be *any* left." Corona coughed.

"You're hit awful bad." Olita wiped at the blood on her back. "You can't ride as far as the camp."

"We're not going that far."

"No?" Olita looked back at him.

"No. We're going someplace else. Closer."

"Where?"

"Diaz?"

"Yes?"

"Lead the way to Mamacita's."

"Sure."

"Not too fast. I'm pumpin' out blood."

At the first sound of gunfire Elena had crawled under the bed in her room just off the kitchen.

Now, as Dawson came down the stairs she stood holding a lamp in the hallway.

"Elena," Dawson said. "Are you all right . . . *usted bien*?"

"*Sí, señor*. Yes . . . *Señora*? . . . Mrs. Walker?"

"She's fine." Dawson nodded.

"And Mr. Walker?"

"He's all right too. Go to bed, Elena. Good night."

"*Sí, señor.*" Elena turned and moved toward the kitchen.

Dawson had detected a look of disappointment in Elena's eyes when he told her that Chad Walker was alive and well.

Thirty

"Place looks like a slaughterhouse," Sheriff Ben Vesper said as he stood next to Chad Walker early the next morning.

"That's what they intended for us," Walker said, then pointed to the charred remains of Charly. "And that."

Dawson had ridden into Pinto at dawn. He woke Sam Mendez who was asleep in the office and Mendez ran to the hotel where Vesper kept a room. The three of them rode back to Walker's Way together.

"Can I wear your gun, Sheriff?" Sam had asked.

"What for? According to Mr. Dawson here, the shootin's over."

They all stood in front of the porch. Walker, Vesper, Sam, Dawson and Lorena. Elena was in the doorway wringing her hands.

"They appear to be Comancheros all right, what's left of 'em," Vesper said. "But why? Where's the profit? Unless they were . . ." He looked toward Lorena ". . . going to take, well . . ."

"I don't think they had any such notion. Just going to burn the place down and us with it."

"I'll say it again. Why?"

Walker shrugged.

"You're lucky," Vesper pointed at Adam, "that Mr. Dawson was here."

"Yeah." Walker nodded. "If it'd been Nueva, he'd've helped them burn it down."

"Hear you two had a little run-in when he came to pick up his possibles."

"He better not come back here again . . ." Walker waved one of the canes toward a corpse on the ground. ". . . Or he'll end up like that."

"Sheriff." Sam Mendez took a dodger out of his pocket. "You think that this Corona fella is among 'em?"

"Don't know. We'll have to take a closer look when we get 'em back to Pinto."

"You want to borrow one of my wagons?" Walker asked.

"No thanks. We'll ride back now and send Tony Amado out with some of the boys to . . . clean things up."

"Well, don't wait too long," Walker said. "They'll stink up the place. We'll cover 'em up with blankets."

"Good."

"I'll get some blankets from the barn," Dawson said and started to walk.

"I'll go with you." Lorena fell in beside him.

"Had breakfast, Sheriff?" Walker asked.

"Nope."

"Want some?"

"I think we better get moving. Come on, Sam."

"Yes, sir."

Vesper and Sam mounted and rode toward the gate.

"Bastards," Chad Walker said and looked around at the bodies of the Comancheros.

"You should have let them burn the place." Lorena said as they walked closer to the barn.

"And Chad?"

"You saved his life, Adam. How does it feel?"

"Maybe I saved yours too."

"You bring death to this place," Mamacita had said when they came into her shack. "I can smell it." And she crossed herself.

"Tell her to shut up!" Corona gritted. "Or I'll shoot her in the belly." He staggered and almost fell. Olita and Diaz helped him to the bed in the corner.

Through the night they had done everything they knew to stop the bleeding. Hot towels soaked in whiskey had helped but blood was still seeping out of the wound at dawn.

From time to time Corona became unconscious, but the pain would wake him again.

"We've got to get a doctor," Olita said. "To take the bullet out and stop the blood."

"He's going to die." Mamacita crossed herself again. "I can smell death."

"Get her away from here!" Corona spat out the words.

"There's got to be a doctor in Pinto." Olita leaned close to Corona in the bed. "I'll get him. Bring him back."

"No!"

"There's no other way. That bullet's got to come out. Diaz will stay here."

"Get her out!" Corona gasped.

"Diaz. Get me one of your mother's blouses . . . or a sweater and get her away from here."

Diaz nodded. "Mamacita. Get on the burro. Go to your sister's place. Stay 'til we send for you."

"Death," Mamacita whispered.

Tony Amado, along with two Mexican helpers in the wagon, rolled out of Pinto heading for Walker's Way as Ben Vesper and Sam walked back into the sheriff's office. Vesper had assured Amado that the county would pay for the funerals, but "keep it cheap," Vesper added.

"What do we do next, Sheriff?" Sam asked when they got inside.

"Next, I'm going to buy you breakfast across the street."

"No foolin'?"

"No foolin'."

But Olita opened the door, stepped inside wearing a sweater, and closed the door behind her.

"Sheriff?"

"Yeah. What can I do for you?"

"You can pay me six hundred dollars." She pointed to the dodger on the bulletin board. "After I take you to Corona."

"Is he alive?"

"Maybe yes and maybe no. The reward's dead or alive, yes?"

"Yes."

"He's wounded. Needs a doctor, but there's somebody with him."

"Comanchero?"

She nodded.

"Why did they hit the ranch?"

"I don't answer any more questions 'til you get him."

"A doctor, huh?"

She nodded again.

"Sam." Vesper pulled open a desk drawer.

"Yes, sir?"

"I want you to go over to Doc Bonner's."

"Yes, sir."

"But put this on first." Vesper handed him the gun belt and pointed to the carbine in the rack. "And take that too."

"Yes, sir!"

Joe Nueva stood in front of Baldy's Bar watching. He struck a match on the post and lit a cigar.

Ben Vesper was in the driver's seat of Doc Bonner's buggy. He wore Doc's jacket, with Olita next to him, and Sam Mendez rode his horse just behind the buggy.

Brad Hatcher on his palomino rode past the buggy from the opposite direction.

Hatcher thought of saying something to the sheriff but thought better of it when he recognized Olita. If she recognized him ... and she had to ... she didn't show it.

After the buggy was far enough away, Nueva hurried

toward Hatcher and his horse in the middle of the street.

"What the hell happened out there?" He looked up toward Hatcher on horseback.

"I don't know. But keep away from me 'til we find out."

"If she talks . . ."

"Shut up, Joe. There's nothing we can do yet. It's her word against ours."

"And Corona's."

"Maybe not. Keep low until we find out." Hatcher heeled the palomino and rode on.

Diaz stood at the open door in front of Mamacita's shack as the buggy pulled up. Vesper and Olita climbed down.

Sam Mendez was nowhere in sight. He had dismounted behind a rock a couple hundred yards away.

"You the doctor?" Diaz asked.

Vesper lifted Doc's medical bag and nodded.

"I said I'd bring him, didn't I?" Olita brushed past Diaz. "How is he?"

"Bad."

"Is he conscious?" Vesper asked.

"Huh?"

"Awake."

"Sometimes." Diaz shrugged.

"Let's have a look." Vesper followed Olita inside and Diaz followed Vesper.

It was the sheriff's intention to take Corona alive if he could . . . and see him hang.

Corona lay in the bed. His eyes were open staring at the ceiling.

"I brought the doctor," she said.

"You did?" Corona looked toward Vesper and, even in his condition, noticed the gun under the sheriff's belt.

"You know I can't live without you," Olita leaned down and whispered.

"And I . . . I can't . . . die without you." From under the

blanket Corona fired twice into Olita's chest. "You dirty . . ."

As she fell to the floor, Vesper's fist smashed into Corona's face.

Diaz drew his gun.

"Drop it!" Sam hollered from the doorway.

Diaz turned to aim but Sam's gun cracked, the Comanchero clutched his chest and he dropped.

Vesper's gun was drawn and pointing at Corona. But the sheriff already knew that it wasn't necessary.

Corona was dead.

As Tony Amado and his helpers were collecting corpses and stacking them in the wagon, both Dawson and Lorena heard Chad talking to Tony about Uriah.

"Here's a hundred dollars. Keep him apart from these bastards and make sure he gets a first rate burial and a solid tombstone. Let me know when you bury him and have a minister there to read over him."

"What do you want chiseled on the tombstone? Name, dates and such?"

"Just say . . .'Uriah. Soldier of His Country.' Got that?"

"Right. 'Uriah. Soldier of His Country.' Got it. And you can bet, Mr. Walker, it'll be first class."

"It better be . . . oh, and one more thing."

"Anything you want, Mr. Walker."

"It's what I don't want." Chad pointed with a cane. "Those chickens."

"How's that?"

"When your two Mexes are through . . . cleaning up here, tell 'em to gather up all the chickens out back."

"What do you want done with 'em?"

"I don't care. Just get 'em out. I don't want any more goddam chickens around here." Walker had turned away and was making for the front porch.

Lorena looked at Adam. Neither said a word.

———

Doc Bonner in his shirt and vest, and of course, his pants and boots, was standing in front of the sheriff's office talking to Brad Hatcher as Doc's buggy came up Main Street with Vesper at the reins and Sam on horseback riding alongside.

Actually, Hatcher had been doing just about all the talking, trying to find out what he could from Doc, but Doc played it tight lipped as Vesper had instructed him to do until they got back.

A few other curious citizens of Pinto, including Joe Nueva, began to gather around the buggy as it pulled to a stop.

Sam dismounted and hitched his horse to the rail. Vesper jumped off the buggy and began to take off Doc's coat.

"Here's your coat, Doc. Much obliged."

"Did it do the trick, Ben?"

"You might say that. By the way, there's three dead ones in the back of the buggy . . . along with your bag."

"What's that?" Hatcher pushed his way closer to try and see what he could, but the bodies were covered with blankets. "Who are they?"

"Comancheros. Somebody go and get the mayor from the bank. I want him to witness this. And Sam go fetch Mrs. O'Donnell. Carry her back if you have to, but get her."

"Yes, sir." Sam was on his way.

"Hope that's all right with you, Doc. This is important."

"Then I guess it'll have to be all right," Doc said while he slipped on his coat.

"Look here, Sheriff." Hatcher turned to Vesper. "I'm a member of the city council and I want to know what this is all about."

"You will, Mr. Hatcher. So will everybody in just a couple of . . ."

"Here comes the mayor now." Baldy pointed toward the bank.

"Good," Vesper said. "Now everyone just get back a step or two."

"Ben." Terrance Swerd pushed his way through. "You been out doing a little hunting?"

"So to speak."

Maureen O'Donnell, flanked by Alma and Sam, made her way through the crowd. Vesper tipped his hat as they approached.

"Mrs. O'Donnell . . ."

"Yes, Sheriff?"

"I want to see if you can identify somebody." Vesper reached into the back of the buggy and partly uncovered one of the bodies. "Is this the man who killed your husband?"

Maureen O'Donnell gasped. So did some of the other people.

"Is this the man they called . . . Corona?"

"Yes," she whispered and nodded, "yes, it is."

"Great thunderin' hallelujah!" somebody shouted.

"Well, then. I guess that makes it official," Vesper said. "All right, everybody this don't concern, clear out. We got work to do." Most of the crowd started to disperse.

"Thank God," Alma said as she put her arm around Maureen O'Donnell. "And thank you too, Ben."

"Mrs. O'Donnell, would you come inside the office? There's a form to be signed."

"Yes, of course."

"You too, Mayor, as witness."

"I'll sign too," Hatcher said.

Sheriff Ben Vesper shrugged and led Maureen O'Donnell through the door.

When the form was properly signed, Vesper looked around at the people in the office, Maureen O'Donnell, Alma Gorsich, Mayor Swerd, Brad Hatcher and Sam.

"I'm instructing that the reward, six hundred dollars, goes to Mrs. O'Donnell."

"That's up to you, Sheriff," the mayor said.

"And there's something else. Sam here is witness." Vesper began to pull a roll of bills and five Double Eagles out of his pocket and put the money on his desk. "We searched Corona and found this."

Hatcher did his best not to react to the sight of the money on the sheriff's desk.

"Amounts to three hundred, bills and Eagles. That goes to Mrs. O'Donnell too. Any objections?"

"Not from me, Ben," the mayor said.

"I guess..." Brad Hatcher nodded toward Maureen O'Donnell, "...that's only fitting. Congratulations, Mrs. O'Donnell, that's quite a lot of money." And quickly added, "Of course it can never make up for your loss."

"No, it can't," Vesper said. "I guess that's all for now. Oh, Mayor, I'd like to come by and talk to you sometime."

"Anytime Ben. You did a great job."

"That is my job." He looked at Sam. "And the deputy's too."

"Deputy?" Sam grinned.

"Since this morning."

"Oh, by the way, Sheriff." Brad Hatcher nodded toward the window. "That woman, the dead one out there. Did she say anything to you..." Hatcher trailed off.

"About what?"

"Oh, about Corona ... or anything?"

"We had a very pleasant conversation."

"I see. Well ... think I'll have a drink."

"Me too." Terrance Swerd smiled. "This calls for a little celebration." The mayor and Hatcher moved toward the door.

"Thank you, Sheriff." Maureen O'Donnell extended her hand to Vesper. "But, that money, I think you ought to ..."

"You're welcome." He took her hand, but for just a moment and didn't let her finish. "I hope this makes things just a little ... well ..."

Maureen O'Donnell nodded. Alma smiled at the sheriff and put her arm around the young woman as the two of them walked through the doorway.

"Do I get to wear the gun from now on, Sheriff?" Sam asked.

"You get to keep it. And the badge. What's a deputy

without a badge? And a raise to five dollars a week. But you still got to sweep up."

"Yes, sir!"

"Sam . . . how did it feel when you shot him?"

"I don't know." Sam shrugged. "He didn't say."

Thirty-one

"And he opened his mouth,
and taught them saying
Blessed are the poor in spirit
for theirs is the kingdom of heaven.
Blessed are they that mourn;
for they shall be comforted.
Blessed are the meek
for they shall inherit the earth."

Reverend Harlow Groves spoke with a deep, caramel voice belying his string frame. When the reverend turned sideways there wasn't much to see, mostly a jutting nose and chin, but that Sunday afternoon his sonorous voice flowed across the hill of the cemetery like the rolling sea.

"Ask and it shall be given you.
Seek and ye shall find.
Knock and it shall be opened
unto you . . ."

Chad Walker became more restless, impatient and resentful as he stood, supported by his canes, next to the tombstone with the inscription he had dictated to Tony Amado.

URIAH
Soldier of His Country.

Walker had expected little more than a two- or three-minute ceremony with a brief prayer and nobody present except the reverend, maybe Lorena and Adam, himself and the body.

But Reverend Groves, who was never one to shun an audience or pass up the opportunity to revel in the sound of his own voice, had announced that immediately following Sunday church services, parishioners were invited to attend funeral services for a dearly departed citizen of Pinto known as Uriah. The reverend didn't mention citizen Uriah's means of departure.

Walker leaned heavily on his canes and looked neither at the reverend who tolled on, nor at the mourners who numbered close to a score. Among them the sheriff and his deputy, the mayor, Tony Amado, Brad and Mary Ann Hatcher and the rest, most of whom never met nor cared to meet Uriah when he lived and breathed.

> "Rejoice and be exceedingly glad,
> for great is your reward in Heaven.
> For everyone that asketh receiveth;
> and he that seeketh findeth.
> There is darkness at noon, but
> you must not give up hope . . ."

Walker was giving up hope that Reverend Harlow Groves would ever wind down.

> "I was eyes to the blind
> and feet to the lame.
> Harken onto the voice of my cry.
> Behold and rejoice.
> For the darkness shall be lifted.
> And the crooked shall be straight."

Walker stiffened at the words and didn't want to listen anymore.

"You shall run and not be weary,
You shall walk and not be faint . . ."

"Put an amen to it!" Walker growled, startling the reverend and those others who heard.

"The Lord giveth and the Lord taketh away." The reverend speeded up. "Blessed be the name of the Lord." He concluded, put on his black hat, turned and started to walk away.

"Just a minute, Reverend." Walker managed to pull a roll of bills out of his pocket, peel off two five-dollar bills and slap them into the reverend's palm. "Here's your pay."

The reverend did not refuse Chad Walker's offering. He even smiled as he walked toward Mrs. Groves who enjoyed the sound of her husband's voice almost as much as did the reverend.

Brad and Mary Ann Hatcher approached Lorena.

"May we express our condolences," Hatcher said. "To both of you. I know you were very good to . . ." Hatcher nodded toward the grave, ". . . that man. I hope everything is all right after what happened at the ranch."

Hatcher had attended the funeral service hoping to find out more about what had happened during and after the Comancheros' attack.

"Sure you do," Walker snarled and turned to Lorena and Adam. "Come on, let's get out of here."

For the next few days at the ranch Chad Walker became even more surly and isolated. He began drinking during the day, something he had never done before.

It started as soon as they got back from the cemetery.

"That pious sonofabitch . . . 'eyes to the blind . . . and the crooked shall be straight . . . run and not be weary . . . walk and not be faint.' What the hell does he know about it . . . or care . . . what the hell do any of 'em . . . Adam, pour me a drink, will you?"

"Sure, boss."

And Walker had Adam mount him onto the pinto. He wanted to ride alone. He rode and whipped Domino to the brink of the animal's endurance and his own.

"He keeps this up, he's going to kill himself," Adam said to Lorena when they were alone.

Lorena didn't answer or show any emotion.

"Terrance." Vesper sat across the desk from the mayor/banker and spoke softly. "I've been thinking."

"About what, Sheriff?"

"About all that money Corona had on him, those bills and the Eagles . . ."

"What about 'em?"

"It could've been a payoff."

"For hitting the ranch?"

"That's what I've been thinking. That . . . and who'd want it done. Anybody make a sizeable withdrawal lately?"

"Ben. You'd better be careful about making any accusations you can't substantiate."

"I'm not accusing anybody . . . just asking. I'd appreciate an answer, Terrance. It won't go any further until I get proof, but it might lead somewhere, or to somebody."

"No, Ben . . . not lately."

"Nobody's drawn out a few hundred in bills and Eagles?"

"Who'd have that much cash around here?"

"Not many, but can you chew it any finer?"

"Sorry, Ben. You know I'd help if I could, even though I don't favor that Walker fellow. But nobody's made any such withdrawal."

"Well, thanks anyhow, Terrance. Guess I'll just have to keep pokin' around. If you think of anything that'll help . . ."

"Sure, Ben, you know I will."

"I don't think much of Walker either," Vesper said as he got up from the chair. "But I think less of burning and killing."

"We all feel the same way about that."

"Good day, Mr. Mayor."

"Oh, Ben?"

"Yes, sir."

"That was a very fine gesture . . . your giving the money to that lady, I mean."

"She's a very fine lady."

Brad Hatcher had kept one thousand dollars in bills and gold coins in his safe at Spanish Bit just in case of an emergency— or in case he needed ready access to cash for a confidential transaction. He checked what was left, seven hundred dollars, and closed the safe as Mary Ann came into the den. He whirled and stood behind his desk.

"Dammit, Mary Ann. I wish you wouldn't sneak around here like some damn Indian."

"Excuse me, Brad. But since it's your poker night in town I just wanted to say good night before going upstairs."

Hatcher, Terrance Swerd, Baldy and a couple other leading citizens of Pinto played poker at Baldy's every Thursday evening and Hatcher usually spent the night at the hotel, sometimes not alone.

"Uh, well . . . good night."

"Brad?"

"What?"

"Did you have anything to do with what happened at that ranch?"

"What the hell are you talking about?"

"I'm talking about your greed and what you said to me the night we came back from there. Or have you forgotten?"

"Yes, I have."

"Well I haven't. You said he'd regret not selling . . . that 'he'd get his.' "

"Did I?"

"Yes you did. Brad, if I find out that you were behind what happened . . . those people might have been killed, all of them . . . if I find out that you . . ."

"What would you do, Mary Ann? What *could* you do?"

"I'd leave you and . . ."

"And where would you go?" Hatcher laughed. "And with what? You don't have a cent to your name. This place and everything in it and on it belongs to me and me alone. It has for a long time. You've signed everything over. You're here at my sufferance and only for as long as I feel like suffering. So just shut up, Mary Ann, and don't ever say another word about it or I'll kick you out with the clothes on your back and nothing else . . . except your goddam cats. Now get away from me until I'm ready for you!"

Mary Ann Hatcher turned and walked out of the door past Marissa who stood there with a tray and glass of milk in her hand.

"Maureen, you sure you'll be all right? That Thursday night poker game usually goes on 'til two and Baldy don't feel like getting up and waitin' on customers whether he's winning or losing."

"Don't you worry about a thing, Alma, I'm just fine. Doctor Bonner says I'm practically one hundred percent. 'Course we still don't know for sure about . . ."

"The baby?"

Maureen nodded.

"Well, I can't help you there, lady, never having had . . . or wanting any of my own . . . oh, I'm sorry . . . shouldn't've said . . ."

"It's all right, Alma . . . but I do want the baby, boy or girl. It'd be a part of Tim that's still alive . . . still with me."

"Well, then, I hope you get what you want, and speaking of that . . . have you thought any more about staying here in Pinto?"

"I have, but I'm still not sure."

"Well, at least now that you've got that money you don't have to be in a hurry about making up your mind."

"I don't feel right about that, Alma. That money rightfully belongs to Ben, the sheriff, that is. I'd like to tell . . ."

"Save your breath, Maureen. When Ben's made up his mind about something, it's set in cement. Dry cement."

"I'm still going to talk to him."

"I'm sure he'd like that."

"What do you mean?"

"Your talking to him ... about anything, except that money. I don't suppose you've noticed he's a big, good-looking fella and ..."

"Alma!"

"Oh, I know it's early for you to start looking around, but it'd be hard not to take notice ..."

"Alma!" she repeated.

"Plenty have, but ..."

"Now, I won't hear another word about it!"

"All right."

"Not another word."

"Not tonight anyhow." Alma smiled. "Good night, Irish."

"Say, Mr. Hatcher, you got a match?" Joe Nueva stood with an unlit cigar in front of Baldy's knowing that Brad Hatcher would ride in about seven for the poker game that Nueva had never been, nor would ever be, invited to sit in.

"Sure, Joe."

"You find out anything?" Nueva whispered.

"About what?"

"That big-titted Olita and what she told the sheriff about ..." Nueva whispered even lower, "... us."

"I don't think she got around to it. She was just looking for the reward, and, Joe ..."

"Yes, Mr. Hatcher?"

"The less people see us together for a while, the better. You understand?"

"Sure Mr. Hatcher, I understand. Thanks ... for the match," Nueva said louder.

After supper Chad Walker had started on his second bottle of bourbon since morning and half of that bottle was empty.

Adam kept trying to leave the library and so did Lorena but Walker wanted them to stay, and dark as Walker's mood was, it could get even darker and more dangerous, particularly to Lorena, if they crossed him.

"Adam, I'm gonna have a couple of those greasers knock down that henhouse and shack. Don't want to look at it . . ."

"Hell, Chad, you don't have to do that."

"Huh?"

"I mean I'll tear it down. I'm through with the corral. Start in the morning."

"Well, they're coming tomorrow anyhow. I'll pay you extra for supervising."

"No you won't. Part of my job so long as I'm here." Dawson glanced at Lorena.

"You've already done more than your job." Walker swallowed more whiskey and smiled. "With that Winchester. But I got some too, didn't I, Adam? I blew a few of 'em to hell's breakfast, didn't I?"

"You did, boss."

"Sure I did. And it felt good too, killing those greasers. Your friend's got the right idea."

"Friend?"

"Custer. General George Armstrong Custer. Killing all those red bastards up there standing in the way of civilization. I'd like to be up there with him getting my share, just like with those Rebel sonsofbitches before they got me."

"Chad," Lorena said. "Not that again. Haven't we heard enough . . ."

"You've heard enough when I say you have and not before." Walker struggled to his feet with the support of one cane while he held the glass of whiskey in the other.

"All right, Chad." She went closer to him. "But ease up, please. You've been so drunk lately you can't even take your clothes off at night."

"Then you'll take 'em off for me!" he barked. "You're good at that, you . . ."

"Chad, please!" She reached for the glass, but he dropped it and backhanded her hard across the face sending her against Adam who kept her from falling.

Adam Dawson was close, closer than he had ever been to hitting the crippled man, as Walker staggered and nearly fell himself.

"Go on, get out!" Walker said, bracing his body against the chair. "I'm going to sleep here tonight, on the couch."

Dawson still had his arm around Lorena's waist and helped her toward the door as her body trembled.

"You don't have to take that," Adam said after he closed the door and they stood close together in the hallway.

"I've taken it before, Adam, and more when he's like that."

"How long are you going to keep on taking it? Because I can't."

"Yes you can." She kissed him the same way she had kissed him when they found the saddle. "If it means us being together, we both can. Just promise me you won't leave. Not yet." She kissed him again and he took her even closer in his arms knowing that Chad Walker was only a few feet away behind the closed door. "Things'll work out." She pulled herself away and walked up the stairs.

At that time as he watched her moving up the stairway, he wasn't sure that things could, or would, work out.

But Adam Dawson knew that he wouldn't leave. Not yet.

Once before Adam Dawson had had to make up his mind whether to stay or leave.

After Washita.

Dawson lay in his bunk and thought about what Chad Walker had said an hour or so earlier. "I blew a few of 'em to hell's breakfast . . . felt good too . . . your friend's got the right idea . . . Custer . . . killing all those red bastards up there standing in the way of civilization . . . I'd like to be up there with him getting my share, just like with those Rebel sonsofbitches."

During the year of Custer's court martial and suspension that he had spent in Monroe with Libbie and with Dawson, the situation on the frontier had gone from bad to bloodier.

Again and again the Kiowas, Comanches, Cheyennes and Arapahos had broken the Treaty of Medicine Lodge, a treaty they had signed but never understood. The white men understood it, but they broke it too, though not with the savagery of the Indians who robbed, raped, captured, murdered and mutilated with repeated regularity.

Sherman and Sheridan decided that they had to do to the Indians what they had done to the Confederacy . . . destroy the enemy's capability to make war. It had to be done in order to clear the plains between the Platte and the Arkansas for the oncoming settlers and the travelers along the Santa Fe Trail. To do it they would have to replace the reluctant General Alfred Sully with a commander who had no reluctance, no hesitation and no fear. The choice was clear. The telegraph was sent.

> Headquarters, Department of the Missouri,
> In the Field, Fort Hays, Kansas,
> September 24, 1868

To General G. A. Custer, Monroe, Michigan

General Sherman and myself, and nearly all the officers of your regiment, have asked for you, and I hope the application will be successful. Can you come at once? Eleven companies of your regiment will move about the 1st of October against the hostile Indians.

> P. H. Sheridan,
> Major General Commanding

Sherman and Sheridan sent for Custer. Custer sent for Adam Dawson. The Seventh was on the march again to the tune of their battle song, "Gary Owen" . . . marching to glory and gore. Sheridan said to Custer, "Now I can smoke a cigar in peace. You have never failed me."

And once again Custer did not fail.

Black Kettle, chief of the Cheyennes who had been defeated at Sand Creek, could not hold back his young warriors. They had been on the rampage all summer and fall and now had repaired to their winter camps along the Washita, secure in the knowledge that the army could not conduct a winter campaign against them in such adverse fighting conditions. But their secure knowledge did not include the bold tactics of General Custer.

Custer with Captain Dawson at his side blasted through snow-blown flats, bounded over frozen banks and treacherous gullies toward the lodges of Black Kettle's band.

Against that November dawn a ball of gold fire ascended then hung fire . . . the brightest and most beautiful of morning stars.

"Charge!" Custer roared and became a Cheyenne legend as "Son of Morningstar."

With sudden savagery, guns erupted and cavalry blades slashed red. Custer, leading the Seventh Cavalry, red scarves crusted white with snow, would let no one get ahead of him in the charge. Half-naked Indians, men and women, streamed out of their shelters, to be torn by bullets and blades, trampled by icy iron hooves. Washita became a human abattoir.

The sound and smell of slaughter, of screams and curses, coursed across bloody blotches of snow catching twisted bodies as they fell and shivered and died.

Dawson and the rest of the troopers had never seen or done anything like it. And like it or not they did it. The killing included anything that moved, warriors, women, children, horses, mules . . . until no warrior was left standing and Custer gave the order to cease firing and spared hundreds of women and children who had clustered against a southern slope.

Inside what was left of the lodges, the troopers found albums, letters and remnants of Bibles, evidence of Indian raids on Kansas homesteads.

Black Kettle was dead along with the young braves who would fight no more . . . forever.

Mawissa, Black Kettle's sister, offered Custer the hand of Princess Meyotzi, a young Cheyenne girl, in marriage as a token of peace. Custer respectfully declined.

But Autie gratefully received and accepted the letter sent to him by his commander, General Philip A. Sheridan.

> *"The Battle of the Washita River is the most complete and successful of all our battles, and was fought in such unfavorable weather and circumstances as to reflect the highest credit on yourself and regiment."*

Later when Sheridan shook Custer's hand he added, "It was a regular Indian 'Sayler's Creek' " in reference to the effective destruction of Lee's army at Appomattox.

But the devastation at Washita had destroyed something else, not in Custer, but in Adam Dawson.

Dawson no longer had the stomach for killing. He had seen and done enough. Too much. He had made up his mind that Washita was his last charge with Autie. He didn't exactly say that to Custer, but Adam did tell him that he was leaving the Seventh and the army.

Custer didn't believe it, or didn't want to.

"It's not over yet, Adam."

"It is for me."

"Listen, someday the white man and the red man can live in peace like the North and the South. But we've got to crush them first, like we did the Rebs. They're the enemy, like the Confederates were, and you know some of them were my close friends at the Point and after. We fought for the Union and against slavery. The Indian ways are worse, much worse than the South. They've got slaves too. They buy, sell, trade and steal women and children like horses. They've got to understand that all that has to change. But believe me, Adam, I know my Indians and they aren't crushed yet.

"Mark my words, they'll all unite with their new chiefs,

Sitting Bull, Crazy Horse, Crow-King and the rest. Sioux, Cheyenne, Kiowa, Arapaho all riding together for one last battle and I'll be there, so will you."

"That's one fight you'll fight without me, Autie."

"I don't want to do that, Adam. Who knows where that last fight will lead to? After that I can quit soldiering . . ."

"And do what?"

Custer just shrugged.

"You thinking about running for president, Autie?"

"Might be fun." Custer smiled. "Other soldiers did. Washington. Jackson. Harrison. Grant."

"I'll vote for you, Autie." Dawson smiled back. "But I'm still leaving."

"Please, Adam." Libbie had been listening and spoke for the first time, holding Custer's hand. "At our wedding I said you were Custer's luck; I still believe that. Don't leave us."

"I'm sorry, Libbie."

"It's all right, dear," Custer said and pointed to the red scarf around Dawson's neck. "As long as you wear that scarf, Adam, I'll be looking for you to come back."

When Adam Dawson rode out alone from Fort Hays, Autie had ordered the regimental band to strike up "Gary Owen."

Even outside the fort walls Dawson could hear the song that he and Custer and the Seventh had marched to.

In his bunk as he touched the red scarf he still wore, he could still hear it.

Adam Dawson knew that, once more, the time was coming when he had to leave.

Thirty-two

Chad Walker, steadied by his canes and wearing a change of clothes and the .44 he always strapped on when he went away from the ranch, stood on the front porch as Lorena walked back from where the two day hands and Dawson were tearing down the shack and hen house.

She had motioned for Pedro, the laborer who spoke English to come away from the work, said something to him that Dawson couldn't hear then walked back toward the house, while Pedro headed for the barn.

Dawson had made coffee in the bunkhouse then went straight to work with the two day hands when they showed up. He wondered why Lorena hadn't said anything to him that morning but thought it best to stay away from her and Chad until one or both of them called for him.

"Adam bringing the buckboard around?" Walker asked.

"Told Pedro to do it."

"Why not Adam?"

"Just didn't want to bother him." She shrugged.

"You sure didn't bother me any last night when you came back into the library. Lorena, you were . . ."

"Chad," she interrupted. "Do we have to talk about it here in broad daylight?"

"Why not?" He grinned. "I thought it was great! Passed out afterward like a bull-head goat, I . . ."

"Chad, just remember what you promised."

"What was that?"

"That you'd stay away from Nueva."

"I told you I would last night." Walker pulled a pint of whiskey from inside his coat pocket. "So long as he stays away from me." He took a drink.

"God, Chad. You've just had breakfast."

"I'm still having it." He took another swallow and put the pint back in his pocket.

Pedro drove the buckboard up near the porch and stopped. Walker made his way to the wagon and started the task of climbing aboard as Pedro jumped off the other side.

Adam, stripped to the waist, but wearing the red scarf came around to the front of the porch as Chad strapped himself in.

"Hey, boss. Where you going?"

"Pinto."

"How come?"

"Ordered a few cases of Tennessee bourbon. Outta be in by now. Getting low on cigars, too."

"You want company? I'll put on a shirt..."

"No, Adam!" Lorena interrupted and she knew the interruption had been too harsh and abrupt, but quickly recovered. "I've got some things to take care of around here, need some help."

"I already got company." Walker held up the pint of whiskey. "You can help unload, Adam, when I get back." Chad pocketed the bottle after taking a swig, picked up the reins and lashed the team. "Heah! Heah!"

The animals took off, hoofs and wheels churned dust.

The two of them watched for nearly a minute as the buckboard shrank in the distance, then Adam moved closer to Lorena.

"Why didn't you want me to go with him?"

"Because," she smiled, "I'd rather you stayed here with me. Wouldn't you?"

He ran his fingers through his hair and wiped the sweat from his forehead.

"Adam." She looked toward the day hands tearing down the shack. "Let them work for a while out there. Come on inside."

"I'm all sweaty."

"So what?"

Chad Walker drove the team like a Roman charioteer, picking up momentum as he hurtled past and carelessly close to a Mexican astride a mule on the road.

"*Chinga!*" the Mexican yelled. "*Pendejo!*"

Walker snapped the reins hard and laughed as he looked back.

"The same to you, greaseball."

"The buckboard made a precipitous turn as the trail curved along the cliffside. The trail climbed and so did the wagon. Higher, higher, with Chad in control until the road topped out, leveled off for a few yards at the crest, then sloped in sharp descent on the other side of Devil's Drop.

Suddenly the wagon punched into the team, then lurched from side to side and again slammed into the plunging animals pulling it.

Walker fought the reins and tried to get the buckboard back under control as it swerved closer to the sheer drop from the rocky strip of trail.

Drained of bravado he hauled on the reins and hollered at the horses ahead. But the crazed animals still charged downward as the wagon bed smashed against them.

"Whoa! Whoa, goddam you! Whoa!" Walker grasped the reins in one hand, reached out with the other and pulled back hard, as hard as he could, on the handbrake.

Nothing. Useless. Dead.

He pumped back and forth again and again on the handle with no effect. The wagon still wobbled from side to side with wheels bouncing and spinning off the ground. Walker gave up on the brake and jerked back with both hands clutching the reins. One of the ribbons snapped loose and Chad lost all control of the galloping horses.

His lips pressed into a tight, thin bloodless line. Veins stood out on his temples and neck. Chad Walker was strapped in. Trapped. But even if he could have unstrapped himself he couldn't have jumped, not with his strengthless legs.

The frothing team, blood-eyed and frightened of the drop, raced closer to the jagged edge of the cliff wall. The buckboard scraped along the rocky wattle of cliffside as wood, metal and stone screeched and sparks flew from the spinning wheel hubs. The wagon careened then slammed broadside against the jutting wall, wavered and tipped onto its flank, bringing down the horses and almost but not quite going over the edge.

It was a twisted, broken mess, with the one remaining wheel still whirling in the air. Both toppled horses snorted and pawed, fighting to get to their feet.

Chad Walker lay meshed under the spring seat, still alive and even conscious. He breathed hard and tried to squirm free. But the buckboard suddenly jerked forward a foot, then violently jerked again farther pulling Walker with it. He fought to keep the seat from crushing the life out of him and yelled at the struggling horses.

"Whoa! Whoa!" But the wagon lurched again.

Walker's right hand groped and finally freed what he wanted. His gun. He leveled it ahead and squeezed the trigger, again and again. There was a snort and last gush of air from each of the horses as each of them stiffened for an instant and died.

Chad Walker relaxed as much as he could while still snared in the seat of the wrecked wagon. He didn't know it yet, but the shots did more than kill the horses.

The three of them had reacted to the sound of gunfire, the brown-robed Padre Ramos and two young Mexicans, Raoul and Andre.

"Somebody hunting?" Raoul looked away to his left.

"I don't think so." The padre shook his head. "Nothing to hunt out here."

"Maybe they shoot the goat we look for!" Andre exclaimed.

The padre hurried off in the direction of the shots. Raoul and Andre followed.

Walker still struggled to free himself as he spotted them coming toward him. They stopped a few yards away from the debris.

"Hey! Hello! Over here!" he yelled. "Over here. Get me out!"

The three were on their way. Raoul and Andre got their shoulders under the broken wagon bed and lifted. They held it up just high enough so the padre could unstrap Walker and help him out from under.

Still on the ground, his face and body bruised and clothes ripped, Walker propped himself on his elbows. He reached inside his coat for the pint of whiskey and found broken glass.

"Well, it could've been worse," he mumbled.

"What did you say, *señor*?" the padre asked.

"Nothing." Walker shrugged. "Thanks. *Gracias*. Good thing you were close by."

"We were looking for a young goat that ran away from the mission."

"Yeah, well . . . you found me instead, an old goat. Seems like I owe you, Padre. I'm Chad Walker."

"I know of you," the padre said.

"Guess you know my wife better . . . Lorena, she comes to help you at the mission."

Padre Ramos looked puzzled.

"Well, Padre, I'd appreciate it if you'll send one of these boys to get somebody and bring back a wagon."

"Of course."

"Matter of fact, I'd appreciate it enough to make a sizeable contribution to your mission."

"Thank you *Señor* Walker, but that is not necessary."

"It is for me. And ask 'em to bring back something to drink . . . and I don't mean holy water."

Thirty-three

The next day Chad Walker's accident was the main topic of conversation at Baldy's Bar and much of the rest of the community of Pinto.

The reaction was mostly of disappointment, disappointment that Walker had survived. No one was more disappointed than Brad Hatcher. Fate had intervened, but unfortunately for Hatcher, not fatally. Not this time.

In spite of Hatcher's instructions, Joe Nueva had approached him as Hatcher came out of the bank.

"Say, Mr. Hatcher."

"What is it, Joe? I told you . . ."

"This'll just take a minute. Would you mind stepping around the corner . . . for just a minute?"

"O.K.," Hatcher said when the two of them were around the corner and out of sight. "What do you want?"

"Oh, a hundred dollars ought to do it until I get that job with you."

"What the hell for?"

"For a horse. You see I'm afoot right now and . . ."

"Listen Nueva, if you think . . ."

"I think I oughtta have a horse until I get that job. You know the sheriff's been asking a lot of questions about Corona and that raid on . . ."

"Listen, you stupid bastard, you can't say anything without implicating yourself . . ."

"I don't intend to say anything, Mr. Hatcher. Hell, I just

want to have a horse in case you've got something for me to do . . ."

"Well, I haven't."

"You never can tell. I can come in pretty handy."

"All right, Joe. Here's a hundred but that's the end of it. No more. You understand?"

"Sure I understand. Too bad about Walker and that wagon. His not gettin' killed, I mean." Nueva put the money in his pocket. "Anytime you got anything I can help you with, Mr. Hatcher, just let me know." Nueva walked away and headed toward Linus McCloud's Livery.

Brad Hatcher watched as Nueva left. He didn't think that Nueva would tell the sheriff anything about the deal with Corona and he didn't like the idea of being blackmailed, but he considered the hundred an investment for future services from Nueva. He knew that Nueva hated Walker as much as he did. Almost as much.

Maybe Hatcher could find a way to get rid of both of them.

Deputy Sam Mendez sat on a bench in the sheriff's office cleaning the carbine when the door opened and Alma Gorsich stepped inside.

"Good morning, Sam."

"Good morning, ma'am." Sam looked up and smiled. "It is a good morning."

"That star looks real nice on your vest, nice and shiny . . . the star, I mean." She smiled back.

"Thank you, ma'am. I just polished it."

"Uh-huh. I see that you're polishing your rifle too."

"No, ma'am. Oiling and cleaning it."

"I see." She looked around. "But I don't see the sheriff. He in the outhouse?"

"No, ma'am."

"Is it a secret?"

"Is what a secret, ma'am?"

"Where the sheriff is."

"Oh, no. I can tell you if you want to know."

"Then go ahead and tell me, Sam."

"By now," Sam took a look at the clock hanging on the wall, "he should be at Mr. Walker's ranch. First he said he was going to stop by and have a look. He should've already done that by now."

"Have a look . . . at what?"

"Oh, the wreck of that wagon. Mr. McCloud's sent some fellas over there to take care of them dead horses that Mr. Walker shot."

"How do you take care of a dead horse, Sam?"

"Well, ma'am, there's different choices. One choice is you could bury 'em. Another choice is you could skin 'em, cut 'em up and . . ."

"Never mind, Sam. I'd just as soon not hear any more."

"Yes, ma'am. Can I tell him somethin' when he gets back? About you comin' by, I mean?"

"I expect he'll be stopping by Baldy's sooner or later, so I'll tell him myself . . . well, not tell him, ask him, might even ask you too."

"Yes, ma'am. Ask me what?"

"About coming over for supper at my place with Mrs. O'Donnell and me some night this week. What do you think?"

"I think he'll do it. I know I will . . . if you ask me."

"Consider yourself asked, but don't tell him about it 'til I talk to him first." Alma started for the door but turned back smiling. "Sam?"

"Yes, ma'am?"

"Just 'cause you're wearing a badge now, don't think . . ."

"Don't think what, ma'am?"

"Don't think that you can get a beer at Baldy's."

"Oh, no, ma'am. I don't drink beer."

"Good. I'll have some milk for you at supper."

"You could've been a widow, Mrs. Walker," Sheriff Ben Vesper said. "He's a lucky man."

"I should've gone with you, Chad." Adam took a step toward Walker sitting behind his desk.

Walker was bruised and sore, but in light of what he had gone through, appeared to be in fit condition and in comparatively good humor.

"Good thing it didn't happen on the way back." Chad smiled. "Would have lost all that good bourbon instead of just a pint."

"I've warned you a hundred times, Chad," Lorena said. "About driving that wagon so fast on Devil's Drop."

"*Two* hundred times, Lorena. Maybe next time, I'll listen . . . but don't count on it."

"Well, I don't think it's funny!" she remarked.

"Neither do I," Vesper added. "There's something wrong, Mr. Walker. Very wrong."

"What do you mean, Sheriff?" Lorena asked.

"I mean that on the way out here I checked that wagon and . . ." Vesper paused.

"And what?" Most of the humor had gone out of Walker's voice.

"The pin on the wiffletree was filed. Bolt on the brake line was gone too. And one of the reins looked like . . ."

"Go on," Walker said.

"Looked like somebody was out to kill you, Mr. Walker."

"Kill me?"

"Chad." Lorena bit her lip. "I should've said something, but . . . I know how mad you get."

"Said what? For chrissake, *what*?"

"That's right, Mrs. Walker." The sheriff nodded. "I'd be most interested in anything you have to say."

"Last night, after . . . after I left you here in the library I went into the kitchen and saw something . . . somebody through the window."

"Who?!" Walker asked.

"First I thought it might be Adam . . . but then I realized it wasn't him. I'm sure of that, but . . ."

"But what?" Walker's voice was louder. "Who the hell was it? Did you recognize him?"

"I can't be absolutely sure . . . that's why I didn't say anything. But it could've been Joe Nueva."

"Nueva!" Walker exploded. "Hell, yes! Who else but him!" Chad pulled a gun out of his desk drawer. "He got sore cause I kicked his ass outta here. I ought to go into town and blow his head off, the sonofabitch!"

"Take it easy, Mr. Walker," Vesper said.

"The hell with that easy stuff."

"Just cool down a minute."

"In a pig's ass! If he comes around here . . ."

"If he comes around here you've got the right to defend yourself and your property . . ."

"And I sure as hell will!"

"But don't go looking for trouble."

"I'll give him trouble with this!" Walker held the gun up.

"Not yet you won't. Not til' I have a talk with him."

"Talk!"

"That's right. I'll find out what I can."

"What the hell more is there to find out?!"

"That's my job. If he did it, I'll make sure he won't get away with it. That's my job too and I'm good at it."

"Well, I'm good at *this* too." Walker held the gun even higher. "You tell him if I see his greasy face around here, I'll kill him!"

The Douglas chair in front of the sheriff's office usually occupied by Ben Vesper currently was occupied by Deputy Sam Mendez. Shavings fluttered toward his boots while Sam whittled on a piece of diminishing wood with the John Henry knife he had borrowed from the sheriff's desk.

The man rode in from the south, dismounted and looped the reins around the hitching post in front of the sheriff's office. The horse grunted with relief when the man stepped off. He was a big man. Bigger than big. A foot taller than

Sam, who, himself was bigger than most, and broad as a buffalo with a face not nearly as comely. He wore a black square brim hat and a plaid shirt with garters around both biceps. His gun hung low and wide within easy reach of his outsized hand. His face was both grim and grimy and likely hadn't been washed this side of the Mexican border. The man moved up toward the door of the sheriff's office. Sam stopped whittling, brushed some of the shavings off his lap, looked up and smiled.

"Howdy. You look like you've come a distance."

"What's it to you, sonny?"

"Huh?"

"I said what's it to you, little boy."

"Oh, nothin'. I was just wondering if I could help you."

"Not unless you're the sheriff."

"No, sir, I'm not. But I am the deputy." Sam smiled again and pointed to his badge with the John Henry.

"Deputy? Hell," the man grunted. "You don't even look housebroke."

"Not very friendly, are you, mister?"

"Nope. And the name's Rango. Frank Rango. You probably know the name."

"Nope."

"Bounty hunter . . . among other things."

"What other things?"

"That don't concern you, sonny. I want to see the sheriff, pick up some fresh dodgers."

"Sheriff's not here."

"Well, I'll go in anyhow . . . have a look." Rango started to move.

"No you won't." Sam got up and placed the John Henry on the seat of the empty chair.

"How's that?"

"I said no you won't. Not until the sheriff gets back."

"Suppose I'm not inclined to wait, sonny?"

"You'll do it anyhow."

"You gonna make me wait, sonny?"

"If that's the only way you'll have it."

By now about a dozen citizens had formed a semicircle in front of the office, not too close, but close enough to witness and listen to the youth's baptism of the badge. Sheriff Ben Vesper had ridden in but stayed at a greater distance still on horseback. Sam never took his eyes off Frank Rango.

"Oh, I'm goin' in all right, sonny, but first I'm gonna take down your pants and spank your bare ass . . ."

Sam's left fist smashed into Rango's nose, his right hand pulled the gun from his holster and the barrel of the .44 cracked against the bounty hunter's skull.

Rango dropped to his knees, teetered with blood gushing from his broken nose, then buckled to the ground with Sam's gun pointed a foot from his face.

"What's going on, Deputy?" Vesper had dismounted and stood on the boardwalk nearby.

"This one says he's a bounty hunter . . . among other things. Wanted to go inside, get some dodgers. Told him he'd have to wait 'til you got here."

"Well, I'm here."

"Yes, sir."

Vesper grabbed the dazed man and pulled him to his feet.

"Looks to me like you assaulted an officer of the law."

"For chrissake!" Rango wiped away blood from his face. "He's the one hit me!"

"With just cause. He's your prisoner, Sam. What do you want to do with him? Lock him up?"

"He'd just get blood all over the place."

"That's true."

"Why don't we just let him ride off and bleed somewhere's else, Sheriff?"

"It's up to you."

"Well, then." Sam reached down, picked up the black hat and shoved it on top of Rango's head. "Mount up . . . sonny."

Vesper, Sam and the citizens watched while Frank Rango did just that. Then the crowd dispersed.

"Good work, Deputy," Vesper said.

"Learned it from you, sir."

"Looks like you improved on it a mite. Seen Nueva around?"

"No, sir, I haven't."

"Keep an eye open for him. I'm going over to Baldy's."

"Yes, sir."

"It appears," Alma said to Vesper as she put the beer on the bar, "that your young deputy can take care of himself."

"And then some." Vesper took a swallow and looked around the saloon at the daytime customers. "Have you seen Joe Nueva around?"

"Somebody said he rode out of town this morning. Yeah, it was his pal Paco over there."

Vesper looked at the four Mexicans playing cards at a table and finished his beer.

"Oh, Ben, I wanted to ask you something, stopped by your office earlier."

"I'm listening."

"Would you like to come over and have supper with us some night this week?"

"Us?"

"Maureen and me."

"Who's doing the cooking?"

"She is."

"Then I'll come."

"How about tomorrow? Say six?"

"Said and done."

"And Sam said he'd like to come too, but don't worry I'll keep him away from the two of you after we eat."

"Don't keep him up all night, he's got to work the next day."

"In the old days . . . so did you." She smiled as Vesper walked toward the table.

"Say, Paco," the sheriff said at the table. "Where's your roommate?"

"Joe rode out of town."

"Didn't think he had a horse."

"Bought one at the livery this morning."

"What'd he use for money?"

"Money."

"Where'd he get that much all of a sudden?"

"*Quien sabe?*" Paco shrugged. "I'm not married to him you know."

"Yeah, but do you know where he went?"

"He went to see Margarita."

"Who's that?"

"One of his *chi-chi*s. Lives over in Golead."

"Say when he was coming back?"

"Tomorrow." Paco shrugged again. "Maybe."

"Then I'll see him tomorrow . . . maybe."

Sheriff Ben Vesper checked with Linus McCloud. McCloud had sold Nueva a horse and saddle, both used, for eighty-five dollars cash and Nueva still had money in his pocket when he rode out.

It wasn't until that night that Dawson had the chance to talk to Lorena alone, and even then he knew it wouldn't be for long. Elena had just left the kitchen to go to her room and Chad was in the library smoking and drinking.

All day she had been avoiding him and even now she turned to walk away.

"Lorena." Adam spoke low but took hold of her arm as she turned. She looked even more dazzling, beautiful and pure, than she had when she stepped naked out of the stream.

"What is it, Adam?"

"You know what *is it*. And so do I. You didn't see Nueva or anybody else out there last night."

"Didn't I?"

"Except yourself."

"You think *I* did it?"

"Well, didn't you? Isn't that why you didn't want me to

go with him? Isn't that why you kept me here?"

"It was because I wanted to be with you . . . you and I both know that Adam, and he's incapable of love the way we love each other. I never loved him the way I love you. I've never loved anybody like this and it's tearing me apart . . . you can believe anything else you want just so you believe me when I say that . . . Adam, you're hurting me!"

He hadn't realized how hard he was gripping her.

"Hey, you two!" Chad's voice came from the library. "What're you doing out there?! I'm lonesome as a coyote."

The two of them kept the lonesome coyote company for the next hour. Walker had suggested a card game but Adam begged off so Walker went to drinking bourbon instead. Adam thought there was something different about the way Chad acted that night but figured it was because of Walker's close call with the wagon. And for the first night Adam could remember, Walker hadn't mentioned Custer even once.

"Say, Lorena," Chad said. "You haven't gone to the mission lately, have you?"

"Not for a while . . . but I will again, maybe next week."

"Uh-huh. Well when you do I want to give you some money for the padre. Seems like a nice fella. I'm sorry he couldn't come with them when they brought me back."

"Yes, so am I."

"How much?"

"How much what?"

"You think I ought to give him . . . he saved my life. That ought to be worth at least a hundred. Don't you think?"

"I'm sure he'll appreciate whatever you give him and put it to good use."

"Yeah, but tell him not to light any candles, I don't go for that."

"I'll tell him whatever you want, Chad." Lorena was getting more uneasy and wanted to talk about something else but Walker beat her to it.

"Haven't found your saddle yet, have you, Adam?"

"Haven't looked lately."

"We thought we'd go look tomorrow, if that's all right

with you, Chad." Lorena glanced at Adam then back to her husband.

"Sure. Hey, friend," Walker said. "You know what you *oughtta* do?"

"What, boss?"

"That waitress over at Baldy's, Alma, she's a little long in the tooth, but still not a bad-lookin' poke hole and she's got eyes for you. You oughtta go into Pinto and put it to her."

"Chad, for heaven's sake!" Lorena blurted.

"Just a suggestion." Walker shrugged. "Thought he might be gettin' a little horny, what the hell he's only human."

"Yeah, well," Dawson rose. "This human thinks he'll turn in."

"Me, too." Walker gingerly twisted his shoulders and rubbed his neck. "Pretty damn stiff and sore. You got to give me a good rub tonight, Lorena . . . all over."

There wasn't anything Adam Dawson could say or do except "good night" and head for the bunkhouse.

That's what he said and did.

Thirty-four

A cynical Texas sky hugged the range of hills and hovered over the desert esparto as Adam and Lorena rode, slow and silent, toward the boulders.

An arcing sun tried in vain to break through the mid-morning haze still blanketing the gray slab above them. The summer storm might or might not come. But not as uncertain was another kind of storm swirling inside the two of them.

A storm from the heavens would be welcomed and salubrious, bathing and replenishing the arid soil.

The other storm, the mortal storm, would not cleanse. It would spill out blood if they let it.

"I can't take much more, Adam."

"Neither can I."

"Last night, he . . . he was worse than ever . . . he made . . ."

"All right, Lorena! You don't have to draw me any pictures, they're already there."

"For you they're pictures, for me they're hell. He's made a world of his own out here. He's never going to leave it and he's never going to change."

"Something's got to."

"Not unless we make it change. You, or me, or both of us. I think he's beginning to . . ."

"To what?"

"Well, maybe to think that there's something between us, you and me."

"Yeah, I kind of got that feeling last night too."

"What're we going to do?"

"First . . . we're going to find that saddle."

She knelt at the side of the graves, the graves of her father, mother and infant brother on the sloping hill, where she too would be buried unless Brad Hatcher carried out his threat to throw her off the land that belonged to her family since before there was a Brad Hatcher.

On the ground beside the purse she had brought with her, were her Bible and the gun that had belonged to her father.

For years she had found solace in the Bible, the source of her endurance and hope. But since Hatcher's threat she had thought more about the gun. It was a sin to kill, to kill herself or her husband . . . or both. But more and more it seemed to be the instrument of her salvation, or at least satisfaction.

She reached for both, and held the Bible in one hand, the gun in the other.

"*Chulita.*"

Mary Ann looked up and found Marissa standing beside her. *Chulita.* Since she was born and until Mary Ann married Hatcher, to Marissa, she had been *Chulita.* Since then, *Señora.* Until now. The old woman's face was calm, as calm as it had always been ever since Mary Ann could remember. From the time Marissa had cradled her in her arms and against her breast. A surrogate mother. Devoted. Loving. Protecting.

"*Chulita*, please. I know what is in your heart."

"You always have." Mary Ann nodded.

"Please. Give that to me."

Mary Ann knew Marissa wasn't talking about the Bible. "Why?"

"Because that is not the way. Not for you."

"I can't think of any other."

"*Chulita.* Give me the gun."

"Oh, Marissa. I don't want to leave here."

"You will not." She reached out and took the gun. "You will be here as long as you want to stay."

"It." Mary Ann looked around. "It all belongs to him now."

"Please . . . try not to worry. I won't let him do anything to you." She put the gun under her shawl. "This is not the way."

"But . . ."

"I am old, *Chulita*. What happens to me doesn't matter. I will take care of you . . . and everything."

Sheriff Ben Vesper walked through the bat wings and looked around. A dozen of the daytime regulars were there including Joe Nueva who was drinking at his usual table with Paco and two more of his amigos.

Vesper walked toward Nueva, stopped in front of him and pointed to an empty table.

"Joe. Bring your drink." He moved to the empty table. Nueva lifted his glass and bottle and followed.

"Hey, Sheriff," Alma called from behind the bar. "You want something?" Vesper shook his head as he and Nueva sat.

"How about a drink on me?" Nueva pointed to the bottle he had set on the table.

"You've been buying a lot of things lately."

"Yeah." Nueva shrugged. "Spendin' some of my hard-earned cash."

"You hear about Walker's accident?"

"Too bad," Joe grinned, ". . . he didn't croak."

"You shouldn't say that, Joe."

"Why not?"

"Because it was no accident and you've got all the makings of a prime suspect."

"Horseshit!" Nueva snorted.

"Don't raise your voice . . . unless you want me to make this official."

"With another crack on the head?"

"Your choice."

"Okay." Nueva took a drink. "What's this crap about a 'suspect'?"

"Everybody knows Walker fired you. You argued. He threatened you or vice versa. He told you to get out and stay out."

"So?"

"So it seems you went back and did a little work on that wagon."

"Bullshit. I haven't been back since."

"You were seen."

"Who says?"

"Never mind who."

"That drifter who took my job? Him?! Hell, he's the one you oughtta be checkin'."

"Why?"

"Cause I know her and what she wants. She craves lovin' and her old man's got no *cajones*. She's a wildcat and I got the scars to prove it."

"Come on, Joe."

"Come on nothin'. He's got her and he's after that ranch. That's why he fixed that wagon and that's why he sicced you on me."

"And you're just an innocent party, huh, Joe?"

"When it comes to that wagon I am."

"All right then, where were you Thursday night, Joe . . . after it got dark?"

"That's easy." Nueva smiled. "Hey, Alma, come here!"

At the boulders Adam and Lorena gave vent to all the pent-up fury and passion that had been building. They held nothing back. They blotted out the world around them, everything that had happened before and everything that could happen later. There was nothing else. No other time or place. Only the naked desire for each other, within each other.

The summer storm did not come.

They ate in silence, Walker, Lorena and Adam, while Elena served supper, with only the occasional table sounds interrupting the quiet until the knock on the front door.

"Who the hell can that be?" Walker growled.

"I'll go find out." Lorena rose and walked toward the entrance.

"Glad you found your saddle, Adam," Walker said when she left.

"Yeah. Me too."

"Lorena sniffed it out, did she?"

Dawson didn't intend to answer and didn't have to as Lorena's voice called out from the other room. "It's the sheriff, Chad."

"Sorry to trouble you at supper," Vesper said as he followed her in.

"No trouble." Walker looked up at him. "Main thing is, did you find Nueva?"

"I found him. But he's not our man."

"The hell he's not!"

"Look, Mr. Walker, if there was anybody out there that night, it wasn't Nueva. Got an airtight alibi. He was playing cards with some of his friends. Game started at seven, didn't break up 'til almost three in the morning."

"Some of *what* friends? A bunch of lying greasers? Call that an alibi?"

"Take it easy, Mr. Walker, my mother was Mexican."

"I don't care what she . . ."

"The game was at Baldy's and Baldy was there. So was Alma, the mayor and Hatcher. Nueva never left."

"Yeah, well, maybe he got somebody to do it for him. One of his amigos."

"Maybe . . . and maybe not. But all the same . . ."

"All the same what?"

"You'd better be careful because somebody *did* do it and they're liable to try again."

"Yeah, well I can take care of myself and you tell Nueva to keep outta my sight or I'll kill him!"

"I already told him."

"Then you've done your duty again, Sheriff. Good night."

The sheriff nodded, threw a look at Dawson and Lorena, then turned.

"I'll see you to the door," Lorena said.

"Thanks, Mrs. Walker, I can find it."

"That's about all he can find!" Walker said as he heard the door close. "Goddam greasers, can't believe any of 'em."

Unfortunately Elena came in from the kitchen carrying a pie just as he said it.

"And that goes for you too!" Walker floundered to his feet using his canes. "I don't want to see *him*, or *you* or his goddam *bastard* you got in your belly . . ."

Elena cowered. Lorena moved between them.

"Chad!"

Walker pushed her aside and shoved the pregnant girl hard. Elena slammed against the wall, dropped the pie, and fell to the floor face first.

Walker had let loose of his canes and Adam Dawson's hands were around him, both to hold him up and restrain any further excitement.

"Go on!" Walker hollered at the sobbing heap on the floor. "Get the hell out and stay out!"

"I'm taking her to the mission." Lorena bent to help the girl to her feet.

"Take her any damn place you want."

"I'll get the other buckboard and do it," Adam said. "She can show me the way."

"Yeah, you do that, Adam. And . . ." He pointed to the fallen canes. ". . . hand me those sticks."

It was almost midnight before he got back. The house was dark.

Adam Dawson had made up his mind. He wasn't going to leave . . . and he had made up his mind about Chad Walker.

Thirty-five

Lorena poured coffee from the pot into a cup in front of Adam as the thick strips of bacon seared in the iron frying pan.

She stopped pouring when they both heard the stairway basket thudding to the bottom.

"Hey, what's going on back there?" Chad's voice called out, then came the sound of the canes and dragging boots, as Walker moved into the kitchen.

"I said . . ."

"We heard you, Chad. I'm fixing breakfast, Elena's gone. Remember?"

"Yeah." He seemed pensive, maybe even a little contrite. But with Walker it was hard to tell. He made his way into a chair. Lorena poured him a cup of coffee and went back to the stove. "Sleep okay, Adam?"

"Uh-huh. You?"

"Didn't even hear you come back." He drank, then let the hot vapor drift up through his nostrils. "Say, Adam, do me a favor, will you?"

"Sure."

"Take the buckboard, go into town and pick up those cases of bourbon I ordered. Down to my last quart."

"I'll leave right away."

"Oh, and my cigars over at the grocery."

"Sure."

"Lorena, you go with him."

"What?" She turned from the stove.

"Don't you have something you can do in town?"

"Well, yes, but..."

"Then go do it. I don't want anybody around today."

"Why not?"

"Because I don't. That's why."

"But Chad, who's going to take care..."

"I can damn well take care of myself!" He flared, then softened. "I just want to be by myself. Got things on my mind."

"Okay, Chad." She looked at Dawson. "We'll go."

Walker put aside the cup, rubbed his forehead and eyes. His head bent downward.

"Adam. You haven't said a word since we left."

Dawson still didn't say anything, or even look at her. He stared straight ahead at the horses and the trail into Pinto.

"You think he knows..." She touched his arm, "... about us?"

"It won't matter much longer."

"What do you mean?"

"I mean I know how to do it."

"How?"

"You'll find out... before it happens."

"When?"

"Tomorrow... he'll be dead."

"Halcón," she whispered

"Paloma," the old man on the bench replied, then opened his eyes.

"The Hawk" and "The Dove." Years ago, unremembered by any except the two of them, he had raped her and they remained lovers for years afterward.

Today he was an old man, bent, with one leg crooked. He had been at the mission for most of the century. Four padres had come and gone, the fifth, Padre Ramos, was still here where "Tio Carlos" still tended his flowers and the vegetable garden and was venerated by young and old as the kind and gentle majordomo of the mission. A man of peace who spoke poetry and told fairy tales to the children.

He looked up and smiled at Marissa.

She stood near the bench in the garden. Tio Carlos's hoe, an instrument he rarely used anymore, but almost always carried, leaned against the small wooden bench.

"Paloma," he said. "You are more beautiful today than in all the yesterdays put together."

"Halcón, your eyesight is failing . . . but you can still hear me whisper your name."

"As long as I can hear the birds, smell the fragrance of the flowers and see my Paloma, I am content."

Looking at the venerable old man everyone knew as "Uncle," Tio Carlos, it was almost impossible to even suspect that he had, early in the century, been known as "The Hawk," the terror of both sides of the border, even before there was a border. The bold *bandito* who rode wild, robbing, raping and pillaging; handsome, dashing and dangerous. Untamable. And while beautiful, dark-eyed Marissa didn't tame him, she fell in love with him and he with her. It was to her he went, bleeding, with bullets in his back and leg. And it was Marissa who saved his life and he promised never to rob or kill again.

Years later a crippled stranger came to the mission, a man who called himself Carlos and later everyone called him Tio Carlos. They met often and passionately, but no one ever found out, and while their passion faded, their love never wavered or diminished.

"Sit next to me, Paloma"—he patted the bench with a gnarled hand—"and wash away the years."

"There is something else I want to wash away," Marissa said as she sat.

"What can I do?"

"Here at the mission, do you keep poison for the rats?"

"With all the cats at Spanish Bit there can't be any rats." He smiled.

"Weed killer might be better. Something to go with wine."

"This wine . . . white or dark?"

"Dark."

"Good."

"Halcón, I have to tell you something."

"No, you don't."

"I'm going to tell you anyhow. Years ago you promised you would never kill anyone again. I'm here to make you break that promise."

"No one has a better right." He took her hand in his. "Just sit with me for a little while. This might be the last time. Then I will bring you what you need, Paloma."

Only the master of Spanish Bit drank wine.

The horseshoe flew, hit the iron rod sticking out of the ground, spun, and settled into the dirt. Ringer.

Joe Nueva and his *compadres*, Paco, Jake and Jamie were pitching horseshoes on the empty lot in Pinto. Nueva had just tossed the ringer but turned his attention in another direction.

The buckboard with Lorena aboard was in front of the depot. There were two cases of bourbon on the bed of the wagon and Adam Dawson came out carrying a third case. He placed it next to the other two and moved toward her.

"I'm going to pick up the cigars over at the grocery. You want to come along or wait here?"

"I'll wait." She smiled. She had been smiling to herself since Dawson told her about tomorrow.

"Be right back."

He walked past the horseshoe players on the vacant lot, toward the grocery store next door. As Dawson got there, Brad Hatcher came out of the open door.

"Oh, hello," Hatcher said. "How are you . . . Mr. Dawson?"

"Good," Dawson said. "Hope you're the same," and walked inside.

Hatcher's eyes went to Lorena on the buckboard and so did he.

Joe Nueva was no longer pitching horseshoes. He stood watching as Hatcher stopped close to the wagon.

"Lorena," Hatcher said softly after looking around. "I've got to see you."

"Take a good look."

"I mean . . . you know . . . like before."

"Why, Mr. Hatcher." She smoothed out the dress around her knees. "I'm shocked! And you a married man . . ."

"Lorena . . ."

"I'm sorry, Mr. Hatcher." She paused and then smiled pleasantly. "But then again . . . who knows? We might even do business together . . . someday." Then louder. "Good-bye, Mr. Hatcher. Give my regards to *Mrs.* Hatcher."

Adam rolled a cigarette as Fabrini, the pudding-faced grocer, put two boxes of cigars on the counter.

"There you are." Fabrini smiled. "Nothing but the best for Mr. Walker."

"Yeah, that's right."

Nueva and Paco had walked through the open door and stood there muttering in Spanish.

"Be right with you, Joe," Fabrini called out.

"No hurry," Nueva said. "Just need some tobacco and cigarette papers." Nueva looked at Adam, nodded, grinned, then started up again in Spanish to Paco. Both men nodded and smirked. Nueva gave Paco a light punch on the shoulder.

"Nueva." Dawson pointed the unlit cigarette.

"What?"

"Something funny? Or something bothering you?"

"No bother." Nueva shrugged.

"Look. I didn't ask for your job."

"It's okay." Nueva shrugged again. "I didn't want the job anymore anyway. You want to pick up my leavings, it's okay." He pointed out the door. "I'm all done with her too."

Adam dropped the cigarette and flew at Nueva, but as he passed Paco, Paco pinned Dawson's arms and Nueva's fist rammed into Adam's jaw.

Dawson booted Nueva hard in the crotch. He doubled over and held himself in agony while Adam jerked free of Paco's grasp and turned to slug him. But Paco stepped back, raised both hands in quick surrender then ran out of the door.

Dawson grabbed the front of Nueva's shirt, slapped him twice across the face and shot a right fist into his jaw knocking Nueva out the door and onto the boardwalk.

Lorena watched from the buckboard and Nueva's amigos stood by as Adam Dawson, carrying two boxes of cigars, walked out of Fabrini's Grocery, stepped over the inert body of Joe Nueva and proceeded toward the wagon. As he walked he wiped the leakage of blood from his mouth with his wrist.

Dawson climbed onto the buckboard, put the cigars on the floorboard and took up the reins.

"Adam." Lorena's hand touched his arm. "Are you all right?"

"Depends," Adam said, "on what you mean." He snapped the reins. The buckboard took off.

Brad Hatcher had seen it all. He waited until the wagon passed then went to Nueva, still dazed and bleeding, who had been lifted to his feet by his *compañeros*.

"Joe," Hatcher said, "I want to talk to you."

"Huh?"

"Come with me." As they walked away, Nueva still wobbly, Hatcher smiled. "Now there is something you can do . . . for both of us."

"Is there something we should do, Sheriff?" Sam asked as he and Ben Vesper stood across the street.

"Seems like everything's been done," Vesper said. "For now. But tomorrow I'm going to take a ride."

It was the best beef stew ever served in Texas, the best Ben Vesper had ever tasted. So he said.

After supper Alma and Sam went into the kitchen, ostensibly to wash the dishes but actually to let Maureen and Ben sit out on the porch and maybe talk about something beside the weather.

"Beautiful night," Maureen said.

"Texas night."

"But sitting here like this does remind me of . . ."

"Of what?"

"Of . . . Ireland."

"Well, same sky." Ben looked up. "Same moon, same stars. I'm sorry that other things aren't the same for you."

"Ben . . . Doctor Bonner says I'm going to have the baby. But I knew it before he did."

"I'm glad for you, Maureen. Will you be staying here until . . . until then?"

"Doctor Bonner thinks it's best I do, but . . ."

Vesper was afraid of what Maureen O'Donnell was going to say until she said it.

". . . I dislike imposing on Alma for all that time. She won't admit it, but I know it is an imposition."

"I've got an idea . . . if you'd care to hear it."

"Ben . . ."

"I've got a ranch not far from here. There's an old Mexican couple running it, a lot bigger than this place. They'd be glad to have you."

"Oh, I don't think . . ."

"I've got a room at the hotel here in town. It's a lot handier in case of trouble. Why don't you stay out there . . . until I move in, I mean."

"Are you planning on doing that?"

"Someday, when I quit the law business. Didn't want to be a sheriff in the first place. Just happened."

"A lot of things . . ." she nodded, "just happen . . . but Ben . . ."

"I know. I won't push it." Vesper smiled. "Course I would have to charge you rent."

"I can afford it, now." She smiled back then turned serious. "Ben, about that money . . ."

"That's been settled. Five dollars a month ought to cover the rent. We can settle other things later."

"Anybody ready for coffee and dessert?" Alma's voice called out from inside.

"I'm ready," Vesper said and looked at Maureen as he got to his feet.

"So am I." She nodded.

He took her hand and helped her up.

"So you gave it to Nueva, huh? Good!" Chad Walker lit one of his fresh cigars and took another drink. He had been drinking ever since Dawson and Lorena came back, through supper and now in the library. "Tell me some more, Captain. What started it?"

"He did."

"Adam knocked him flat on his back," Lorena said. "He was still out when we left."

"Sorry I missed that."

"I don't think," Lorena went on, "that you'll be seeing any more of Mr. Nueva around here."

"You know, Adam," Walker took another drink, "I been trying to figure something out about you."

"What's that, boss?"

"Just this." Walker looked at Lorena then back to Dawson. "What in the hell *aren't* you good at?"

"A lot of things." Dawson smiled.

"I don't know about that." Walker let the blue smoke spiral out of his mouth. "Never saw a drifter like you. Educated. Rode with Custer. Good with cards, with a rifle, with his fists . . . hell what *haven't* you done?"

"Well, I haven't been able to beat you . . . and Domino."

"That's right!" Walker nodded with satisfaction.

"Not yet."

Lorena leaned forward just a little and listened, trying not to look at Dawson.

"What's that mean?" Walker smiled. "Still think you can do it?"

"Well, for one thing, I've never raced you using my own saddle."

"You think," Walker was now laughing, "that would make a difference?"

"It might."

"A *saddle*? Never heard that before."

"Maybe you're right. Probably wouldn't make much difference."

Lorena became afraid Dawson would let it drop but Adam knew how to play this game with Walker too.

"A saddle!" Chad Walker wasn't going to let it drop. "Hell, Domino and me can beat anything with four legs. Anything that can't fly."

"Guess so."

"Guess?! Why the hell don't we find out?"

"Well, if you want to."

"Sure I do! But let's make it interesting, what do you want to bet?"

"Bet?"

"Yeah." Walker settled back in his chair. "What have I got that you want?" There was an edge to his voice.

"Trouble with that is," Dawson's voice was calm and even, "I haven't got anything *you* want."

"Yes you do. One thing."

"What's that?"

"I'll bet you one month's wages . . . against that red scarf."

"Well, I don't . . ."

"Ha! There is something you're afraid of, otherwise you'd bet."

"All right. It's a bet."

"Good." Walker finished his drink. "When?"

Lorena finally looked at Adam and held her breath.

"Tomorrow's as good a time as any," Dawson said.

"First thing in the morning." Walker came to his feet using the canes and started toward the door. "Come on, Lorena. I'll need a good rub tonight."

"I'll be right up, Chad. Soon as I clean things up and put out the lamps."

She waited until she heard the sounds of Walker hauling himself up the stairs in the basket then went to Adam, put both her arms on his shoulders. He looked straight ahead past her.

"The race tomorrow," Lorena whispered. "That's what you meant?"

He nodded, barely.

"How can you be sure?"

"I'll make sure. I'll fix it."

"How?"

"With one of the straps on Domino." Dawson spoke as if he were planning a battle attack, but without emotion. "When I bump it, that stallion'll go crazy . . . drag him hanging by one leg . . .'til it's over. I'll see to that."

"I know you will. It'll work, Adam. I know it will."

"So do I."

Thirty-six

Adam Dawson stood in the barn next to Domino. The stallion was out of his stall and saddled with the special rig. Adam patted the animal's mane and tugged lightly on one of the straps. He had finished the work he had set out to do.

But he wasn't quite finished. There was something left. Something inside of him, something in his brain, or heart or soul. Something that made him hesitate.

> "Relax, Yank. We're on the same side."
> "The war's over."
> "I'm Lorena. Chad's wife."
> "He's taking Nueva's place."
> "Welcome, brother Adam."
> "Plenty of everything handy here. I'm glad you came this way, Captain."
> "Don't waste your life."
> "Good advice. Take it."
> "The eagle suffers little birds to sing."
> "I named him after you, Gallant Man."
> "Let's not find the saddle, yet."
> "You're practically part of the family."
> "I never should have hit that bull's-eye."
> "He's used me . . . like a saddle. God, I feel dirty, Adam."
> "There's a place where I go. I want you to come with me, Adam."

"*There is no art to find the mind's construction in the
     face ... or body.*"

"*You're lucky ... that Mr. Dawson was here.*"

"*You saved his life, Adam. How does it feel?*"

"*Blessed are the meek for they shall inherit the earth.*"

"*There is darkness at noon but you must not give up
     hope.*"

"*The darkness shall be lifted and the crooked shall be
     straight.*"

"*Ease up, Chad. You've been so drunk you can't even
     take off your clothes.*"

"*Then you'll take them off for me.*"

"*Things'll work out.*"

"*Not unless we make them.*"

"*I'm all sweaty.*"

"*So what?*"

"*Looked like somebody was out to kill you, Mr.
     Walker.*"

"*I think it could have been Nueva.*"

"*He's incapable of love the way I love you.*"

"*He's beginning to think there's something between us.*"

"*Adam, hand me those sticks.*"

"*Not if I leave.*"

"*You want to pick up my leavings, it's okay.*"

"*We'll never be together while he's alive.*"

"*I know how to do it. Tomorrow he'll be dead ...
     dead ... dead.*"

"*How?*"

"*Drag him with one leg ... 'til it's over. I'll see to that.*"

"*I know you will ... I know you will ... I know you
     will.*"

Adam Dawson was standing next to the appaloosa when Lorena came out of the kitchen door.

"Thought I heard you." She smiled.

"Where's Chad?"

"Still upstairs." Lorena looked at Adam's horse.
"Where's Domino? I thought you were going to bring him."

"I'm not going to do it." Adam spoke softly and looked straight at her.

"Do what?"

"Kill him."

Lorena stiffened.

"You've killed before," she said.

"But I've never murdered." Adam went toward his horse. "Tell Chad I said good-bye."

She moved to him, turned him around, and looked like she rose from hell with her hair on fire.

"Adam . . ."

"No, Lorena! You're good . . . better than good. You had me on the gallows with a rope around my neck and I almost stepped off. Almost . . ."

"Adam, think a minute . . ."

"That's what I did."

"Great!" She spat the words out. Bitter. Berating. "He's got no legs and you've got no spine. Gallant, hell. Gutless!"

"What was wrong with Nueva?"

"Nothing!" she gritted, " 'til you came around!"

"Well," he started to turn again, "I won't be around any-more."

The porch door slammed open like a rifle shot. Chad Walker stood against the doorway, a cane in his left hand, a gun in the other and black hate in his eyes.

"No, you won't be around! Neither one of you!"

"Chad!" She took a step.

"Stand still! Goddammit, just stand still!"

"Chad . . . it was his idea . . ."

"Sure it was."

"Chad, just let me tell you . . ."

"There's nothing you can tell me that I don't already know!" Walker was unsteady on just one cane. He pointed the gun at Adam. "And you! My good Yankee friend. Fought in the war on the same side . . . the only one I ever trusted. More than trusted. I thought you were different than all these other bastards . . . and you . . . you were going to kill me."

"Maybe I was. But I didn't."

"Well, I'm going to kill you."

"Not today."

"Right now!"

"No, Chad. I'm going to step on that horse and ride out of here."

"Not unless dead men ride."

"Then it'll be in the back . . . but I don't think you'll do it. I couldn't kill you and you won't kill me."

"Why not?"

"Because, soldier . . . this is your last chance . . . to end the war."

Adam Dawson turned and stood straight and still, offering a perfect target. His back.

Walker's gun still pointed. He leaned on the cane with his left hand, eyes locked on Adam's back. His gun hand trembled. His fingers tightened, about to squeeze. But his shoulders shuddered, then sagged.

He dropped the gun and steadied himself with both hands on the head of the cane, his eyes looking at the ground.

A loud laugh broke the silence.

Joe Nueva stepped from around the porch still laughing as he came closer, right hand touching the butt of his gun.

"What a couple of daisies! Lorena, you sure can pick 'em." Nueva stopped laughing and walking. His eyes centered on Dawson. "You, *drifter*! Pretty good with your fists, huh? Let's see how good you are with a gun."

"Why?"

"*Why*? Why do you think I came here?"

"I told you before, I didn't want your job, Nueva . . . or anything else."

"But you took it!" He looked at Lorena then back to Dawson. "You took everything you could get your hands on . . . told the sheriff you saw me that night . . . told him I tried to kill that cripple." Nueva pointed at Walker. "That's why!"

"Did I?"

"If you didn't, then who did?"

Dawson's expression didn't change. He didn't move or take his eyes from Nueva.

"Joe . . ." Lorena didn't think Dawson would say any more but Walker might say or try to do anything.

"You?!" Nueva rasped.

"Joe." She took a step. "No! I swear!"

"You 'swear.' You . . ."

"Get outta here, Nueva!" Walker blurted. "Get off my land!"

"Shut up, you stupid cripple son of a bitch!" Nueva snapped. "You don't know what the hell is going on! I screwed your wife. So did Hatcher." He pointed to Dawson. "So did *he*! So did everybody! You're nothing but a crazy, castrated sonofa . . ."

"NUEVA!" Walker screamed, tried to move ahead and almost fell. "I'll kill you!"

"With what?" Nueva grinned. Then laughed. "That cane?"

Chad Walker lunged for his fallen gun. He staggered, lost the cane, stumbled and sprawled onto the porch, writhing in agony.

"Cripple sonofabitch." Nueva's laugh turned to arrogant contempt.

The gun was just a few feet from where Walker had fallen. His face twisting in pain and humiliation, he started to crawl.

"You move one more inch," Nueva drew his gun, "and I'll shoot you first."

"No you won't!" Adam said.

Nueva whirled at him and fired. Not fast enough. Adam's gun was already smoking. Joe Nueva clutched his chest. He turned toward Lorena. His lips trembled trying to say something. Whatever it was never came out. His eyes closed. He moaned. Joe Nueva dropped.

Dawson holstered his gun. Not fast, not slow, he moved toward the horse.

"No!" Lorena shrieked.

He mounted the appaloosa. Lorena ran to him. She

clutched at Adam's leg. Clawing. Not letting go as he turned the animal and started to move.

"Adam!" she cried. "Take me with you! I don't care about the money . . . or anything . . . I can't stay here . . . I won't!"

"Then don't."

"Adam . . . you and me . . ."

He dug into the horse's flank. The appaloosa responded. Faster. Still dragging Lorena as she fought to hang on.

"Adam . . . what am I going to do?"

The horse moved even faster. Dawson never looked down at her.

"You'll think of something."

The appaloosa started to gallop, dragging her until she had to let go.

"Lorena . . ." Chad Walker called out.

She fell to her hands and knees, sobbing in the dirt.

Dawson reined in his horse close to Sheriff Ben Vesper on his mount.

"I don't know how much you saw, Sheriff . . ."

"Just enough. Keep riding. And Dawson, on your way out, say good-bye to Brad Hatcher."

On a hillock, just outside the gate, Hatcher waited astride the palomino. Neither man spoke or looked at the other when Dawson rode past.

Things had not worked out the way Brad Hatcher had planned. But it was not the end of the world. Brad Hatcher would ride back to Spanish Bit, have dinner, plan his next move and drink some red wine.

Once again Adam Dawson rode lonesome slow. Pinto, Walker's Way, Spanish Bit were all behind him. The sun on its downward arc began to dip toward the haze of the western horizon.

He reined up, took out his silver watch but not to look at the time. He turned it over, read the inscription.

Adam
Come on, you Wolverine!
Autie

And remembered ... "It's not over yet, Adam ... I know my Indians ... they aren't crushed yet ... mark my words, they'll unite with their new chiefs, Sitting Bull, Crazy Horse, Crow-King and the rest. Sioux, Cheyenne, Kiowa, Arapaho all riding together for one last battle and I'll be there, so will you."

"Please, Adam. At our wedding I said you were Custer's luck ..."

"As long as you wear that scarf, Adam, I'll be waiting for you to come back."

After Washita Dawson had vowed never to kill again unless his life depended on it. He had come close to breaking that vow. But he had made a choice. Now he had to make another choice.

Adam Dawson put the watch back into his pocket. He took off the red scarf, thought of tossing it away, leaving it behind in the desert. Instead he folded it and tucked the red scarf into his saddlebag.

Adam Dawson rode West.